Advance Praise for *A Matter of Geography*

"They were neighbours - Christians, Jews, Muslims, Hindus - till Bombay's religious violence tore their community apart. What is the meaning of 'home' to someone who has emigrated? Can love conquer geography? *A Matter of Geography* elegantly explores the ever-changing human relationships within the cosmic framework."

-- Sylvia Fraser, author of *Pandora* and *The Rope in Water*

"With a richness of details, Jasmine D'Costa, gently and insightfully, through the eyes of childhood innocence, lifts the veil on a tumultuous time period in India where violence and religious hatred swept through a peaceful, diverse and tight knit community, forever altering the lives of its inhabitants. More than ever and in difficult times, *A Matter for Geography* is a much-needed glimmer of hope."

-- John Calabro, author of *An Imperfect Man* and *The Cousin*

"Jasmine D'Costa's *A Matter of Geography* is a brave commentary on the place many of us carry in our hearts as home. It leaves us with the question, is there a true sense of shared belonging or are some Indians more equal than others?

-- Shagorika Easwar, Editor, *Desi News* and *Canada Bound Immigrant*

A Matter of

Geography

Library and Archives Canada Cataloguing in Publication
D'Costa, Jasmine

A Matter of Geography/ Jasmine D'Costa

Issued in print and electronic formats.
ISBN 978-1-77161-246-3 (softcover).--ISBN 978-1-77161-247-0 (HTML).--
ISBN 978-1-77161-248-7 (PDF)

I. Title.

PS8607.C68M38 2017   C813'.6   C2016-907568-0
                                                   C2016-907569-9

This novel is entirely a work of fiction. The names, characters and incidents portrayed in it are the work of the author's imagination. Any resemblance to actual persons, living or dead, and events is entirely coincidental.

Published by Mosaic Press, Oakville, Ontario, Canada, 2017.
MOSAIC PRESS, Publishers
Copyright © 2017 Jasmine D'Costa
Printed and Bound in Canada
Designed by Courtney Blok
Cover Photo: Maya D'Costa
Author Photo: Mary Perdue

ONTARIO ARTS COUNCIL
CONSEIL DES ARTS DE L'ONTARIO
an Ontario government agency
un organisme du gouvernement de l'Ontario

We acknowledge the Ontario Arts Council
for their support of our publishing program

We acknowledge the Ontario Media Development Corporation
for their support of our publishing program

Funded by the   Financé par le
Government   gouvernement   **Canada**
of Canada   du Canada

MOSAIC PRESS
1252 Speers Road, Units 1 & 2
Oakville, Ontario L6L 5N9
phone: (905) 825-2130

info@mosaic-press.com

A Matter of Geography

Jasmine D'Costa

mosaicPRESS

To my angels at crucial times of my life: My brother Bennet, Philomena, Avita and Fr. Zbigniew Kozar.

Prologue

Bombay slept in a soft collective snore that summer night of 1968, quite unmindful of the many homeless souls looking for a place to sleep; some foraging in bins, others just giving up and dying. In the National Park at Borivali, near the far north of Bombay, the trees wrestled with each other in tight-wooded abandon, their leaves purging the defiled city air that streamed through their flutter. An occasional roar from the Lion Safari enclosure disturbed the silence; and somewhere in the deep interior, a flying stag beetle noisily took flight in search of a mate. All seemed right with this world except for one young panther cub, lost, wandering in search of its mother, unafraid, its path through the brush defined by the chatter of monkeys and birds that warned of its approach. Finding a bus parked in the small clearing on the edge of the woods, it sauntered up the stairs, lured by the slow rhythmic snore so like the steady heartbeat of its mother, and lay close to the driver who used the bus as his little home.

Very early, around four a.m., a faint reddish dawn steadily diffused dark clouds into the horizon at the north end of the park. A cock crowed from somewhere over the hills where tribals lived, keeping livestock, chickens, and growing their own vegetables for sustenance. Crows cawed in response; monkeys chattered restlessly. An almost subconscious challenging clamour sounded all

1

at once: The clanking of milk bottles being delivered to the blue wooden milk booths that dotted the sides of the roads; people lining up for milk, some dropping a stone to mark their place in the queue while they returned to bed for that extra five minutes; the loud clatter of pots and pans being washed in a million sinks around the city; cars, taxis, and trucks rushing downtown before it crowded. In that second of light, heat, and alien sounds, dewdrops slid down a million leaves heavy with dawn.

The bus driver stirred lazily, woken by a sharp ray of sunlight hitting his eyelids. It was a moment before he became aware of his companion. Eyes popping, he stared at the two-foot-long cat, his mouth opening and closing soundlessly as a fish—no bubbles, just spittle that had dried in a white pathway down the left side of his mouth. He sat upright and slowly stood. Mercifully for him, the door was on his side of the bus. He kept eye contact with the panther as he attempted to back slowly towards the exit, much like a moonwalker floating unaided by gravity, or a yogi on a magic carpet. It can hardly be said that he succeeded. The cat, now on its feet, kept a steady distance between them, advancing as slowly as he retreated. As soon as he reached the door, he turned and ran, frantic, towards the park gate, his hands waving in the air, shouting, "*Vaag, vaag*—tiger, tiger," his heart jostling with the words in his mouth.

The panther stretched gracefully at the door, alighted too, and casually strolled in the direction of the city. Forest officials, now alerted, closed the main gate of the park—a meaningless gesture, as the gate was merely symbolic, more a way to prevent humans from entering without the ticketed fare than to lock the animals within. To be fair, 114 square kilometres of forestland could hardly be fenced in.

The panther took the path that led out from the undergrowth on one side of the park gate. Weeds, tall and still green from the recent monsoons, twisted in the slight morning breeze but offered no resistance, bowing gracefully to let the panther through.

The crowds on the city streets, unconcerned about rubbing shoulders with each other—men, women, children pressed close—stopped in curiosity to watch the bus driver run, certain a drama was soon to unfold. And so it did. Toward the left side of the gates, someone on the outskirts of the crowd spotted the large cat emerging from the bushes. Mesmerized at first, they stared, their index fingers in some disco-like flash dance, pointing at the creature. A nervous businessman in the middle of the crowd, standing on his toes to see what was happening up in front, threw his hands upwards, screaming, *"Hey Bhagwan, vaag, vaag*—Oh God, tiger, tiger,"* terror written in the tremolo of his delivery. This cry triggered a mad scramble, and in moments, wild masses of bodies tried to run in every direction. It was pandemonium. The screeching tyres of vehicles caught unawares sent up the smell of burnt rubber. The crowds now screamed in several voices, tones, and pitches, but mostly those of panic: *"Vaag, vaag*—tiger, tiger, tiger!"* Those whose view of the panther was obstructed followed the direction of the dispersing crowd, joining in the chorus..."*Vaag, vaag, vaag!"*

The panther—who at first, just curious, stood there in wonder, never having seen such a large number of people in its own haven—blinked. It moved its head in all directions, and at one time even peered up at the sky as if to understand why these strange animals were fleeing like they had just seen a lion. The panther, now alarmed with the direction of its own thoughts, instinctively followed the direction of the crowd and noise, bounding behind them though it did not know what it was running away from. In an inevitable consequence of one not understanding one's strength, the panther knocked dead a child in its path. The frenzy stepped up several notches as people tried to break into shops that had not yet opened their doors, some of them shattering the glass windows in desperation, others running into open doorways of apartment buildings.

When the forest officers were finally able to get through this commotion, they took aim at the animal.

Weird, thought the panther as it felt the sharp prick of the arrow, and now quite sure about whom the crowds were running away from, I am only protecting myself, before it lost all consciousness.

"…(human nature being what it is) will, at some time or other and in much the same ways, be repeated in the future…"

- Thucydides
The History of the Peloponnesian War
Translated by Richard Crawley

Chapter One

Over a hundred stony meteorites hit the earth near Kirin in Northeastern China on 8th March, 1976, the day Anna was born. That is how I remember her birth. I went with Mother and Father to the hospital to see the newborn girl of our neighbour and friend Mr. Fernandes. There she, bundled in a flannel blanket, very white and pink, looked up at me, smiling—our own 6 lb. meteorite from some distant star, lighting up the room and, from that day, our lives. She lay blissfully unconscious of her narrow escape from the forced sterilisation campaigns sweeping the country in the year preceding her birth and the new, more rigorous birth control policies that had been enforced in India. They say extraordinary women are born in the leap year, as if the preceding three years' extra six hours were cumulated and added to the leap year in expectation that it would need more time to accommodate the events written into its fate.

Sunday, the twelfth day of October 2008, I sat staring at the big china centrepiece in the middle of Mother's oval dining table. Two white cherubs on either side of an intricately carved knob spat out recycled water, fountain-like, into the white collecting bowl at the bottom. The white silk dupion tablecloth had white cutwork embroidered corners and sparkled like new, though it had been part of her dowry. My mother, Isabel, knew how to preserve the pristine nature of all that she owned. She knew, too, how to send a message. Her eight-seater dining table was just one of Mother's numerous ways of telling me she looked forward to the larger family that of course I would provide: wife, grandchildren, etc.

You know genuine bone china when, held against the light, you can see your fingers through it. And you know the sounds of nervous tension when you hear the clear, bell-like tinkle of cup playing with saucer. I set my cup down, fearful of doing Mother's bone china severe damage despite its reputation of 'high mechanical strength.' Smells of delicious pulao, mingled with the curls of chicken curry being prepared, sailed forth from her kitchen.

Isabel silently pushed the chicken to and fro in the pot, frying the flesh in green coriander and mint paste and alternately whipping the bowl of curds to top it with. Her silence, unusual, meditative, almost nervous, made me wonder who was more affected by Anna's pending arrival. I looked at her and decided it would be good for my nerves to go to the airport early and wait there, rather than in this contagious nervousness.

The news had come about a month earlier on 14th September 2008, a Sunday morning, just a little after eight, when all the world appeared to be bursting at the seams. Somewhere in the South Atlantic Ocean an iceberg had calved, bursting from a small fissure into two large islands of ice; no doubt, to be further calved into a hundred small icebergs and ice islands, pushing the waters, causing the waves to ripple and travel outwards, to burst ashore.

In Bombay, the weather, despite the pundits' predictions, burst into a response, pushed somewhere from a distantly related rupture. Heavy clouds burst into thunderstorm. The footpaths suddenly expanded into a steady flow of umbrellas bursting into the street, spilling over from the sidewalks with mysterious people huddled beneath. I reluctantly watched from my bedroom window. The window had burst from its seams too, no longer fitting flush in the framework that had warped with the weather. And not so mysterious, the figure of my mother, bursting out of the seams of her blouse, hurried into the recesses of the building where I lived.

Tribes such as the Garos of Assam, some races along Lake Ashanti and the Gold and Ivory Coasts, or others such as the Iroquois in North America, are matrilineal societies where the women rule over namby-pamby men, urging students of social theory from the time of Bachofen to ponder this female dominance. I, however, with characteristic male assertion borne from a long line of patriarchal ancestors, had declared myself independent of my mother.

But for now, I gave up my Sunday with a sigh. Don't get me wrong; I loved Isabel, but her attempts to coax me into marriage were sufficient cause for apprehension. On the other hand, if one had to be reasonable, what was one Sunday in the lifetime of a male when a beloved parent visits, braving the elements? No doubt an urgent appeal was coming my way, wrapped in a bio of the "very lovely girl who, though I have not met, seems so nice, look Peter, look at her photograph."

"Peter," she said, not stopping to gain her breath, "take this bottle of pickle and put it in the fridge." She shoved a bottle of mango pickle at me as she wiped her feet on the doormat to remove the muck of the street before entering my apartment.

"And don't put your fingers in the bottle, you will spoil the pickle—it will not stay," she added as I opened the lid to get a whiff of the red, deadly looking thing, which I admit I loved.

"So Mum... Sunday morning? Must be important ... Surely, not just to hand me pickle in the rain?"

"Peter, I wish you would exercise your manners towards your mother too. Get me a cup of tea and first, get me a towel."

I guessed she was going to take her time getting to the point. I could see a long morning ahead of me, perhaps stretching into lunch.

"Tea." She paused, her eyes scouring the ceiling and all the corners of my living room for that unwitting spider web, or the table cover of dust, or the stray fragment of paper on the floor, ready to critique Premibai's housekeeping. She was still grappling with my independence though I had moved out of her apartment over ten years ago.

"Tea is the gift of God himself." Sighing, she put down the cup I'd handed her and picked up the towel to dry her hair.

"Anna," she said from behind the towel, "is coming from Canada. She has inherited some property in Mangalore—she's there as we speak—but she will be living with me for a week. She arrives in Bombay a month from now."

Pulling into the airport car park, it struck me that it looked like the big manufacturing unit of Toyota or some super-big Japanese car manufacturer, or just a giant bird's nest, with flying aircraft landing and taking off in loud, thunderous whooshes overhead. It brought back a familiar feeling of excitement: Travel, the unknown beyond, and perhaps the excitement of seeing Anna, all a heady rush. I stood in full view of the arriving passengers and, a bit too late, wondered if I should have brought a placard like the ones the tourist operators stood with, pushing their way in front of the waiting crowd to pick up strangers they had contracted with but not knowing what they looked like. How much of travel involved resting one's faith in strangers.

Her hair was curlier than when I knew her. That was my first thought when I spotted her. Taller, fairer, older, but still those loving, gentle eyes. I needed no placard. Her scent, familiar yet strange, disguised by some foreign perfume, her walk still the same, stopping a few feet away from me, looking at me direct, then smiling, walking slowly, building to a quick trot and she was here in front of me. Anna, Anna...

I had never hugged Anna. Young boys do not hug young girls. But right then it seemed logical as I held her, blowing into her hair, swinging her around and around and doing it with careless abandon. We laughed, our hands sliding over each other's, putting distance between our bodies all the better to take each other in, till our fingers hooked to hold our balance and we kept turning around, the laughter of our childhood bubbling through and not a thought of our separation...my anger...my resentment.

"Peter, Peter, you look so well, handsome as ever, and my dear friend...Isabel, where is she?"

"Where do you think, Anna? She is killing the fatted calf for you!"

She only smiled then, somewhat shyer than before. "I did not know what to expect after all these years."

Lightly, our hands released each other and I grabbed Anna's

bags and led her out of the terminal. We drove along the highway towards home, Anna looking out the window, eagerly taking in the scenery, as if she needed to fill her body with its memory despite the squalor, the foul smells, the humidity that hit us. As we got out of the car, I could see Mother, pulling her head in after having stuck it out of her window for a good 30 minutes, I imagine, looking out for us. Anna jumped up and down, waving.

"Isabel, Isabel, I love you," she shouted.

Isabel, who had wiped her face to take off the traces of snuff, now opened the door and opened her arms, engulfing Anna. Anna pushed her away, her hands on Isabel's waist still. Jumping with almost child-like excitement she said, "Isabel, Isabel, my Indian mother."

Isabel could hold it no longer. Over the years, Mother had become soft, and now she sniffed loudly and tears streamed down her face. "You know how devastated we were when you left. We spent a long time trying to get over the separation. We were family, Anna."

"We are family, Isabel," she said, kissing Mother.

Chapter Two

"There are two ways to be fooled. One is to believe what isn't true; the other is to refuse to believe what is true."

- Søren Kierkegaard

I can only begin from the end. Not the end of my story, but the end of our lives as we knew it. Anna's family, the Fernandeses, and mine were neighbours in Billimoria Building. Though we were neighbours, we grew up as one family. But all that changed the day we saw the Muslim bakery on fire, that December of 1992. Dad, who worked as a Police Inspector in the Nagpada Police Station, had warned us that there was some kind of trouble fomenting, but its magnitude took us all by surprise.

The previous evening, on the 8th of December, Mohamed Farooqui, who lived in room no. 26, several rooms away from us, got stabbed. When I call them rooms, you will have guessed that these apartments were small, with no separate bedrooms as in the flats inhabited by more prosperous families. Two strangers, not from our neighbourhood (where we knew every resident either by name or face), followed Mohamed as he returned from the small but flourishing hardware shop he ran. Sometimes his son, Ali, would sit in for him, but I don't think Ali made such a good fill in, being only sixteen and more interested in anything other than hardware. Fortunately, this was one of those days when Ali stayed home, and so he escaped his father's fate.

Waylaying Mohamed as he reached the junction of Nesbit Road and St. Mary's, nearly home, the two strangers asked him whether he was Mehmood. "No," he said, unsuspecting, volunteering more information than asked for; he pointed to his room on the second floor. "I am Mohamed. I live in Billimoria Building, there, the window with the sheets hanging out to dry." At which they stabbed him, screaming, *"Mussalman, suvar*—Muslim pig."

Anna, who spent much of her time at the window, for she suffered from asthma and felt claustrophobic within the small confines of their apartment, witnessed the stabbing. Shaking till her teeth chattered and gasping asthmatically she pointed and gestured as she told her father, "They k-killed him, they killed h-him."

Mr. Fernandes, peering past Anna out the window, caught sight of the backs of the two men running away from the bleeding Mohamed down the silent, deserted street. He rushed over to us in room no. 18, two doors down the verandah of the second floor, and both Dad and he raced down the stairs. In a normally crowded street, under normal circumstances, crowds would by now have surrounded Mohamed, cogitating on what best to do, talking to each other, sharing notes on the happening. But this, we realised, not being normal times, Mohamed lay there alone, huddled and bleeding on the desolate street. Dad and Mr. Fernandes hailed a passing taxi and lifted Mohamed between them, hauling him into the back seat. Both of them sat in front with the driver. They took him to the J.J. Hospital, very close to where Mohamed ran his business.

Later that night Mohamed died. Just moments before, he opened his eyes and called for Mr. Fernandes, who stood at the foot of his bed. Mr. Fernandes mistook this sudden spurt of life as a sure movement to recovery. Mohamed then enunciated clearly, though weakly, *"Mehroonisa aur Ali ka khayal rakhna*—watch after Mehroonisa and Ali," and then, as we Catholics say, gave up his spirit.

We did not connect that event to the larger situation until the next morning, when someone torched the Muslim Bakery.

It had been almost fifteen years since I picked up the book that's sat in my drawer looking forsaken but as fresh as when she gave it to me. Anna's neat notebook lay under my socks and undergarments in the top drawer, covered in brown paper with a white label, much like those we stuck on all our notebooks in school.

She had tied it with red string, securing it with a neat bow on the top of it. Every time I glanced at the book I felt anger tic under my eyes. An anger that never went deeper because I allowed barely a moment to pick out what I wanted from that drawer, pushing it shut before succumbing to any unwelcome desire to read it. But with Anna's imminent arrival announced by Mother, I looked at the diary once more, for a very long moment...Anna had always wanted to be a writer.

With trembling hands I untied the thread that bound the book and opened it randomly. Clutching at my chair, I lowered myself mechanically, words flying at me as if I'd opened Pandora's box; the evil in our lives bursting out from my repressed memory. It was as though it were just yesterday that our lives had been turned upside down. Anna's words brought it all back—the year that I turned 21, an adult and yet so much a child.

On that fateful day in December of 1992, as we rushed to the window and watched the fire brigade noisily hurry down our street to rescue a burning bakery, I first learned that Ali was Muslim.

For all the sixteen years of my life, there were only two kinds of people in our world—the Catholics and the non-Catholics. In the Catholic school that I attended, there were the Catholics who sat together for the Religion period, and while we discussed the gospel or other issues that kept us being 'good Catholics,' the non Catholics moved over to another classroom for a separate lesson in Moral Science. I never was inquisitive enough to ask what they actually taught there, but really, that was the only time we knew anyone was different from us.

A burning bakery can wipe innocence. It is no accident that they stabbed Ali's father the night before, we were soon to realise. That bubble of innocence that was once opaque now became transparent, giving us a glimpse into a world that soon would be ours; like drawing heavy curtains open and looking out with surprise and a bit of difficulty at the world out there in bright sunshine. That day, we looked at our neighbours differently. Who were they? Ali was Muslim. The

Surves on the first floor in room no. 16 were Hindus. Ms. Eze-kiel, a Jew, a very mysterious Jew. Mimosa? We knew nothing about her except what she told us. She'd escaped from Burma and lived here as a refugee, till she met Paddy and married him. Paddy, Irish, tall, red-faced, and most of the time drunk, had stayed here even after the British left, making him in-congruous in the neighbourhood. He'd later gone the way of most drunks—cirrhosis of the liver, leaving his widow with no means whatsoever. Mimosa did some odd jobs, baby-sat, and often went scavenging from neighbour to neighbour enquir-ing what they had cooked for the day, mostly in a very refined tone. But more than these personal details, our neighbours were Hindu, Muslim, Jewish, Anglo-Indian, Indo-Burmese, and we were Catholics. In a sense, I understood how Adam felt after he ate the apple. Suddenly Eve was a woman and they were naked.

Daddy said we were all the same and Mummy, silent and thoughtful, looked infinitely sad. Mummy generally never looked sad. She says she did feel this way once before: She had a pet pig, or so she thought. She bathed her pig, talked to him and she sat on his back as a child playing pretend Cow-boys and Indians. Oh my God! Is that how the word piggyback came to be used? Anyway, she even gave him a name—Balth-azar, after one of the Magi. Lots of bonding with the pig later, she realized that Balthazar was no pet but bought as a piglet to be fattened in time for her First Holy Communion party. That was the only other time Mummy was really sad, or so she says. Seeing her shake her head from side to side made us all sad. We always reflected Mummy's feelings on most things.

That day we became more Catholic than we had ever been in our life. Mummy took out a box of religious treasures—little crucifixes, miraculous medals, rosaries that sparkled, scapulars and such-like, which we had received over the years from Don Bosco's church in gratitude for the charitable do-nations Daddy made regularly. They were kept away, almost like reserves for a rainy day. Our rain had arrived in torrents.

Mum opened the box silently and first took out the 'mi-raculous' medals and laid them aside. She then reached for the crucifixes, strung them on black cords and passed them around the circle we had made around her, instructing us to wear them prominently outside our clothes. Even Daddy, used to meting out the orders, silently put the cord over his head and adjusted the cross outside his shirt.

The Marchon family from room no. 19 never went to church. They said they were Catholics, and I suppose they were. What with names like Joe, Mili, Miriam, etc. But they did not go to church. Mummy strung all the crosses she had in her box and sent Daddy with them to the Marchons, who lived in what we considered a House of Sin for more reasons than their lack of church attendance. Mummy knew they would not have crucifixes to hang around their necks.

WE ARE CATHOLICS, our crucifixes announced.

Chapter Three

"The reason why certain intuitive minds are not mathematical is that they are quite unable to apply themselves to the principles of mathematics, but the reason why mathematicians are not intuitive is that they cannot see what is in front of them..."

- Blaise Pascal

In the telling of my tale it may seem I am rambling, for all you want to know is why Anna left us to go to Canada. The larger events of sectarian violence, being Catholic in a Catholic neighbourhood—almost a Catholic ghetto—the very fabric of our lives in Billimoria Building, its residents, even its structure—all of these seemingly minor details conspired against us. Trust me when I say it is all important, it all adds up, these seemingly irrelevant larger and smaller issues.

The Mahabharata and the Ramayan were my favourite stories growing up.. It played on TV at a time when all we could see was an occasional Sunday Bollywood movie or a late night Charlie Chaplin, or *Here's Lucy*. Programming shut down at 11.00 p.m., only heightening our fascination with the TV. The Mahabharata aired on a Sunday morning; all of us faithfully went to church, listened to the gospel and the readings from the Bible and the homily, secretly waiting for the service to end. We then rushed home to settle down to the Mahabharata—almost ironic, for even the devout, most conservative of Catholics were totally hooked on this Hindu mythology of gods, greater and lesser, and of men, brave and cowardly.

Not just our lives but the very social structure adapted to the Ramayan and Mahabharata. We no longer went next door to talk to our neighbours, nor were we occupied in the special Sunday lunch, a family affair around the dining table. We sat with our plates in front of the television, focused on the screen, with not even a glance at those sitting around us. Some neighbours who did not have a television would come over to the homes that did, to watch. In that sense, sharing did still happen. The cricket matches, the Commonwealth games, the Asian games and the Sunday movies were times when neighbours did sit together, but focused on the television and not on each other.

The Ramayan and Mahabharata, came with the promise of endless stories, of stories within stories, of a hundred thousand verses, of relationships of love, of war, of magic, and a world of India that was within our blood. Our stories were woven around it, our proverbs, phrases, culture, and philosophies fed upon these epics and shaped our narratives. Our world filled with its magic, heroes, love, family; we fashioned our sensibilities around it, engulfed. Matrons of superior reserve broke down in tears, cheered, and laughed along with the story. Many a friendship on the suburban trains sprung up discussing the latest episode.

It was only reasonable that when, in 1990, the festival of *Rath Yatra*, the procession of Ram's chariot, was announced by one of the political parties, we were excited. Though I was eighteen at that time, and Anna but thirteen, we, in our almost naïve, cloistered view of all things non-Catholic—viewed in a light of distance, awe, and fairytale-like quality—welcomed this, unaware of its political motivations. We could relive our favourite story. A larger-than-life drama, played on the Nation's stage and through the streets; its grandeur appealed, its drama excited. Every wall in Bombay displayed graffiti: CHAL AYODHYA--Come to Ayodhya—SHILANYAS LEKE—With Your Brick. Like the posters that announce films or advertisements to everyone who passes, it announced the impending drama.

Our vocabulary did not stretch beyond a smattering of Hindi words, to be understood and spoken only at the Hindi class in school; they were not part of our life of English words, reading, speaking; of Shakespeare, P.G Wodehouse, Charles Dickens, Laurence Oliver. We even dreamt in English. In learning to speak, read, write in English, our thoughts and cultural understanding were imprinted with English thought; our grammar from Wren and Martin had phrases, authors, philosophies of living, loving, and the world as seen through the English authors we read. Just as Alexander's empire was confronted with Greek assumptions, the Greek way of life, so was our immersion in the British way. A community, to be functional, must have shared expectations. Did we? We lived in a world cut out from a very large part of the country that was impacted differently, lived differently, had different assumptions that we in our bubble had no knowledge of despite being born in Bombay and having lived here our entire lives.

Perhaps you will forgive me here when I admit that *"Shilanyas"* was not within our comprehension. We thought this was a mela, a large fair. I recall being puzzled at the slogans. Unexplained, no small print, no riders, just a slogan we spent no time thinking about, carrying on with our little misconceptions. People raised their eyes to the constant reminder painted on walls and pillars all over their cities and towns. Reluctantly tearing their gazes away from the television that brought the stories of heroes and gods and family and magic and miracles, they knew that their destiny, their duty, their karma and dharma, in order to be a true Hindu, was to join this movement to restore a temple in Ayodhya, where Lord Ram was born.

My friend of later years, Dr. Apte, a social worker and a very devout Hindu—very chauvinistic about Hinduism, I believe—would religiously go every Sunday in khaki brown shorts to train in the camps of the RSS, a Hindu nationalist organisation, to be a good Hindu and defend the faith and the country. Crusaders defending the faith without armour, wielding sticks, in clothes grown men should never wear; I have never understood how a bunch of bony men with flared khaki shorts, sticks, and some unskilled exercise routines could do a better job than the Indian Army. For in my mind, logically in a country that was democratic and primarily Hindu, did they need to defend Hinduism? Were they under attack? Would I trust them to defend me? Or was I part of the enemy?

Dr. Apte lived a distance from my home, but I met him on the train one afternoon when, after leaving the college early, I found a seat next to this very bony, ascetic-looking man. He sat calmly looking at the world, in direct contrast with my disgusted state of mind after having taken part in a heated discussion started by a very obnoxious colleague, Ms. Raikar, in what was ironically called the Teachers Rest Room, and stomping out. Having a good way to go before reaching our destinations makes friends of the most unlikely of men. Dr. Apte spoke English, enunciating every syllable very strongly but always correctly. A very interesting chap, self assured; even when he did disgusting things like dig in his nose, he acted like it was the most pleasurable, socially acceptable activity that nature demanded. Almost like pushing one's hair from one's eyes or loosening one's collar. In many ways, though I did not know it at that time, he would assume an oracle-like quality in my life.

Our train had stopped midway between stations because of an accident on the track ahead—generally the reason for many a lasting friendship among co-travellers on the suburban trains. Dr. Apte and I refused to do the undignified thing that most of the passengers had resorted to—jumping onto the track and walking along it to destinations unknown. Both of us knew that joining the desperate march would save us very little time. We decided our time could be better spent with a book till they had cleared the tracks. I opened L. E. Dicksons' *History of the Theory of Numbers* and all at once was absorbed in a world of definition, certainty, and comfort. Dr. Apte, leaning under to better to see the title of the book I was engrossed in, spoke from somewhere down below. "Ah! You are reading Mathematics?"

This is the marvel of the Marathi language or perhaps just of Dr. Apte. Most of his questions were rhetorical. *Jevtos ka?* Are you eating? That's when he saw me eating. *Or Padtos ka?* Are you reading? if he chanced on me doing so. There have been times he has entered my bedroom as I slept, shaken my foot peeping out from below my sheet, waking me up and asking, *Zoplas ka?* Are you sleeping?

I answered, "Yes, I teach Mathematics. And you? I mean, what do you do?"

I had planned to sit in with my other teaching colleagues in the staff room, but found myself suddenly sucked into conversations I wanted no part of... The most annoying Ms. Raikar, a colleague I took pains to avoid, had once again steered us into the *"Amche*

Mumbai—Get the outsiders out" debate.

Somehow these debates triggered the worst in me. On this day my mind was already reeling with Mother's announcement of Anna's arrival. Provoked as I was at the least hint of the events that had separated us, this conversation had brought up feelings I thought I had no time for.

My annoyance rising, my own tolerance tested to the utmost by now, I escaped the staff room to go home and rest amid the anonymity of the city. I stopped on the way to buy a sandwich.

"How do you want it?"

"Very hot, and put a piece of cheese too."

The sandwich stall was a small glass case atop a stand that folded at the end of the day—or perhaps at the end of the proprietor's cucumbers and bread—and accompanied him home, pushing and jostling to enter an already swelling train.

Finding myself outside the railway terminus, sandwich in hand, I looked up at this marvel of architecture, Victoria Terminus—newly named Chatrapathi Shivaji Terminus. The spinal cord of Bombay, its tracks run up the long back of the city, its stations, set vertebrae-like every few kilometres as it heads North, carrying to and fro the millions of faceless, nameless flesh. In this robotic city there's no time to look up at the sky, yet up there on the top of its dome, the statue of Progress reaches for the heavens. Somewhere in the foundations of its Gothic grandeur is hidden the remains of what was once a temple of the local fisher folk, dedicated to the Goddess Mumbra Devi. Commerce stamping out the spiritual. Mumbra Devi, the goddess after whom they reportedly want the city to be named...Mumbai. Not even the gods can stop the wheels of this city turning.

Moments later, as if a tsunami, the crowds swelled out of the terminus, stopping all lanes of traffic as they pushed their way across the street. I moved against this tide of bodies without noticing the sweat and grime that rubbed against me: my space ending somewhere between my dermis and epidermis. I entered Platform No. 1 and into the 5.30 Chembur train; my body taking its direction from its own involuntary movement of habit, my mind dazed. Chatrapati Shivaji Terminus it was now called, but Victoria Terminus it stayed...and Mumbai? Bombay it shall remain for me!

Do not the names of our streets and railways and our hills and valleys reflect and place our history? Would we have located the Garden of Eden long ago, had not a stream of vain ancient politicians wasted useless moments renaming it?

Amche Mumbai, indeed! These name changers... Throwing out the name Bombay in the need to supposedly throw out all that is British. It was in essence throwing out the very basis on which this city was built—tolerance. These activists, perhaps not even born in this city, want to lay claim like every acquisitive man in history, finding new and modern ways to do it! Take that repulsive Ms. Raikar... she was born in Ratnagiri.

Every now and again are born men who must leave their mark on the world, conquer it. Alexandrian, but rendered impotent by the democratic regimes they find themselves in, they set about raising enemies and bogeys among men of religious and ethnic differences, spurring hatred. History is rife with them, and it is on the histories of their own minds that they lean for validation as they change names and lay claims on land and building.

Damn you, Anna.

Stepping out of the train is as involuntary as boarding was—out of one's hands, so to say. Pushed out by the crowds alighting at the station, I find myself inadvertently at Dockyard station and with a robotic mindlessness walking down the slope to the road, taking the left turn towards Mazagaon and St Mary's Road where we lived, Anna's family and mine, for many years of our younger days.

Proportions are relative to one's own size: big, small, tall, short, nothing definitive. Walking down these streets at this moment as an adult, what had seemed like a huge avenue when we were still sucking lollipops had now miraculously diminished to a one-lane road. Since those days, I'd shot up to just an inch or two above six feet. Everything has dwarfed around me, everything but the events of our youth, which had, like the fluttering wings of a butterfly that creates tidal waves across oceans, loomed large in our life, engulfing who we were and designing our histories.

I looked at the small lane, Gangabowdi, which had fired the imagination of our young minds during the endless summers we spent listening to the stories Joe, our neighbour, told us: the street where ghosts and spirits abided and lost souls wandered in search of whatever lost souls search for. Walking past the road that led up to Mazagaon Hill, Bombay's reservoir, and the gardens on it, I passed the old tram terminus and turned down St. Mary's Road—walking down history...our history, like the history of the world, written in blood.

Somewhere down this road, Billimoria Building, the home I could never leave behind, stood innocent-like, common, dilapidated, its paint worn out, its shadow filling the small, now overcrowded street. Within its crevices still lingered the best memories of my life, making the worst memories in its folds take an unforgettable place in my experience. Cheap wooden barriers now replaced the formerly wrought-iron, intricately designed balustrade that had framed the verandah that wrapped the tenements and linked them together in a designed embrace, joining lives like one giant, affectionate arm.

I headed to the second floor, tracing my way up the wooden stairs, each worn in the center, outlining our footsteps, sometimes light, sometimes heavy, but always overlapping as we trampled up and down, occupied with daily living.

The building was unchanged otherwise, as though time had stood still, except it was more worn out, more silent, no children's laughter. The same Shahabad stone that paved Bombay's footpaths—wherever there was space for a footpath—still paved the floor of the first-storey passage. It was still the same wood, over a hundred years old, the same wooden banister, polished, not with any artificial lamination, but with the many hands that clutched it to walk up and down, the seats of children sliding down in playful excitement.

I stepped onto the second floor, where we'd lived for more than twenty years of my life. The second floor was the superior floor—not just in height, but also in flooring, the size of apartments, and the people. We lived there—or I should say we had lived there, because most of us who lived there once were now scattered. The second floor was now predominantly Muslim. Our little Catholic universe swallowed by a black hole, disappearing only to surface in splinters in places unknown, separate, reborn, recreated.

I walked through the door of the passage on the right that led to the verandah and the apartment where I'd lived with Mum and Dad, the side of the building where Anna and her family had lived. The wall at the head of the stairs separated the passage from the common toilets. To keep the accountability and maintenance manageable we had divided the families between the toilets. Three families shared a toilet, locked it and held a key, to prevent those who did not maintain it from using it. Ironically, the doors to our apartments were kept wide open most of the day and latched from the inside only at night when we slept. A narrow passage, enough for one person to stand in, insulated the toilets from the main passage wall. Its design seemed indifferent. Why would anyone design three families to one toilet? The building's alleys and passages must have been a designer's nightmare after a bilious night of hot food and opium. Yet, in its forgotten folds you could find memories of love, sacrifice, and blood.

To our little childish minds the main passage at the head of the stairs had seemed large; sometimes it doubled as a basketball court, cricket field, handball field, soccer field, and everything in between. It was our dance floor, our party room, our conference room, our life. Now, as I stood surveying it, it could be not more than 15 feet in length and 8 feet in breadth.

The verandah faced out to St. Mary's Road and the building opposite. All that happened out there happened in full view of the residents of the building in front and those on the street who, perhaps taking leisurely strolls to the church, glanced upwards in our direction. However, what happened in the passage between the toilet and the wall, and in the main passage, was private as private could be in a neighbourhood where everyone knew everything about everyone else.

I walked along the verandah and stopped outside no.18; I looked out at the road, recalling those ominous events of December 1992 when our lives changed. I watched the children in the building across play badminton in the yard and felt a lump climb in my throat and stick in my Adam's apple. The three coconut trees in the dirt-packed ground of Billimoria Building swayed in the breeze of that quiet evening, the events they had witnessed all those years ago seemingly forgotten.

Epimetheus, forgetting the warning of Prometheus to accept

no gifts from Zeus, married Pandora. Would that the world been different—would the history of man have been different? Would mine have stayed in some forgotten abyss never to surface? I cannot answer, for the deed was done. Mother's announcement had moved me to open Anna's notebook, which, akin to Pandora's box, had let loose these butterflies in my heart and the groundswell in my head, leaving it throbbing and painful.

Do grown men cry?

Chapter Four

"The price of apathy toward public affairs is to be ruled by evil men."

-Plato

Nothing disgusts me more than the utter naivety of the sort that cost us our world all those years ago.

"This Catholic apathy will be the death of you all," Dr. Apte said, shaking his bony head when he realized I'd been ignorant of the Hindu Nationalist movement sweeping the country in 1990. How would I know, I defended myself, when I lived in a strongly Catholic neighbourhood, attended a Catholic school and college? I'd been eighteen at the time—girls, parties, and study were more a part of my world than religious politics.

Still, looking back, why did we not know? Were we indifferent, impervious, or plain stupid? Was our bubble made of latex?

"Don't you understand that this was not about religion?" Dr. Apte said. "It was about giving the people a common enemy to unify them, putting fear in their hearts and getting into power. If you are apathetic and do not keep on top of things, you will find the Catholics are the next target. Who will they turn to next after the Muslims are done in, or when people tire of seeing them as the enemy?"

We sat in silence for a very long while as my mind turned back to the announcement of the Rath Yatra, the graffiti covering the walls of Bombay.

Sangh Pariwar, Dr. Apte explained, the organisation at the forefront of the movement calling for *Hindutva*—*Hinduness*—and India for Hindus, gave a call for Ram *Shilas*, consecrated bricks, to lay the foundation of the Ram Temple in Ayodhya, the site, they claimed, where Lord Ram was born.

We'd been steeped, as I mentioned, in the in the Mahabharata and Ramayan, so knew that Ayodhya was Lord Ram's birthplace. "But is it the same Ayodhya?"

"Reportedly so." Dr. Apte shrugged. "History that depends on word of mouth will as such continue to validate all later-day records."

Hindu Nationalist organizations like the VHP and the RSS delivered several hundred thousand Ram *Shilas*, consecrated bricks made of 'local earth,' to villages and towns all over. The bricks, wrapped in saffron cloth and consecrated by the *pujaris*, priests, and village elders, set in motion processions of the faithful all over the country carrying this offering and converging in Ayodhya. The organizations also distributed earth dug from Ayodhya to the villages and towns in the country to unite all Hindus as one nation.

Almost 200,000 villages sent bricks. Around the country, about 300,000 pujas of the Ram *Shilas* were performed and almost 100 million people joined the various processions that carried the bricks to and from Ayodhya. *Mahayagnas* and meetings were held, spurring the frenzy—"though, needless to point out, you slept through it all," Dr. Apte began his story.

"In my village in Jaigad I led the prayers and the consecration of the brick. On the designated day, I carried the brick wrapped in saffron cloth and with my friend Joshi, we took the bus to Mumbai, and from there, a train to Ayodhya to build the the Ram temple, on the spot where Lord Ram was born. This, you know, was not as simple as it sounds. A mosque stood on that very ground. I suppose you know about the Babri Mosque, at least?"

"It changed our lives..."

"Well then we won't get into that," he said, flicking his hand dismissively.

At this point he opened a small cloth pouch, pulled out a paan leaf and spread slaked lime over it as though the lime were butter. Then he began to fill it with various little goodies—tobacco, arecnut, little this and that, every other thing that makes up a paan. Tilting his head he pushed the whole bundle into his wide open mouth in one move and, keeping it at that angle, continued. "On October 30th in 1990, I went with my Ram *Shilas* to the Babri Masjid as planned. We did not have a place to stay nor did we pay for the train journey. We expected that it would be provided for; that is how little we were really prepared for this day. We believed that all Hindus would be part of this and there would be ashrams open for us."

He seemed agitated now. He began to chew more forcefully, and I was thankful for the distance between us, expecting at any moment some red fluid to fly from his mouth.

"We went to the site directly. The crowds had converged outside. Tens of thousands had arrived on the spot and I could not get to the front. I stood at the edge of the crowd, which was just as well, because when it got ugly I was able to run from the scene faster than others, with little physical damage to myself. The crowds chanted:

> "*Jai Shri Ram, bolo Jai Shri Ram—Hail Shri Ram,
> chant Shri Ram
> Jinnah bolo Jai Shri Ram—Jinnah chant Shri Ram
> Gandhi bolo Jai Shri Ram—Gandhi chant Shri Ram
> Mullah bolo Jai Shri Ram—Mullah chant Shri Ram.*"

Dr. Apte got lost in the nasal-toned chanting, quite unaware of his surroundings, for we were sitting in the Chembur gardens not very far from where I lived. Embarrassed, I looked around to see whether I knew anyone from those who, now disturbed or curious, looked in our direction. Some seemed even ready to join in. Dr. Apte, however, owned the world he lived in.

"The chanting stirred a frenzy in us *karsevaks*, volunteers. It is a strange thing, this mob energy, almost magic, compelling. The chanting reached a crescendo and some of the *karsevaks*, growing emotional, beyond the limits of civility, defaced tiles on the mosque. One enthusiastic *karsevak* who had come well prepared, or maybe belonged to a group that had pre-planned their course of action, actually went as far as flinging a can of orange paint on the wall." At this point he matched the visual with action; unashamedly, he spat the red fluid the paan had generated from his mouth into the bushes near by.

In need of fresh sustenance after such a long spell of speech, he took out the small pouch from his pocket once again. The pouch matched the underpants that peeped slightly above the belt of his trousers—striped, perhaps stitched from the same material. He opened the pouch slowly, as if it provided rhythm for his contemplation and helped his recollection of the details. He stuffed the paan leaf once again and popped it into his mouth. As the paan began to turn red, he kept chewing, then needing to talk, he tilted his head backward at a 45 degree angle to contain the red spittle that threatened to drip onto his shirt front.

"The Chief Minister of Uttar Pradesh, the state which housed the epicentre of all this action, and where the Babri Masjid stood, gave a 'shoot on sight' order to the police and paramilitary force who were called out at that time. The police who came to the spot went up to the Mosque first, prayed, and then opened tear gas and fire. We scattered in all directions. I and some of my friends, and a whole devout bunch of Hindus who had made the trip to vanquish the enemy—the present-day Muslim—found ourselves in dire danger of being shot down by the paramilitary. We ran into a small side alley, frightened for our lives.

Out of nowhere, as if by magic, the doors on the street opened for us, and we were taken by the residents into their homes, protected and fed till all quieted down."

Dr. Apte paused and gave a small shudder. Deciding that the *supari* had reached a point of optimum utility, he turned around and spat it once again into the nearest bush, possibly reducing the life span of said bush by several years.

"This is not all, Peter. I am ashamed to say that all those living on that street were Muslims. You can imagine my anger and shame when I realized this. We'd been raised from the time we were little children to believe that these were our enemies. We spent years hating them. Really, when you stop to think of it, with hindsight I can say that these Muslims who we hated so much had no hand in the history of the Moghuls who destroyed our temples. They were perhaps victims too, converted by the sword, or by some other chance shared their religion. I lost all trust in the VHP and the RSS. They cheated us."

"So what did you do?"

"After we got back home, I realized what a fool I had been; I, who thought I was educated and well read, smart and all knowing, had been tricked. Never, I decided, never would I ever believe them again, nor any other who teaches hatred and divisiveness."

He sighed. "And yet I at times forget their disingenuity, and get swayed when the call is given to protect our religion." It was a dilemma even I as a Catholic could understand—one's upbringing shapes one's whole identity. How can you ever truly escape who you are?

Chapter Five

The one calculation I don't care if they got wrong is the days of the week. One more day to the week and our year would be an eternity. And even if it is a cliché, I say thank God it's Friday, I'm happy for the weekend. Thirty-seven, single, living alone in my two bedroom apartment in Chembur is not the right recipe for reminiscing about the past.

I have worked for the last ten years in St. Xavier's College at Dhobi Talao, teaching mathematics: numbers occupy a large part of my day. I like certainty, calculated risks, clear concepts, and exactitude. Turning down a job in a bank that offered more money, I'd stuck with my academic view on life; not having to test my concepts with practice was more comfortable. Money occupies the mind, leaving no place for sensibilities and reasoning. It also occupies time. It makes you forget that there are other things to do, people to love, life to be lived. Teaching has not made it any better though. Zombie-like, I acquired all the trappings of a successful man: the car, the apartment, a club membership—which I hardly ever use—designer clothes. The much sought after bachelor. Have I attained the "life to be lived, people to love"? Something stops me every time I look too closely at life outside my work.

I watched the spider rappel down my ceiling and made mental notes to admonish Premibai tomorrow. Surely there is way to stop them proliferating, like sweeping cobwebs and killing the life in the middle of it.

I am attacked by spiders. They multiply indiscriminately, weaving their webs around our normal lives, not sticking to the shadows and corners they are supposed to lurk in. I shake my head—clearly Isabel's obsession with cleanliness is rubbing off on me. Or maybe it's Anna's visit making me aware of the cobwebs that have obscured the past.

Anyway, I have to read on. Read Anna, so to say. I could never admit to my callousness should she ask me—that I'd put the book away when she first gave it to me, too distressed to read it, too pained, too angry with her for making us miss her. Abandonment is a strong feeling. How used one gets to people, and how forsaken we feel—most irrationally.

I flip the pages through the years. Not much ever happened in the apartment building, not even in leap years, but we met, talked, fought and loved each other in an almost inevitable way. We residents had meetings for everything—Christmas, New Year—everything was a meeting. We had story meetings, play meetings, meetings to discuss the landlord... I flip the pages, wondering where to begin. I spot the year 1990 on top of a page and linger there. It was the start of events that changed our lives.

1st December, 1990

Late, around midnight, Dad pulled out the typewriter, a Remington he bought along with a Pitman's manual when I was ten. He'd ordered us to practise typing — "a very good skill to have." It was "steel grey," Dad every so often corrected our notion that the colour of the typewriter was black.

Tonight, Dad set two buff colour sheets into the carriage of the typewriter and inserted a carbon paper in between.

Earlier, around eight p.m., Isabel D'Souza, our neighbour and the wife of Inspector Joseph D'Souza of the Byculla Police station, had slipped down the dark stairs and hurt her ankle. "Good thing she did not break her back," Dad said, hammering at the stubborn 'a' with his right index finger as he pounded out a letter to the residents of the building calling for a meeting to discuss installing a light on the stairs.

Nothing could really break the back of Isabel D'Souza, I was sure. She lived in room no.18 with her husband and their son Peter, our brother and friend. Inspector Joseph worked long shifts, most of them at night, so much of Isabel's time was spent in our home. Big, tall, sturdily built, Isabel moved to and fro from our home to hers at all times of the day or late evenings to pass her time. She kept an eye on us when Mother was at work, and Mum, eternally grateful to her, said, "I can go to work only because of Isabel. I know she watches out for you."

Sometimes she arrived at dinnertime. Our dining table was too small for the entire family and so Dad and Mum ate after we four children finished. Francis, my little brother, watched for Isabel. He hated the vegetables that Dad insisted he eat, and as soon as Isabel came in, he'd plead with her to eat them. If she hesitated, he stood on his chair and stuffed vegetables into her mouth. Isabel, laughing and protesting weakly, would eat them and then give Francis a kiss before she went to the living room to see Dad.

But that day she limped as she went in.

"What happened, Isabel bai, sister?"

"I twisted my ankle, bhovoji, brother-in-law. If there were lights on the stairs I would have seen the banana peel, but the passage is so dark and so are the stairs. I don't know why the landlord won't clean the building or install lights!"

"Isabel bai, I will take up the matter," said Dad, who was ever ready to embrace a cause.

'What I don't understand is, why throw a banana peel on the stairs," Mother interjected.

"Joseph comes home late too. I worry for him. And if Peter should fall and have an emergency, what would I do? I have only one son."

"Bai, if you have a problem and Joseph is not at home, you can call me."

"Thanks, bhovoji."

Isabel was indeed our second mother, bound to us not by blood but love.

One of the few graduates of her day, vocal, presentable, yet a stay-at-home wife, Isabel, my dear mother, seemed to challenge logic. While Mrs Fernandes, simple, unambitious, worked in an office in the city as a stenographer, mother, educated, trained as a teacher, stayed at

home. Another of life's contradictions: Mrs. Fernandes, four children
to mind—reason enough to stay home; on the other hand, four children to feed. Dad, liberal man of the world, would have loved Mother
to work to occupy herself while he worked long hours; while Mr. Fernandes, conservative, would have loved to have been the sole provid-
er. But life has its way of dodging expectations.

With Mother, I think it was about me... or perhaps Janet, the
sister I lost. I suppose lost does not describe it. To lose someone or
something you first have to have it. I never did meet my sister. Her
death happened before my parents conceived me, or even conceived of me. Isabel, then a teacher at St. Mary's High School not
far from where we lived, had gone to school as usual. It was the school
that all of us in Billimoria Building—i.e., the boys—would attend. Or, I
guess I should say, all the Catholic boys; Ali, our Muslim neighbour, went
to Anjuman Islam, though it was twice as far from us as St. Mary's. The
Surve boys from the Hindu family on the first floor went to the municipal school a few steps away; finances, I suppose, being the uppermost
concern of Mr. Surve; and the Marchon boys did not go to school at all.

Mother went every morning to teach at the school and came home at
lunch break. Grandmother, who lived with my parents then, looked after
Janet, who had turned four that year. My understanding and knowledge
of the episode came, strangely, from Joe Marchon, our neighbour. Mother and Dad never spoke about it, neither to me nor between themselves,
at least as far as I was aware. But I knew it grieved her still. In the corner of
our living room stood a tall armoire of Burma teak wood, carved in a rose
design by hand and finished with melamine polish. The armoire, though
large, held only mother's clothes and private treasures. In the three drawers on one half of the inside, never left unlocked, she kept a part of herself
away from both Dad and me, claiming privacy in our little apartment
that could ill afford to allow exclusive domains. In one of these drawers,
she kept locked Janet's photographs, and on occasion, I have chanced
upon her, sitting in the armchair beside it, gently stroking the pictures
as she flipped through the pages. She would shut the album and never
let me look at them. Isabel could not always be understood, but I believe
that locked in those memories were an unshakeable sadness and guilt
that she bestowed upon herself, and which jostled with each other to
surface in quiet moments of solitude.

Joe, of course, had no such reservations toward silence. Ever ready to tell a story, truth or fiction, he recounted how Janet, sitting on a chair, quite inexplicably slid down and fell one morning, hitting her head on the floor. She lay there bleeding profusely. Those were the days when telephones were for the wealthy: for those who could afford to pay a deposit to the telephone company, and then some more to a lowly clerk in the telephone office, and then to his boss, or the minister of communications, and then to the wireman and electrician, to connect the instrument to your home. Though Dad was a police inspector and was expected to make money on the side, his Catholic conscience stood firmly in the way. So Grandmother did what the rest of the world does without a telephone. Desperate, and panic-stricken because of all the blood, she rushed to Joe Marchon next door. Joe, also without telephone, ran down the street to get mother from school.

Cutting out Joe's embellishment of the story, his emotions as he ran, the heroic dodging of traffic, and so on and so forth, Mother rushed back and took Janet by taxi to the J.J. Hospital on Mohammed Ali road, about 3 km away. Janet came home bandaged, and when she woke from her sleep the next day Mother realized that she had lost sight in one eye. Isabel gave up her teaching career to take care of her daughter. She blamed her ambition for her daughter's loss of sight. But that did not help; as if that was not enough, we lost Janet the next year very suddenly and unexpectedly from a blood clot that travelled to her brain. Apparently, her concussion had gone undetected. It sent Mother into shock. She descended, I am told, from sorrow and guilt to shocked sorrow, guilt, and painful depression.

Guilt is a strange thing. It gets hold of you and eats up little bits of you every time you pay attention to it. It stands out there, a hungry carnivore, ready to crawl through your insides, gnawing and nipping at every opportunity, irrespective of the event. Though I make it sound like something external, it really is personal; it cannot be verified or proved scientifically, nor can its dimensions be quantified or standardised into formulaic equations across random populations. It is just the freedom we have as humans to choose how we experience within ourselves the events in our lives or how we accept our histories. Mother's guilt, really, was her own freedom to choose what she experienced. The responsibility of actions or her failure to act and her choice of guilt to cope with the loss was purely hers. No one really blamed her. In a very Freudian way—and may it be recorded here that I have no qualifications to judge or analyse her, but nevertheless will—she carried "survivor's guilt," the guilt of being alive after Janet's death. Dad's choice of experience, on the other hand, was one of sorrow, but also one of practicality. How did he deal with Isabel? How does a man deal with a depressed wife, how does he liberate her from guilt? He could not resort to psychoanalysis, which was as yet not very popular. This was not a neurotic guilt but tied in with a choice she made. How could a psychologist answer the question on the meaning of life, of living and dying? Perhaps they could bring things to consciousness, but would that help her forgive herself?

A man of action, Dad came home more regularly, took Isabel to church whenever he could, and then did what Dad did when he solved our problems. He replaced my favourite teddy with a new one when I, on losing him, was inconsolable; if mother complained of a tear in her dress, he went out and bought a new one: fuzzier, cuter, more expensive. And therein lies the story of my birth a year later. Perhaps Dad had a point there. It saved mother from going into deep depression.

Mother, I think, secretly replaced Janet with Anna, as Janet became a shadow in her mind; I think it is in the playing with dolls, dressing them up and combing their hair, that lies the root of a woman's longing for daughters. Sons, on the other hand, are messy, and they wear the same kind of clothes daily, sport short hair, no ribbons and frills. So as much as Mrs. Fernandes was thankful to Mother for babysitting her children, Mother bonded with the Fernandes children like her own, especially with Anna. It fulfilled a mutual need. We, Mother and I, spent most of our spare hours with the Fernandeses, till we really were just one big family. And though mother called Mr. Fernandes "brother-in-law," we were not blood relatives. Dad's job as a police inspector took most of his time and his hours were uncertain. Mother depended on Mr. Fernandes to help her with men's jobs when Dad was away. Dad appreciated this arrangement with very little jealousy, if any; it took the pressure off him. Mr. Fernandes was too Catholic and very in love with his wife—Dad saw no threat. Besides, how does one have an affair in such a public neighbourhood?

I spent all my play hours with Ivan, Susan, Anna and Francis. Growing up with them perhaps was the real formation of my sense of self worth. They adored me and looked for wisdom from me. I was older than all of them, just two years older than Ivan, but five years older than Anna.

Amazing how age differences narrow as one grows older. Anna, who was half my age when I was ten, is now thirty-one. By the time she left for Canada, she was sixteen; a woman, an equal, enough for me to be furious with her, and furious still. But for a long time she was just a little sister, an adoring puppy I took for granted.

"We should put lights on the passages and stairs so that one can see where one is going," Mum suggested.

"It is the landlord's duty," Dad insisted.

"You know Billy will do no such thing, and this will carry on till someone is seriously hurt. Besides, I want a light so that I don't feel scared when the children come home late."

"Well, I will take on Billy," Dad said, turning sideways and banging his right index finger on the typewriter. I guess he ran into an 'a.'

"I just want a light on the stairs," Mum said.

At this point, Anna shifted gears and moved over to talk about Billy.

Since I was often unwell, I spent many a school day at home, standing on the balcony, bored and watching the street like today. Though it was mid-morning, the light was low on this monsoon day. My chin resting on crossed hands on the balustrade, my eyes followed Billy as he got off the bus with an unhurried gait. He wore white pyjama trousers and a loose shirt that he took off as he entered his little den.

A bald Parsee, Billy, the landlord, came every day to the room he retained for himself on the first floor. He filled the room with books, comics, and piles of newspapers. I never understood why. Peter said, tongue in cheek, that he had stealthily decentralized an archive, but of course the truth being Billy needed to hide them from his wife. Some piles touched the ceiling.

I went down to the first floor and sat across from him. He was clothed in only a jabba, a white muslin undergarment, with a thread running across his chest and neck and under one arm, almost like the sash beauty queens wear, if a sash could be a thread.

"Hello, my child. Didn't go to school again?"

"No, I'm not well."

"Well enough to sit here, though?"

"Yes. I just took my medicines, but I spent the night awake. My asthma comes only at nights." Then I plunged into saying,

"Billy, you can be a better landlord."

He gave an indulgent half smile and continued to read his newspaper.

"Billy, why don't you clean up the compound? It's so dirty. We could play there if it was clean."

"I don't dirty it, child."

"Yes, but we have no waste disposal. How can we do it?" He didn't look up from his paper.

"How about the toilets?" I persisted.

"What about the toilets?"

"The roof leaks and we have to take an umbrella to the toilet. It's quite a balancing act to hold the umbrella and squat and do all we have to do."

"You're young, child, it shouldn't be so difficult for you."

"How about the others?"

"For now we'll just talk about you. If they've a problem and talk to me I'll discuss it."

"Billy, you are very mean!"

"OK. I'll show you I'm not mean." He hobbled to the balcony outside his den, leaned on his walking stick and shouted, "Bar-wallah!"

The waiter in the restaurant on the main floor, right below his office, stepped out on the pavement and shouted back, "Kya mangta hai, saab—what do you want, saab?"

"One chai and one plate kebabs."

When the tea and kebabs arrived, Billy poured tea into a saucer and gave me the rest in the cup. We sat eating the kebabs and I sipped my tea silently. The silence was soon broken with loud bubbling sounds of Billy slurping his tea. He put down the saucer and said,

"We Parsees are very generous. Even in death, we give our bodies to the birds."

Chapter Six

Leaning back, I pushed my head on the couch and stretched my legs in front of me, knocking down a cup under the centre of the table. Did I place it there? Above me, near the ceiling, a fly struggled in the spider web. With a sigh, I changed my spot; going into the spare bedroom that doubles as my study, I sat where I could not be distracted by the odd cobweb. I kept my books here, lining all the walls: Blaise Pascal, Descartes, Hans Kung, books on the Holocaust, Mathematics, the complete leather-bound set of Encyclopaedia Britannica, and of course, P.G. Wodehouse. My writing desk, my collection of music CDs, long-playing records, spools of tapes, and art work kept me company. I sat on the rocking armchair that my grandmother left me, ancient, but Mother's meticulous preservation was reflected in the shiny polish of the lotus carved on the back rest. Anna's book lay open on my lap and I looked around with a sense of self...A man without a wife can take much pleasure in his hobbies and the things he owns.

Billimoria Building was not the cleanest of apartment buildings. The exterior paint was long since gone with the monsoons lashing over decades of unchanged weather; the balustrade, wrought iron, looked as wrought iron should, but the floors outside the general areas had dirt of the ages embedded, such that one could not see the black and white stone under. The ceiling, high, wooden, unpainted and with occasional spider nests that escaped the agile lizards' tongues, had here and there a pigeon's nest, some abandoned and some renewed. The toilets we shared with our neighbours quite increased our intimacy—standing in queues if the toilet was occupied by your neighbour, discussing the length of time they took or the kinds of sounds that emanated from behind the locked door, giggling, laughing, unconcerned that we may have embarrassed the occupant; yes indeed we were very intimate, almost a lifting of the seventh veil. It was also where I learnt relativity—i.e., the length of a minute was relative to which side of the door you were on. Sometimes our conversations and sense of fun descended to the level of Anthony's flatulence—a detail that is ordinarily kept private, only to be aired in one's marriage. Though I must say, nothing in Anthony Vaz's married life was much of a secret. The thin walls between room no. 15 where he lived and room no. 16, the apartment of the Fernandes family, ensured that privacy remained an elusive concept.

In a meeting on the second floor—one of several meetings we frequently held—it was decided that Anthony Vaz's family, the Fernandeses, and us would share one toilet. The Marchon family, the Olivera family, and Mimosa shared the next, and it went down the line, three families in a row to the next. Ours was the cleanest. Mr. Fernandes tiled the toilet with white glazed tiles and we contributed and paid Soni, the *methrani*—sweeper—to clean the toilet daily. The others in the building did not have a tiled toilet and the floor was coarse concrete, which became black over time. The landlord had no hand in cleanliness, maintenance, or waste disposal. Billy, so disliked by the tenants, cared nothing about his popularity. He came to his office and collected the rent, which I must admit was small and absolutely impossible to raise each year since, I suppose, as far back as from when the building was built. Our rents never did catch up with inflation, and Billy self-righteously pointed this out whenever anyone was indecent enough to complain.

Anna was the only one of us who shared private time with Billy.

Well, what can I say but that it was so like Anna? She had a trick of viewing the world through her own lens and placing it in some Anna logic.

I remember a time I was fourteen—Anna would have been about nine—and I came home from school, running up the wooden stairs two at a time, reaching the top a little out of breath. There was Anna, hanging upside down from the door frame of the passage, her feet wedged between the bars, using them as a hook. She had blocked the passage and I had to stop.

"What are you doing?"

"Looking at the world."

"What world?"

"The world, the air, the people in it, my thoughts."

"Why upside down?"

"Kalyug," she said.

"Kalyug? Anna, do you want to explain or will you just let me through?"

"My teacher said that this is the Age of Kalyug: the world is upside down. Good is bad, bad is good, our thinking is upside down. I want to see how the world looks right side up."

We saw Billy as mean, selfish, and idle. Everyone spoke of him with distaste. We saw a very dirty man reflected in our crumbling building, dirty compound, and the poor toilets. Billy himself lived in a bungalow somewhere beyond civilization; somewhere in some suburb that none of us knew of. It would take up an occasional summer night, arguing about where Billy lived. Sometimes we spent the evening speculating on the state of his home and his toilets, and sometimes we discussed his wife, Roshan Billimoria. She, in contrast to Billy, was a very fashionable Parsee woman, a bun on the top of her head, always very dark red lipstick and stiletto heels. She would come once a year, I suppose when Billy had not given her the previous month's rent, and would sit in his chair, call for the bar-wallah, and ask him to go from room to room demanding the rent. She made no conversation with any of the tenants, and we had no doubt her manner was disdain rather than reserve. So in our more vicious moments we disparaged her—"Roshan, what do you know; 'ray of light,' ha, ha." We imagined Billy's life at home with this 'light' of his life, and the tenor of our discussions veered between sympathy and wicked glee.

But Anna did not see him through our lens. She saw only the good in people, and why not? Ironically, Billy, who hated Mr. Fernandes for his attempts at unionisation of the tenants—mostly failed attempts, but nevertheless attempts—was always kind to Anna. Everyone was kind to Anna. Expecting Billy to do anything for the building, however, was carrying naiveté to the extreme...

The naivete we showed back then continues to disturb me, so forgive me if I repeat myself on how we carried on in a very solid enclave shielded from the reality around us, almost obtuse in the way we led our lives. Over and over again it spins in my head, especially in those moments when I encounter the triggers to my deepest despair: the paranoia of religious differences, of man's cruelty to man, and the lack of ability to understand events except with hindsight...Have you been deceived by a lover because you refused to believe her inconstancy even though it stares you in the face? And when she walks out on you, you wonder how you could have missed the signs and red flags? Revisiting the history of events, we pick on every look, every small sign, every twist that should have alerted us, and hate ourselves for not being suspicious, for taking no notice of all the road signs, and then finally for our own stupidity. Self-loathing...that's what it is. I find it hard to absolve myself or forgive ourselves collectively.

Though Dad was a police inspector, we still lived in a very protective bubble, away from the rough and tumble, engulfed by Mother and the Fernandes family. Bad was out there, somewhere, and sinning happened, like lies and disobedience to our parents; but sex, drugs, violence, theft happened almost in fantasy, in unreal worlds outside our perimeter, in the movies or in the Marchon household.

It was past midnight and Anna's book lay open on my lap. I imagined that she was already here now, not a month away. Right there under the lamp she stood: not Anna the child, but Anna the woman. And she—she tearfully said she was sorry for abandoning me, loving me as she did. She begged me to forgive her, to take her in my arms, to console her and tell her all is well. And I lovingly forgave, held her and kept her there right beside me where our hands and thighs stayed against each other, cell for cell matching our shared connection. But there was only that sixteen-year-old, bright-eyed optimist she was before Mohamed's death and the events that followed in 1993 caused her to leave, pushing my lids down, coaxing me to sleep...

We spent so many years without a light, going up and down the stairs in the darkness, but when Mother slipped on the stairs and hurt her ankle, we felt it was indeed essential. Surprising how significant a light on a stair can get, as we discovered on that gruesome day in 1993.

Chapter Seven

They say that the sun rises every day. But of course it is not about the sun but the earth rotating around its axis. Did it stand still during the night? Because I woke in dark daylight. The windows banged loudly, as if out there a lost stranger was seeking to enter. Sheets of opaque rain curtained my windowpanes, obstructing my view of the world. Wafts of morning coffee hung heavy, trapped within the closed doors and windows of my apartment, a signal that Premibai, at least, was at work, undeterred by the storm. I walked into the living room still clad in my pyjamas, and got horizontal on the couch waiting for her to bring my coffee to me. Leaning back, I noticed the ever more complex web woven by the spider, now clearer with my eyes wide open and alert; rainbow colours reflected in the threads belied their lethal intent.

I struggled with my images of Anna. That tall, slim girl with her two pigtails and shorts...childlike, woman-child, innocent, loving...what did she look like now, as a woman? Anna, my childhood playmate, the only girl boxer, matched with a different sparring partner every time. These boxing bouts made the boys shudder. Fights with Anna bordered on desperation. The boys, working hard not to lose to a girl (and thus be roasted till the next fight), attacked her with such purpose. But Anna never complained, and fought back as desperately as them—more, I suspect, from fear that we would shun her, refuse to let her play with us, than from courage.

Do you understand how disturbing it got every time I slid into my memories? Perhaps today I should meet with Dr. Apte before he left for the long weekend to Jaigad. I had yet to fully grasp the circumstances and turmoil that set in motion the events that separated Anna and I. But for now, coffee and Premibai...

As if reading my thoughts, Dr. Apte dropped by for breakfast. Without much ado, he lowered his bony behind into a chair opposite mine, took off his shirt, folded it carefully and draped it over the sofa back next to him. He rubbed his palms together, almost as if satisfied that he had accomplished his goal for the day. His manner ever smug, he leaned back.

"Ah, Peter! How is life treating you?" Then without waiting for an answer, he called out to Premibai, who was busy in the kitchen.

Premibai, who had already set the pot for coffee in anticipation of Dr. Apte's demand, appeared through the doorway smiling, as smug as Dr. Apte, tray in hand, cups tinkling on it as she made her way to the coffee table to set it down. She smiled at Dr. Apte while she awaited further orders, which he delivered immediately after the first sip of coffee, sending her scurrying back into the kitchen to execute the loud demand for breakfast—generally *poha*, beaten rice, favoured so much by my Maharashtrian friend. I recall going to Jaigad on his invitation for the weekend. We ate *poha* for breakfast and a different variation with yogurt for lunch, and then for tea we had a sweet variety of the same thing. Our specialty, he said. Anyway, he ordered, in the offhand way one orders servants, "Premibai, *mala poha paheje*—I want *poha*." Thinking of these two individuals, a Brahmin Maharashtrian and a low-caste Gujerati, and their smug certainty of themselves and their roles in life, I could not but speculate that were Premibai educated, were she a Maharashtrian, were she Brahmin, they may have found each other attractive, perhaps even suitable for marriage.

Premibai merely smiled at the orders, quite pleased she did not have to deal with an indecisive employer, and went into the kitchen, her mood near recovered by now after my admonishment over the spider and the teacup. She did not take kindly to my suggestion to keep the house clean—why don't you keep the cups on the table, *saab*? she'd countered.

"Peter, I am leaving for Jaigad. I won't see you for the next two months. I have to tend to the mangoes in my orchard. It is a very crucial growth period during the rains. My *nalike* sons will neglect it and I will lose income on it. So I decided to spend the morning with you."

"I will miss you, Dr. Apte. I wanted to discuss with you some issues that are engaging my thoughts right now. I thought I had time."

"We do have time; I leave only this evening. The rain is not good to travel in and I could have lunch here. Ask Premibai to make *dal*, lentils, and *bhindi*, okra, for me. You know I am a vegetarian."

Not ready with my questions as yet, I considered that perhaps I needed the weekend with Anna, or at least the notebook, first. I pondered on how Dr. Apte would react to my silence. He would be perplexed that I would want to do something other than take advantage of the opportunity to listen to his words of wisdom. Incomprehensible! I, on the other hand, would find it hard to justify rejecting his offer just to be on my own, reading a teenager's diary, as I guessed he would characterize Anna's journal.

I searched for those questions that I had told myself I would ask, the holes in my understanding that arose while reading Anna's journal. "Dr., I wonder if you could tell me what makes Hindus of today resent Muslims. I mean, on a micro level, why would, say, a person like you develop a dislike for a Muslim? Is it about a personal bad experience you had with Muslims? I mean, did some Muslim hurt you and you cannot let go and have applied the experience across the board to all Muslims?"

"Ah, my best friend, Naqvi, is a Muslim. I have had only good experience with my Muslim neighbours." Dr. Apte turned away, picking up the small vase on the table in front of him and examining it closely.

"But you did say that you grew up to hate Muslims. Surely it must have been something within your experience of them?"

He looked up at me somewhat accusingly. "I must insist that I do not have anything against them. But of course I must say that it is easy for me since I do not have daughters. If I did, I would not want my daughter to marry a Muslim. Otherwise, I do not have anything really against them."

"Why?"

"Firstly, if you know us, Indians don't like to marry outside our community. But then if it must be so, even a Catholic is more acceptable than a Muslim."

At my hesitation, he added, "Though, not meaning to offend you or anything, but Catholics will want our daughters to convert. Still, we do not have a uniform civil code in India. This personal law stupidity allows Muslims to take four wives. I don't want my daughter to marry someone and be one of four. We want our children's happiness."

I laughed. "With due respect for your feelings, Doctor, how many Muslims do you actually know who have four wives?"

He smiled. "Put that way, I admit, none. But look at the possibility. They can; and they are not bound morally and legally like the rest of us."

"But then, my friend, I know many Hindus who are not faithful to their wives and have mistresses; for that matter, so do those in other communities. I admit that social taboos and legalities are a deterrent, but then, really, I cannot think of anyone I know with four wives, can you?"

"Peter," he said patiently, even perhaps a trifle indulgent, as towards a marginally unintelligent child. "Do you agree that all of humankind is racist in some form or the other?"

"I would say yes to that."

"Yet we called it *apartheid* in South Africa. That is because it was enshrined within their constitution, if you get my drift." He hooked his index finger and tapped his forehead, a gesture that he used to condescendingly request that one use one's brain.

"We were also," he continued, "brought up to think that Muslims were dirty. Their homes were dirty and if you see the localities where they live..."

"Gosh! Walk around Bombay, Doc. This is a dirty city in many places, but it only reflects the income group and the availability of waste disposal and toilets. Just bad urbanisation!"

"Ah, you are giving me logic. I am speaking of the perceptions we grew up with. There is nothing real about reality except the way we see it." He had raised one hand halfway, his open palm waving in the air like a silent applause or a gesture gospel singers are wont to do. "What we see is defined by our retinas, the angle of the light, the distance we are from the object, and all that. How do I know whether my retina has the same dimensions as that of someone else viewing the same scene? Does not the majority define the rightness of my vision and validate it?"

"Surely once you grow up to an age of reason don't you change that opinion? Human organisms are structured to learn and unlearn at will."

"We are flooded with our day-to-day lives and we blindly follow convention, unless of course we are confronted with some overwhelming motive to change." His eyebrows meeting, his head cocked to one side, he pondered awhile. "Maybe something earth shattering such as falling in love."

At this juncture, he took out a small pouch tucked in his pants and began making a *paan*, choosing from other little boxes that contained diverse fillings, and then folding it into the shape of a samosa. Stuffing it in one go inside his mouth he began to chew loudly.

His words sparked a memory for me. "I'm reminded of the times as a child when I visited my friend Deepak's home. His mother graciously presided over our meals and served us. At first I thought she was being very caring, but nevertheless, we wanted her to leave us alone to talk our boy talk. Not much later, I discovered she did not want me to touch their spoons; one day she pre-empted my attempts to do so, explaining that she would rather serve us than we serve ourselves. We were sixteen, certainly old enough to serve ourselves. Do Hindus think we are dirty too?"

"Peter, you eat pork and beef. That's why they don't want you to touch their vessels; besides, we Hindus bathe in the morning and you people bathe in the evening. It is also a possibility that they were Brahmins. As you know, we Brahmins are particular on who touches our utensils."

"Weird. We didn't like vegetables growing up, but we didn't think that a vegetarian shouldn't touch our utensils."

"Don't get angry. You can touch the utensils in my home, Peter."

Chapter Eight

Strange patterns danced on the wall and ceiling cast by the floor lamp in the corner. My own shadow on the ceiling was gigantic, unrecognizable, dancing, mocking me, daring me to equal its dimension, fit in its mould, match its reality. It curved along the wall adapting to the angles and moved up on the ceiling, taking part of me in a different direction, unable to break through the walls, distorting, bending, and yielding to its confines.. One can hide, change one's shape, but there is always the shadow. I once read about the airplanes that cannot be seen, because of their coating or some such thing. But children look down at the road and point to its shadow—"Mummy, a plane"—while their mothers search overhead and worry about a child who sees non-existent things.

It was nightfall. Beyond curtained windows, the woodworm screeched in drunken madness; mosquitoes, troubled by the shrillness of the woodworm, flew madly, searching for blood to soothe the whirring in their heads. The occasional rickshaw honked, heralding a life of struggle—people returning late or hurrying to the station to get to work in time. In the distance, Bollywood played a tune on some chawl loudspeaker facing outwards into the neighbourhood rather than inwards to entertain those at the party. Look at us, look at us, we are enjoying our miserable lives, it shouted out to the neighbourhood that was trying in vain to sleep. Spiders rappelled down to places where unsuspecting prey genuflected over grace in anticipation of dinner.

My bed, polished Burma teak wood, with a rose-carved headboard that matched the armoire, had Isabel written all over it. One year, overtaken by bed bugs, Dad insisted we get rid of the bed. Mother, shocked that he could be so cavalier about something that had been in her family for sixty years, went silent for a week, pulling up the cotton mattress obsessively, searching for the buggers to kill. She went to Mr. Fernandes; as always the fixer of things, and above all Isabel's champion, he took on the project of cleaning the bed—*even if I have to kill them one by one with my bare hands, Isabel*—and salvaged the family heirloom.

My eyes caught the chequered pyjamas laid out on the coverlet by Premibai. That is new... Whatever...

I took Anna to bed with me, continuing from where I'd left off, in the midst of December 1990, and the incident with the stairs.

But now, this evening in our living room, the sounds of typing ceased to be a tik, tik, tok, tik. Dad was getting frustrated with the uncooperative 'a.' He had to roll up the paper to erase the mistake he had made.

"Damn," he said, as the paper tore. He looked at us watching him and then silently rolled the carriage of the typewriter and adjusted a new set of paper and carbon. He resumed typing. Dad typed fast, tik-tak-tik-tok it went, depending on the word, but every time he hit an 'a' he stopped and, ignoring Pitman's instructions—Do not lift your fingers from the keys—he raised his hands and tapped the stubborn key. His irritation mounted.

"One would think this is a simple one-page letter, easy to type — but so trying!"

"I just need a light," Mum repeated.

Dad kept typing. At the end of the page he sighed, shut the typewriter, put a plastic dust cover on it, and we all went to bed. It was only minutes before Dad, mouth open, snored vengefully—almost like he was attacking Billy in his sleep.

Billimoria Building ran two hundred feet along Nesbit Road, took a bend at the intersection, and ran another fifty feet on St. Mary's Road like a giant L. Not far from where we lived, a stable housed horses that during the day pulled carriages for the tourists. Now they clopped up and down with their owners who, after a day's work and feeding, took a nightly stroll down our street. The regular stamp of horses on the tarred roads sent my imagination soaring to Rudyard Kipling's "A Smuggler's Song":

If you do as you've been told, 'likely there's a chance,
You'll be given a dainty doll, all the way from France,
With a cap of pretty lace, and a velvet hood—
A present from the Gentlemen, along o' being good!

Five and twenty ponies,
Trotting through the dark—
Them that asks no questions isn't told a lie—
Watch the wall, my darling, while the Gentlemen go by!

I crept up to the window after I heard Dad snore and watched for the gentlemen to go by, imagining bootleggers and highwaymen in the small street where we lived. I sat on a little round table waiting, and when I heard the stamp of the horses I ducked down. But were there gentlemen as the poem promised? Oh, never. Only the old cobbler who lived in a little tenement opposite, hammering into leather, his back at right angles to the pavement, making shoes till the first crow of the cock as the faint light of dawn showed in the night sky.

Anna's habit of sitting Miss Marple-like, looking at the street and everything around, brought us up to speed on various things that happened in the night. The horses, Ms. Ezekiel's groceries, lovers in the night from the neighbourhood, she saw it all. She saw the stabbing of Mohamed Farooqui in the thick of the events of December 1992, she saw the old cobbler decapitated as he bent over the shoes he was hammering, a martyr to his work, unconcerned about the events that were sweeping around us at that time—we were not the only insular people on that street. Most people want simplicity. They live for the day, struggle endlessly for the survival of their family, earn for their education and food, and then die, sometimes needlessly, believing they did their duty.

In January 1993, a month after Mohamed was stabbed, when we thought everything could be left behind and we could pretend it never happened, events once again swept us in an unexpected direction, telling us that we really had no control and that our choices would continue to be redefined by fate or by the larger society we lived in. Nothing could protect us; our shared expectation of life could only make us insular, stratified, cut off from others who had a different ideology; but larger events affect us all. And though the street resumed its regular drum minus the beating of leather, minus the bent figure opposite hammering into it, and though we went on with our lives, our futures were foreshadowed by events that sucked us out of apathy and unwillingly into the country in which we lived.

Chapter Nine

"Le Coeur a ses raisons, que la raison ne connait point; on le sait en mille choses (The heart has its reasons of which reason knows nothing: we know this in countless ways)."

- Blaise Pascal

Particles of unknown matter from an unknown universe sailed in through my window, riding on a blinding ray of light from a sun that woke me up to its brilliance. September is a strange month in Bombay. It rains, it doesn't rain, not being sure whether the monsoon winds rising from the southwest breezes are spent on their way to us, or whether they will pass over in a burst. But this Sunday morning in September was meant for lazing and reading in bed. I sprawled head down—a more restful position than looking at my walls, which often brought to my attention the detail that needed caring. Resting on the Sabbath was as old as the history of God himself.

But it was not to be. The light, wafts, and sounds of a Chembur morning; the smells from the fertilizer plant clashing into the giddy smells of traffic, cooking, and coffee—they worked my nostrils, triggering the hairs inside to quiver restlessly like the paddy fields in the wind; they shattered my eardrums and fluttered my eyelids to wakefulness, thus pushing my limbs out of bed.

The church, Our Lady of Perpetual Succour, was not far away. Despite the languor that overtook my Sunday mornings, I often contemplated going to church to pray, embarrassing though it was for me. Spending most of my twenties and early thirties in Bombay's Irani restaurants, intellectualising about all things, including the existence of God, it was almost shameful to make this visit with intentions and an agenda. My views have bordered between the devout and atheist, settling in my moments of doubt to being an agnostic.

Here and now, I desperately wanted to believe in the existence of a God created by the Catholics; one that accepted the disbeliever, one that rescued you, and one that granted boons, protected and loved you and above all forgave you these departures from him. A God that would make my hapless desires a reality. Anna would be here a week from today, and I was torn. I did not want to judge by feeling, but by reason. My mathematical training needs the logical reasoning, the principles it conforms to, slow, methodical and not intuitive, getting to the bottom not by sentiment corrupted by our families and the company we choose to keep. I reject 'feelings' as a basis of conclusions. I have rejected the heart as a basis of scientific understanding, as the beginning and the basis of personal relationships. I have, in essence, rejected love.

Unseen, two drops of coffee had stained the dark patterned shirt I wore, a reminder of the haste in which I gulped my coffee before I set out down the street. The devout church-going Catholics crowd the small Chembur street I lived on as they walked along dressed in their Sunday best, synchronised by the clock and the chimes of the church bell. A Catholic street, if streets could be religious. I smiled inside my mouth, somewhere around my epiglottis, causing a small cough that I released into my clenched fist.

"Are you well, Peter?"

"Ah, getting a cold?"

"Nice to see you, Peter, nasty cough!"

Everyone on the street knew each other and I smiled once more, but openly. The land here, which also houses a convent, the school, and the church in addition to the residences, was endowed by The St. Anthony's Homes Co-operative Society Ltd., whose founders had obtained this land from the government and ensured that the area developed into this Catholic conclave in a once not-so-popular suburb of Bombay. I too, had moved here to be in a Catholic neighbourhood. I wonder if that makes me parochial. But it was comforting to live around people you understand—not necessarily those you like.

"Good morning, Mrs. Menezes, your roses are in bloom this year."

"Peter, how is your mother?"

"Peter, I would like to introduce you to my friend Ada's daughter. I think she is just the girl for you."

"Nice dress, Yvonne, you look charming."

We shared the same ethics, schooling, faith, and resultant expectations. I knew what they expected of me, what they expected of themselves, in a larger sense, and that was comfortable. Yes, it created islands—but what else can take away our fears?

So here I stood as I always did, outside the very crowded church. Latecomers, mostly men, crowded the doorway. The high ceilings permitted us to feel that we were looking in and joining the service. Most of the men stood there looking bored, preoccupied, observing the women in front, or just distracted. I joined in the prayer and the Mass, but when the congregation sat down to listen to the homily, I walked out, as I have always done from the time I was eighteen. Instead, I sat in the Udipi restaurant not far from the church and asked for a chai, *pani kum*—less water, more milk. Suddenly the doorway of the church cleared and the laws of physics applied. Matter cannot be destroyed. It moves from one state to another. Or perhaps osmosis, from a higher density to a lower. The restaurant filled up with like-minded men who, avoiding the homily, were either smoking or having a tea. I understand that there have been discussions on whether a loudspeaker from the church should be placed in the restaurant...

We entered once again when the congregation rose for the prayer that followed. Our timing was perfect. The priests there kept the clock consistent—you know the priest, you know the time...

"The Lord be with you."

"And with you also."

"Let us give thanks to the Lord our God."

"It is right to give him thanks and praise."

I will give you thanks and praise, oh Lord, I added silently, thinking of Anna.

Back home, I ate the mutton biryani Premibai had cooked. Sundays are for special fattening foods, one would think. Premibai runs through the oil bottle like it is water, even on weekdays. I pinched the rolls of fat around my stomach as I settled down to the meal. Premibai ate her lunch at my home, so the menus were aligned to what her palate desired for the day. I had very little control. I loved my vegetables crunchy but she had problems chewing with a mouthful of dentures, so veggies were really mushy. "She is the maid not your wife," Mum said, when I complained. "I have asked you a hundred times if not more, if you have not found yourself a wife, I would ask around for you, but you refuse to see women. I don't know what has bitten you."

No, only the heart knows what the heart knows, but you know Mum. Mother knows it all.

I took the notebook with me to the living room once again, sat myself down with Anna on my lap and let her talk to me.

Early next morning Mum had left for work. Dad sucked his stomach in to button his trousers. Finally done, he handed Ivan the typed sheet.

"Ivan, give this notice to all the houses on this floor. Make sure you give it to the parents and not the children. You can give it to the Surves downstairs, and you may leave out Miss Ezekiel."

All we knew about Miss Ezekiel was that she had a bright flower-patterned dress that, one unfortunate day, she hung on the clothesline, a tired old rope tied from one pillar to another outside her apartment. Sammy, the eldest of Joe Marchon's sons, held it against his body, modelling it for us. He had pinched the dress and was on his way to sell it wherever he could.

Not much later, long, crackling angry sounds from the room below floated on the hot, light air of the day.

"Kek, Kek, Ke." The angry sounds got louder. To our ears, everything she said sounded like "Kek, Kek, Ke." So that is what we called her.

Peter said, "Ah, Kek-Kek-Ke is missing her dress, I bet!"

We all ran onto the balcony that wrapped the building to look at Miss Ezekiel's first-floor apartment. We hoped we would finally get a glimpse of her. Diiiisappointed! Through the crack of her slightly open door the sounds came in spurts, but we could not see her.

All the fourteen-year-olds, Conrad and Gordon, the Cabral twins and Carlton Marchon, holding their noses, chorused, "Kek, Kek, Ke."

I felt uneasy. Bad enough Sammy had stolen her dress, but here we were, making fun of her. I had gotten over the habit of reporting all this to Mum, but I still worried about the right and wrong of it.

I walked away along the verandah, silently wondering what to do. Outside Mimosa's room, in the passage near the stairs, Sammy was trying to sell the dress to Mimosa, holding it up against her body—"it suits you, Mimosa, just your colour." Mimosa chided him in mild, polite tones. Her silky ponytail shook from side to side and she wagged her finger at him. "No," she said. "No. And you should be ashamed taking someone's dress and trying to sell it to me. Besides, I do not wear used clothing." Sammy put the dress down on the empty drum outside her apartment, put one hand on her shoulders, and with the other, he covered her mouth and ushered her inside, trying to get her to stop.

Seizing the opportunity, I grabbed the garment and ran downstairs to Miss Ezekiel's apartment. The angry "Kek, Kek, Ke" was still coming through the slightly open door. I pushed the dress through the door's crack. Still hidden behind the door, she grabbed it with the hand that showed a ring on it.

"Sorry, Miss Ezekiel, the wind took your dress off the line and into the compound. I just retrieved it."

"Kek, Kek, Ke," she said softly and closed the door. I could hear three bolts slamming.

I stood there staring at her door. Up on the door frame at the very top of the left side, a piece of carved wood that looked like a toy rolling pin gazed back at me. Peter, who knows all kinds of things, told us that Jews put it on their doors so that when the angel of the Lord comes to slay the sinners, he will spare those within.

There must have been more to Miss Ezekiel than met the eye. I feel a bit ashamed at the times we knocked on her door, and the endless irritating things we did to get her to come out into the open, mostly when Anna was not around. She never did, and we never saw Ms. Ezekiel. When Anna was little, she tattled on us to our parents, so we kept her out of all these forays until she finally agreed to keep it to herself. But she always wrote little 'sorry' notes, or sometimes cut up old Christmas cards to make her own cards and pushed them under Miss Ezekiel's door. We laughed at Anna's niceness, but she just smiled, undeterred. We did not know at that time how significant this little gesture would turn out to be.

Ms. Ezekiel spoke to no one. She never came out of her apartment. Isolated, avoided, it was hard to tell whether she kept away from us or we from her. I personally think she avoided everyone. Neither Dad nor Mum knew anything about her. She had lived there long before they moved in and had preceded every family living in Billimoria Building during my stay there. Much later, I read about World War II and the Jewish genocide, something that we never felt in India or internalized as part of our history, or perhaps it had happened here too and we had curled up in our bubble. Visions of Ms. Ezekiel suffering and escaping torture, or some such thing, sometimes popped into my head. She lived in fear or was just deranged, damaged, whatever. But our behaviour towards her could only be classified as unkind. Perhaps all children are indeed cruel, or perhaps we as children were, for we could only have exacerbated her fears of "they are coming to get me" when we knocked on her door and ran away. Is that innocence? I mean, children's lack of awareness when they mete out cruelty to adults...

One night Anna, who spent most nights at the window suffocating with bouts of asthma, saw the horses stop under Ms. Ezekiel's window. A basket was lowered down the window by bony hands (Anna swears she saw a ring glisten on the ring finger) and the horseman put a variety of groceries into the basket. The bony hands pulled the basket in, almost frenetically. Needless to say, it set Anna out on a new interest— what did Ms. Ezekiel shop for? Who was she married to? So we made up our own stories. We sat in a circle one idle evening, each of us defining a line in Ms. Ezekiel's life as we structured her secret existence from the depths of our collective imaginations.

Anna began:

"Once upon a time was born a very beautiful Jewish princess..."

"American Jewish princess," said Francis. This sparked a small argument.

America does not have royalty.

What do you know?

More than you, you fool.

You're a fool.

No you are the big fool.

Anna shooed them and ordered in gentle tones: "Just continue."

"She had long tresses, golden hair and fair."

"Her tresses curled down her back, and she laughed like a brook over smooth pebbles."

Brooks don't laugh.

Oh don't be literal.

"One day an evil toad disguised as a handsome Jewish banker asked her to marry him."

"She fell in love the instant she saw his false moustache and slick suit."

"'Yes,' she said, 'yes, yes, yes.'"

"So she married the evil toady banker, and went to live in the middle of his pond."

"One stormy night he was gone..."

"And she screamed so loud that her hair fell off, and only the few wisps were left, grey and dowdy."

"She could not face her family and friends, snobs them all..."

"So she came to India, and found Billimoria Building..."

"Where she lived happily ever after."

"With a bunch of kids," I ended, trying even then to redeem us, "her especially never being able to have one with the toad."

Chapter Ten

"All men should strive to learn before they die what they are running from, and to, and why."

- James Thurber

First day after the weekend, college has been hectic—Mondays are always trying. It is not just about the weekend or about the work. It is about acclimatization: Stepping out of one bubble into the next, or moving between lifetimes. As I looked at the columns of the courtyard with students buzzing around, ignoring its stone pillars, granite floors and the lush plants strategically growing to add man's version of nature's touch, I wished I taught something as frivolous as literature or psychology. Students of mathematics are so serious about the subject that they hang around seeking to ask questions both inside and outside of the lecture halls. Sure, they are so like me, but that is the problem, isn't it? I hate to see someone like myself. Oh! That came out wrong... Maybe I want the unknown, the incomprehensible; the predictable does not challenge; it makes life purposeless; dulls the senses and makes us happy...there is something very fashionable and attractive in seeming discontent...

Ms. Raikar sat in a corner of the teachers' common room, talking to her phone. I suspect there was nobody at the other end—she was so antisocial. I hate cell phones and almost unreasonably I extended that feeling to her.

I felt uncomfortable here amidst these people I have worked with over the years. I ask the eternal question a man who finds himself alone in his ideology asks—Is it me or is it them? I was restless, waiting to solve that differential equation...or discover that unknown variable which made the equation more complex.

I got away early and walked down the road to Victoria Terminus to take the train. Just outside the court, a legal advocate rushed up to me bowed in an almost a subservient tilt. For a moment I thought he wanted a handout but he asked me how he could help me—*An affidavit? Domicile? Certification of true copies?* This is what they call 'education by the wayside.' Lawyers who have gone through school, college, graduated and then done their law training are not much different from the man who sits outside Madame Cama hospital with a weighing scale, asking for fifty paise to weigh you. And those ear cleaners on the pavement across...people actually sit in front of them on the street and have their ears cleaned. From trimmed feathers to needles, their tools of trade would put off even those less fussy than me, but they seemed not to ever want for customers. What people do for a living never ceased to surprise me. And more surprising, and inexplicable, were their smiling faces and their focus; a functional equation to solve.

Pushing through this sandbox of people to cross the street to the terminus; stepping onto the train—the unwelcome closeness of wet, sweaty bodies, the stale smell of synthetic clothes that do not breathe, stale breath, hair that you can be reasonably sure doesn't belong to you escaping into your nostrils, tickling your ears; the reversal of the big bang, matter imploding on itself, swallowing into its black singularity all that is compressed within.

At my destination station, I rushed past the crowds on the street and up my apartment building stairs. I turned the key in the lock, stumbled into the room and finally breathed—not being the first man, nor the last, to sink into the comfort of home. Premibai had made the *chai* with a dash of ginger and put it in a flask to keep it hot, a habit with her, to save me making tea for myself. Stretching out on an armchair after a hand bath from a bucket of hot water mixed with savlon, antiseptic, to take off the fingerprints of the city, I settled down with chai and Anna. Flicking through the pages, I searched for the page where I last stopped, then picked up the delicate china cup Mother had given me from her collection and sipped my chai—a man who had earned his comfort.

Dad had called a meeting: Billimoria Building must have a tenants'
association. The leaky roof, the waste disposal, the water supply, the

dark passages and stairs, the dirty common facilities and nooks—all to be dealt with by the landlord. Oh, and the outside of the building, last painted long before I was born.

"Dad, how about Joe Marchon?" Ivan asked, still waiting around for more instructions.

"Leave him out. I will tell him myself."

Joe Marchon lived in No. 19 with his family. Dark, dapper, with very white teeth, he always bounced when he walked, trying to seem taller than he really was. He was forty? Fifty? Sixty? We did not know. We knew he was old enough to have fifteen children. Did he really have fifteen kids? He said so.

Waiting for Joe on a summer evening, we did a head count: Sammy the chor, the thief; Shirlen, Carlton, Miriam... We only got to twelve. The other three were dead, Joe explained. But none of us, not even our parents, knew anything about them.

Peter said, "Fifteen? Poof. Just another Gangabowdi tale."

When we were not visiting our grandfather on summer holidays, we often spent our nights after dinner huddling outside No. 19 waiting for Joe. Today was another such day. Dinner done, we converged onto the balcony where the summer night breeze had cooled the stone of the balcony floor. Eight of us—Peter, my brothers Ivan and Francis, my sister Susan, Carlton and Miriam Marchon, huddled together in a tight ring. Ali, who hardly ever played with us but always came to listen to Joe, sat outside our circle. We giggled in anticipation. We also shivered slightly, wondering about the Gangabowdi ghost.

Gangabowdi was a dark shadow in our minds. We clutched each other as we walked through eerie shadows and abandoned houses on either side of the road that had unpainted wooden awnings and wooden steps. No living soul walked there. Its only sounds were the whisper of the wind and the rustling of leaves. A large well—bowdi—marked the end of the street like a sinkhole from nowhere. Bowing over it, a fig tree wailed like a tormented woman in the rain, her tears mingling in the eternal spring of the water down below. Sunlight could not find its way here and in its perpetual dusk, the spirits of lost souls wandered aimlessly through the houses and the shadows of the street.

We heard quick footsteps on the wooden stair as Joe made his way up to the second floor where we sat on the verandah outside his apartment.

Joe looked happy. He loved his waiting audience. Of many a night, he whispered dramatically about the Gangabowdi ghost, and 'let the cretins have nightmares.' We, on the other hand, giggled and nudged each other, asking questions, looking scared at appropriate moments, urging him at others. The younger ones quivered and clutched each other in a show of fear; the older ones quivered with irreverence. Many hours were spent in disbelief and laughter, but we were nevertheless a captive audience and came back night after night for more.

Today, Joe crouched low, looking into our eyes as we sat on the floor.

"I was walking at midnight down Gangabowdi road..." He rubbed his palms together, a smirk on his face. Unhurried, he waited a few seconds before he went on. "It was misty but warm... I could feel a chill pass through my stomach..." He hissed at this point, with his finger travelling in circles around his stomach. "And then..."—a long pause, as he looked at us one by one around the circle—"I heard it."

Our fists clenched in our laps.

"A woman selling toffee." He held his nose and let out a shrill nasal cry. "Tof-fee, tof-fee."

Our hearts turned to ice as we sweated in the sultry evening air.

"I saw the toffee stand and went to buy some. It was a large thali, flat plate, of aluminum, set atop a wicker stand in the shape of an hourglass. Do you know what I mean?" We did—the kind you see with the hawkers selling buddi-ka-bal, old woman's hair, a kind of candy that came in white strands. "Know that?" he asked once again, waiting for our response.

We nodded.

"A cold breeze whistled near my ears..." Now he began to make long, low whistling, rasping sounds. The sound effects always enraptured us as much as the story.

"I pulled down my cap to cover them and shut out the frightening sounds that seemed like a mixture of wind whistling and a baby crying, if you know what I mean."

We didn't, because his rasping grated on our nerves, quite unlike the cry of a baby, but we kept silent, holding our breaths, waiting for him to go on with his story. He whistled through the gap in his teeth, looking at us one by one around the circle, then continued:

"She stretched out one hand for the money as she handed me a packet. Her fingernails, long, discoloured, turning inside at the tips, made me push my cap back to look at her face."

He stopped once again for a good minute, making us shift uneasily. We knew the best, yet to come, would be some far-fetched unearthly fabrication, yet we shivered in fearful anticipation.

"Suddenly the mists cleared...as if the wailing winds had lifted them to some unknown land." A long pause once again and, standing upright now, his arms stretched apart over his head like the crucified Christ—or maybe Barabas would be a more appropriate simile. He turned and attempted to look at the far horizon, not very far, for it stopped at St. Mary's Road, the buildings opposite limiting his view.

"The stand was there, but there was nobody behind it..." He took a long look around the circle. Francis shivered and huddled closer to me.

"I dropped the packet of toffee like the hot stuff it was and strolled away down the street, whistling like nothing had happened." Joe rubbed his palms together, looking satisfied.

"Why were you there in Gangabowdi on a dark and misty night, Joe?" Peter asked.

"The spirits beckoned me," he replied, never at loss for an answer. "You see, I was born in a veil."

Joe defied definition. He represented everything that we were brought up to despise or avoid. If there were only the Ten Commandments to keep, as we thought, they should be easy to remember. Joe broke every one of them like they did not exist in his memory. There was no good and no bad, so perhaps it was about quantity not quality. He lived his life without shame, without law or rules, just invented the day with each day.

I feel reasonably sure he lied about his jobs as much as the number of children. His life was one bad novel. If the heart said, here is a bad story, evidence played out the truth. Most times he was away on a "business trip," he actually spent it in an 8' x 8' cell in the Arthur Road jail. If not for Dad asking us to keep it quiet, we would have broadcast his secret in our very public sharing of all that happened within the precincts of Billimoria Building. But Joe was our story teller and as story tellers go, especially when television was not an option, he was most sought after by us. Our parents, on the other hand, kept their distance.

The reasons were multiple and no secret to us. When I was little, every morning at about 6.00 am a cock crowed somewhere from the depths of the B.I.T. chawls a block away, waking all who must wake at that hour, and barely two minutes later the baker entered the premises of Billimoria Building to deliver fresh bread to our doors. He carried two deep straw baskets, a bit worn from use, strung on either shoulder. Barefoot, sprightly, each morning the first knock on our door was Abu. One basket weighed down with bread for all the tenants of Billimoria Building counterbalanced the other that held the daily bread supplement of the Marchon family, thus preventing him from tipping over.

The butcher who visited us every morning with a basket made of straw, different from that of the baker—a curious huge V with handles on the top loaded with twenty-two pounds of beef—unloaded all twenty-two pounds at their door. The rest of us ate meat only on a Sunday, sometimes alternate Sundays, and bought ours from the butcher's shop on St. Mary's Road, very near the church. We just could not afford that luxury.

Huge bags of clothes went to the dhobi from room no. 19. Huge bags of clean clothes came back each day. Our clothes were washed at home by a maid who worked for many homes, and we ironed them ourselves. We settled our bills every month, but the Marchon household, averse to maintaining a daily or monthly account, postponed their payments for some convenient date in the future. And oh boy, were they generous! Strangers, friends, their friends, all kinds of people constantly dropped by; some stayed the night, others spent the day or several days, and some stayed with them for months. Food flowed, and sometimes Miriam would bring out a plate of tomatoes stuffed with mince, since we were not allowed to enter the apartment. The food that came out from their kitchen was amazing to us who were used to traditional Mangalorean cooking–being immigrants to Bombay from Mangalore–and we hoped she would do it more often.

"I am expecting my inheritance," Joe explained to anyone who made immediate demands for payment. Like in the cigarette advertisement, the Marchon family lived life king-size. This carried on for many years, until the year Anna was born. The inheritance never came: at least not by then.

Have you ever waited for a bus for a very long time in order to take it just a short distance away? Say a ten-minute walk away; you wait ten minutes for the bus and think, 'Heck I should have walked.' Now you have to make the decision whether to walk or to wait. You think, 'Well, the bus has not come for ten minutes and so it may come shortly. If it comes within ten minutes I will still be ahead.' So you wait the next ten minutes and think, 'Now that I have invested twenty minutes in the wait, perhaps I should wait a bit longer...' and you never hear about the accident on the road that has cancelled all services.

The tradesmen, though now close to bankruptcy, were afraid to stop delivery and cut their chances of ever being paid, but bordering on panic, they began insistently demanding payment from the Marchon family. Soon, the butcher and the baker, who were the most affected, were no longer able to work on credit with their suppliers, and having no cash, they camped outside the Marchons' door from morning till the street lights went on. This was both embarrassing and dangerous for Joe Marchon, who left home when the cock crowed over in the B.I.T chawls, and long before the sun peeped over the horizon. He returned only very late at night, treading lightly on the stair, not so much as not to disturb the neighbourhood, but in fear of lurking creatures or unpaid creditors. This cat and mouse game, as Mr. Fernandes later described it, carried on for over a week. Then one day, at about nine in the morning, we all converged on the verandah, drawn by the piercing din. The baker, sobbing loudly, was banging his head against the wall and the butcher was shouting profanities in Hindi, hitting the wall with his fist. It did not need much investigative skill to find out the reason for this commotion. The Marchon family had disappeared! In their home was Lulu, Joe's eldest daughter, and her husband and their two sons. No, they did not know where the Marchons were...no, why the hell should they know? No, this is our home...who are you? We did not buy anything from you...we are not connected with the Marchon family...

The baker, I am told, the more susceptible of the two, killed himself. The butcher, who worked on credit, had internalized a valuable lesson and disappeared too, leaving a trail of creditors looking for him. The Marchons stayed away for seven years, returning when I was twelve. By then the butcher, baker and all the other creditors had given up hope, killed themselves, disappeared or just started life afresh.

Gordon and Conrad Cabral never came to story-telling nights.

Though they were our playmates from No. 3 on the other side of the L, they were no longer allowed anywhere near the Marchon children. Two summers ago, as we usually did, we gathered to walk to Mazagaon Hill. The Hill, two blocks away near the old tram terminus, stood on top of a reservoir with several little gardens that were like a maze. Each little hedged garden had a gap for entry and exit. Our summer holidays started in April and went on till June, and we spent at least one day a week in the gardens. Every Thursday all the children from the buildings in the neighbourhood would run in the late afternoon to reserve one little garden to play in.

Most days Shirlen and Miriam Marchon did not come with us. They were older and were more interested in boys their age and in dating. Susan and I, on the other hand, did not dream of dating, because Dad would throw a fit. "You will marry whom your Mother and I choose," he reminded us at regular intervals.

That summer Shirlen and Miriam decided to come to the gardens with us. We walked down Nesbitt Road with clusters of children racing to grab a garden for the evening. Gordon and Conrad ran ahead while we ambled along, knowing we did not need to rush—our advance party would secure our garden.

Along the way, Shirlen and Miriam, whose dresses were too short and necklines too low, flirted with the boys from the building down the road. Miriam stuck out her tongue at them and slowly moved it over her lips, and Shirlen put both her palms under her boobs and shook them.

We were embarrassed. Susan held my hand and pulled me ahead.

"Don't look back," she said. "If anyone sees us with them they will think we are part of this." We sped ahead, quite ashamed to be seen with them. We pulled down our skirts to make them longer, and Susan pushed up her t-shirt to cover the tiny V at the top.

Meanwhile, the boys from the other building flirted with Shirlen and Miriam, and soon they caught up to us. The four of us walked up the hill to the garden Gordon and Conrad had 'caught' for us. That day we played langdi—lame woman. We split into two teams, there being so many of us. Gordon and Conrad were made captains of the two teams and they were given an opportunity alternately to choose their team. Shirlen and Miriam were the last to be chosen and they insisted in being in the same team so Gordon let go one player and took them both. Both teams stood in a circle. One team sent in a catcher and the other sent in two runners. The catcher hops on one leg, trying to tag a runner. If the hopper gets tired, another player from the team hops in. When all the members of a team finish hopping it's the other team's turn. The game ends when everyone gets tired.

Miriam and Shirlen, however, were peeved. The boys from the other building kept booing them every time they were in the ring. Unfortunately Gordon's team lost, and our silly cries of victory—"We won the game! You won the shame!"—did not help Shirlen's and Miriam's mood either. As dusk fell upon us we began to move towards home. Dad had some strict rules: "You must be home before it is dark."

We started down the winding path from the hill. The boys from the other building followed us, still booing Miriam and Shirlen.

Shirlen, now sorely tried, turned on them and, rolling her fists in the air, said, "You have balls without gravy!"

"Booooooo."

Miriam and Shirlen were now both planted in the middle of the path, fists in the air, shouting, "Balls without gravy!"

"Booooooo."

"Balls without gravy."

"Booooooo."

"Ballswithoutgravyballswithoutgravyballswithoutgravy....."

"Booooooooooooooooooooooooooooooooo..."

That night, Gordon and Conrad, fighting at home, kept shouting at each other, "You have balls without gravy!"

"No. You have balls without gravy!"

After which, Mrs. Cabral walked down the corridor knocking on all the doors, leaving out only No. 19, and recounting the events of the day, told all our parents never to let their children play with the Marchon children.

Chapter Eleven

That was far from the most damning reason we were not allowed to enter the Marchon household. Much more went on there, not all of it legal. To our very Catholic sensibilities it was the House of Sin. In the almost peaceful and quiet Mazagaon, the Marchons' apartment seemed a hotbed of international crime. Pimps, drugs, highway robberies, strippers, and smaller crimes like dancing, when the rest of us were discouraged from such frivolity, abounded.

Unbeknownst to most in the building—for our parents might have organized to kick them out—Mrs. Marchon and her daughters carried on a lucrative business. But their unsavoury reputation outside our awareness never deterred gullible young men from hanging around the girls and even proposing marriage. Perhaps it even enticed them. The result was a puppy fest. Boys hung around, crowding the stairway and the pavement in front of the building. There were occasional arguments and fisticuffs, presumably over the distribution of favours, but most of the time they were too absorbed in trying to look their attractive best for the girls.

But it seemed these boys had no chance. The year I turned fifteen, every evening a sleek, racy car zoomed into our street that had, forever since I had known it, been trafficked only by trucks and horses at night. Honking loudly for Shirlen and Miriam, the car, its roof down, driven by a loud, flashy man with a huge crystal on his ring finger, several gold chains around his neck, and a printed silk shirt, blared loud music. Though the man always came by to pick them up at night, he wore shades on his eyes to complete the picture. The car seemed filled to the brim with young, beautiful women, necklines at their waist, a criss-cross of legs, arms, and breasts, voices laughing in gay tinkling tones, as they waited down there for Shirlen and Miriam, who took their time to doll up for the evening. We all hung out of our windows to watch this little tableau played out each evening, and on many an occasion had to put up with Shirlen and Miriam tittering about Bobby picking them up, Bobby this...and Bobby that!

Shirlen, the prettier of the two, with full lips softened with light pink lipstick and large eyes that sat on a very soft face, was the more popular. Most of the men that hung around the Marchon household and at the bottom of our stairs were hung on her. While Miriam had her own following, she did not have the same charms as Shirlen, nor could she match the number of young puppies that wooed Shirlen.

Mr. Fernandes did not like this development. He had Susan and Anna to consider. His daughters should not have to pass, as they went about their daily business, a bevy of hot males who were in all states of arousal. But nothing could be done and no known laws seemed to have been broken. The Fernandeses added this to their petitions in their daily family Rosary: 'God, please let Shirlen and Miriam find a good match.'

Prayers of the faithful never go unanswered...my mother and Mr. Fernandes would vociferously testify to that! And indeed, it was not much later that the Fernandeses' petition was heard. Amit happened. A sailor, first engineer on a shipping line, tall and handsome as most Punjabi men are wont to be, he seemed like the answer to the prayers of the Fernandes family.

Amit's family lived in the North of India; how easy to be tempted in a city where you find yourself young, handsome, rich and alone! Mother, of course, expressed her view on why young men should live with their parents till they are formally introduced to the young women they are to consider for marriage—preferably by the parents. Young men were susceptible to the temptation of a woman. This poor boy did not have his parents' guidance when he most needed it... I must admit we did of course imagine the part of rich and plump in the pocket, more our own building up of an imaginary story with lack of adequate information about this very happy stranger who had become part of the wall decor in our passage near the stairs.

"She is perfect. She is all the woman I want," Amit told Dad one day when he encountered the puppy standing against the wall in the passage and nodded politely, saying, "Waiting for someone?"

We watched, every day, Amit blow kisses from across the street. Amit dismal. Amit ecstatic. Amit in every stage of emotion, completely in thrall to Shirlen's favours. She frowned, she laughed, she smiled, she blew kisses; any amateur lip reader could see him say, *I love you:* A veritable romantic silent movie. Shirlen, for her part, was smitten, flattered, delighted, thrilled, charmed; the attention from someone with the presence of Amit had moved her upwards on the social scale. From the small-time Romeos that hung around the entrance of our building waiting for her to grace them with a glance here, a smile there, a pout, and sometimes a kiss, to this very well employed, educated and good-looking young engineer, she had indeed moved up. Up until now, sex had ruled high with her admirers; this was different.

We had to put up with the endless, "He is so handsome, so clever!"

Nothing makes a woman more attractive than when she is on the arm of another man. The courting of Shirlen revved up. Desperate puppies knelt when she passed them on the stairs, some offering rings, others just pleading for a glance.

Any young man who finds himself competing with an assortment of other suitors pre-empts their pretensions with a proposal. Amit knew this. Shirlen was so flattered into saying yes that she waited for nothing. Amit wanted to marry her, thus raising his attraction in her eyes. No details were asked of Amit, no meeting with his family, no background checks, none of the safeguards mother would have subjected me to, nor the Fernandes children, under similar circumstances. Besides, with her kind of background, what did she really need to check? Amit was so obviously not an axe murderer...

The news of Shirlen's marriage caused a lot of excitement in Billimoria Building, but Mr. Fernandes was the happiest of us all. "At least now the disappointed buggers will go home to their mothers," he said, adding, "Hope that Miriam gets lucky too."

Amit was not destined to have the extended honeymoon he had expected; summoned back to join the ship he worked on, he had to sail out in less than a week after the wedding.

"Women do not live alone in India; you will have to stay with my mother or yours, but I will soon take up a shore job," he promised, "and we can have our own home."

So Shirlen chose, like any woman given the option, to stay with her mother rather than leave Bombay and live in Chandigarh with her mother-in-law, a stranger she had never met.

Once again, as when Amit courted her, we encountered the heavy petting in the passageway as we made little sorties to and fro with reports back to the others. All kinds of scenes were being played out there: "I will miss you," *muahhh*, "I will be back, darling," *muaaahh*, and so on and so forth; the kissing, loud muaahs, silent explorations of Shirlen's throat, hands groping under her blouse, squeezing her breasts unashamedly, all were conducted in full view of those passing up and down the stairway. And in between, curious young eyes peeped hungrily, an education in boy-girl relationships. None of this was part of our lives except in the occasional English film screened in the St. Mary's auditorium as part of the summer holiday club for children. Shocking though it was for us, we were all secretly excited. I think in some way we all formed our ideas of love from this performance in the passageway.

Finally, the black and yellow cab drove up to the entrance of the building. All the windows along the curve of Billimoria Building were filled. Leaning over the sill, we followed carefully the ensuing farewell. Across the street, even the old cobbler put down his awl and peered through his glasses at the spectacle.

The cab driver got out and took one small suitcase that contained Amit's belongings (none of the wedding gifts that were perhaps slowly dwindling with Sammy in the same house). Shirlen, sniffing loudly, clung to him like a limpet in the rain, as if afraid of being washed off. If Shirlen looked like hell, Amit was an epitome of pity. Squealing, his body shuddered in spasms as if in some forgotten Chinese torture.

Finally, the cabbie, who had spent the last fifteen minutes polishing his rear view mirror, honked several times to get their attention. He had made sure to turn down the meter the moment he had set out from home on being summoned by one of the Marchon boys. Amit, ever the well-trained shippee, saw Shirlen into the cab first then climbed in himself. The cab set off toward the docks, where they'd say their final goodbye. Only when the driver turned into St. Mary's Road did all heads abandon their posts at the windows. Once again the hammering of leather interspersed with honking traffic and loud music from the B.I.T. chawls resumed, bringing us back from our reverie of love, babies, and the happy-ever-after.

As far back as Hippocrates, and even as early as biblical times, the recognition that the blood is the carrier of chemical messages that affect mental and physical health is evident: Julius Caesar felt its influence when he distributed land to Cleopatra's children. Romeo felt it with his Juliet, driving them to death. All lovers, both those who made it into history and those who didn't, were probably programmed by the same kinds of hormones coursing through their blood as those that directed the next few hours of our own much-smitten Amit.

Saying his goodbyes to his new bride, he boarded the ship. Shirlen's tears were now dried and she turned on her heels, seeing that there was nothing much left for her to do there. Amit high-fived a few colleagues, set his bag on the deck, and looked out onto shore till he could no longer see Shirlen's back retreating down the road in the low light. He turned, picked up his bag, and proceeded to put it in his cabin. He spent the next two hours trying very hard to get into the swing of things. Not unlike our own detested Mondays, spending so many months on shore had made him a bit averse to the long days at sea that he faced before him. The Arabian sea, once blue and appealing, now looked muddied and rough, and the stars in the sky were obscured by the glow of the city lights. The changed situation in his personal life made this scene even more depressing, and anxiety sped into a rousing sense of need, his testosterone activated by his new marriage. It is amazing how one can be single with no one to love and never feel lonely. But the arrival of a loved one on the scene of one's heart makes loneliness feel like a part of one's body is being torn off.

An hour before they could set sail, the love-stricken puppy grabbed his duffle bag and ran ashore, his hormones shouting, I can't, I can't, I can't ...my heart won't let me...

Amit took a cab back to Billimoria Building, where he expected to be reunited with his wife of very few days. As the cab cruised down Carnac Bunder, he did not notice its blocked streets, nor that the cabbie had taken a circuitous route. So strongly was he in the grip of his hormones that he noticed nothing beyond his nervous excitement the entire journey. The cab stopped short of the entrance, and within seconds, he was running down the street to Billimoria Building.

He ran up the wooden stairs two at a time, turned in the passage and pushed open the door. But Shirlen was not there. We heard through the thin walls his troubled, disappointed voice asking, "Where is she, Mum?"

"Colaba Causeway, shopping," we heard her reply.

"Oh, oh," Isabel, privy to most details provided by Dad, said knowingly, "this is not good."

We stood at the window watching him run out on the street, hail a cab and heard him shout, "Colaba," to the driver, almost like he was kicking a spur into the sides of a horse. We could hear every expletive and every impatient inflection in his voice as we prayed silently for Shirlen. *Damn, every red light is on today, faster, faster, where is she...* went swirling in our heads as we mentally followed his path. As the taxi drew near the roundabout opposite the Regal Theatre, he saw her. *God, she is beautiful. She looks sexy dressed like that... Hello, hello, what is happening here... what the hell is that man doing with her... why won't she let him go...?*

He stopped the cab in front of the Regal, handed over fifty rupees—"Keep the change," he said—and darted across the road, dodging the traffic. The rest of the story is from Shirlen's own account of that evening. Walking up to her, he silently took her hand. Shirlen, who had been very accustomed to living as she pleased without question, felt the initial small flutter of panic die quickly.

"Come home," he said gently. They caught another taxi outside the Regal Theatre.

"Mazagaon," he told the taxi driver.

"Which way would you like to go, sir?"

"Any way you wish to take but just get us home," he said distractedly. He held her close in the taxi, then drew her head onto his shoulder while he stroked her hair silently. But instead of heading home, he took her to a friend's apartment. His friend had sailed that day on the very ship he had abandoned. Despite his scramble to get off the ship, Amit had thought to borrow his key in anticipation of his need for private time with Shirlen.

He ushered her in gently and took her in his arms... kissed her passionately...licked the mole under the lobe of her left ear. "Take this off," he said, tugging at her clothes. She unbuttoned her dress, as she seductively jiggled her breasts at him. (Shyness not being Shirlen's domain, she jiggled her breasts as she recounted the events to us). Amit walked around switching on the lights, quite unfamiliar with the switches; he turned on every switch in the room as he watched her undress.

"Lie back on the couch," he said gently.

She lay there a long while, looking at him.

"Amit, you have switched the iron on."

"Why yes." He switched it off, unplugged it, and began to coil the wire round the handle, slowly matching his step with the action.

"I love you," he said in a quiet voice, walking towards her. He sat down beside her, stroked her left breast gently and then, with an equally gentle movement, he took the iron and singed her breast with it.

She screamed in agony while he repeated the motion with the other breast ... and then her right thigh and then her left. She could now only whimper with shock but soon the horror of the scars that it would leave overrode the horror of his actions; searing more than the burn itself.

He put the iron down, took a bottle of coconut oil and tenderly applied it on her burns.

"I love you," he said.

When they returned home, a hysterical Shirlen recounted the episode to her brothers Bruno and Oswald. Much turmoil resounded through the second floor of Billimoria Building. Banging, clanging of pots and pans, loud noises, yelps, and screams emanated from the Marchon household for the next hour. Finally, at the end of the hour Bruno and Oswald dragged a bruised Amit by the collar out into the passage, screaming, "If we see you anywhere in Bombay, you will have to change your name to Bob; yes, because that is what you will be doing—bobbing in the sea without your hands and legs."

Chapter Twelve

That was no empty threat from Bruno and Oswald. Early in January 1982, about eight years prior to Shirlen's disastrous marriage, when I had just turned ten, shocked disbelief hit the good God-fearing Catholics in Bombay. It would not be exaggerating to add horror and fear to the emotions felt upon hearing that Fr. Justin D'Mello, the parish priest at a small church in Igatpuri, a small town on the outskirts of Bombay was found murdered, his head battered, left to die in the aisle of the church. It hit the headlines, and all Catholics, hardly believing any crime could happen to, or be committed by, them, talked of nothing else: "Can you imagine, *men*...Catholics?" "...that, too, a Catholic priest, *men*..." "The world is not safe anymore, *men*..." Men being used in the same way man is used in colloquial English spoken in some of the colonies.

Investigations led to the sacristan, who had disappeared with the box of offerings and some of the artefacts of the church. The police traced most of the artefacts: the monstrance was discovered in a house down Nesbit Road and the chalice in the Marchon household. Oswald and Bruno were taken into custody one night as the building slept. Despite the thin walls that separated the rooms, nobody heard the proceedings. Mr. Fernandes showed Isabel the report the next morning in the *Times of India*. Buried inside the paper on page five, a two-inch column gave the barest details of the arrest. Isabel already knew of this, of course, from Dad. So now she nodded her head too and fro and made pretence of hearing it for the first time. "Yes, Mr. Fernandes?" "Oh my God, Mr. Fernandes!" She even giggled at the revelation that she was living next door to all the action... Mother's sense of humour triumphed over her conscience. She *hmm, hmmed and ah, ah, ahed* as he spoke. *A chalice in the House of Sin...maybe they will be converted...or they will offer curry instead of wine*—she continued to giggle, quite amused by her own joke, till Mr. Fernandes, who had been looking self-righteous as he showed her the paper, soon saw the humour in the situation, too.

Of course, with the typical cruelty of children, "So where is Oswald?" we asked Miriam when she came to play with us that day. "He's gone abroad," she promptly replied. Talented! Yes, talented actors they were, the Marchons. We sniggered when they were not with us, and I suppose they knew. But they had developed a coat that was impenetrable, knowing that this was their lot.

Oswald and Bruno were released with a light sentence for robbery, while the sacristan was given life imprisonment. The Marchon boys remained undeterred, but they grew more careful and more polished as they continued their life of petty crime.

Chickpea—as Joe lovingly called his wife, Mili—only stepped out of the apartment once a week, when the light was low and no one could see her; then, she stood leaning on the railing looking across the expanse of the compound at the road. She was taller and much larger than Joe and, apparently, had been the beauty about town before she married Joe. In the words of Mr. Fernandes, she was "a Queen Bee, surrounded by all these drones hanging around, languishing, waiting for her. They buzzed around her," Mr. Fernandes added and gave a short laugh, satisfied he had said something quite witty.

Mili was ahead of her time. She dared. She dared to raise a bold eye at the young men in Mazagaon...She dared to look good, though she was not a classical beauty. She dared to flirt, when women were demure. She dared to walk unchaperoned...she dared everything. She was available—that certainly was her greatest attraction. Young men hung around the corner of the street at 7.00 each morning waiting for her to pass, wondering who she would look at that day. Who would she favour, they wondered, as they adjusted their bow ties, and carefully patted the stiff, coiffed puff in their hair.

Her life as a young girl seemed no different from Shirlen's or Miriam's. I suppose those girls never had a chance, born to Mili, who never knew any different; their destinies were defined far before they were born. Mili's upbringing with a single mother of very modest means combined her attractions with pragmatism. Alighting on a plastic flower and dipping into its depths to extract honey, she eventually married Joe, who, much like Shirlen's erstwhile beau, when faced with competition wasted no time merely dating, and instead proposed marriage to her.

Watching Mili wordlessly look out into the night, I sometimes wondered about her. Did she deliberately avoid company? What did she think of, as she looked out into the silence? Was she unhappy, did she want a different life? Did she consider that her life could have been very different if she had not married Joe? Did she long for the days when men danced around her, or had she found her home with Joe? These were all unanswered questions, because she never confided in anyone—at least no one we knew. But one has to say that she ruled that household. Joe and the children never dared to cross her. It is difficult to know what hold she had over them—perhaps just being mother was powerful enough.

That was all we knew of Mili except for one very intimate detail. One summer afternoon on a Sunday, like every Sunday after a heavy lunch, our parents ordered us outside the house: "It is the only day in the week we can have a siesta, so don't disturb us." We, as usual, met in the passage near the stairs. Carlton, the youngest Marchon, joined us with little pieces of coloured paper cut out of old greeting cards and magazine covers; he sold them as tickets for twenty-five paise to any kid who had saved or could produce the fare. He escorted the ticket holders into his house one by one, to see Joe and Chickpea snoring in bed, with Joe's hand inside her dress, cupping her breast.

Chapter Thirteen

Anna's parents consulted with Isabel the day Mrs. Cabral visited them to insist that they stop their children from mixing with the Marchon kids. Certainly, the House of Sin and its inhabitants were a source of worry to the Fernandeses. Susan, Ivan, Anna and Francis were young and susceptible and could easily be led astray by unholy influences.

Isabel, how can we expose the children to such an environment? Should we ban them from playing with the Marchon family? How do we explain why? Children ask questions, you know. These questions flowed alternately from Nattie and Mr. Fernandes, as though they had already discussed the issue and not agreed on the answers that had presented themselves.

We were in the living room, Mother and I, and though I was eighteen, they looked in my direction when they spoke of children. It did not seem odd to Mother that they included me in this general dilemma they faced with Susan, Ivan, Anna and Francis. Isabel, whose opinion Mr. Fernandes respected, decoded the issue:

"We have several factors to consider. On the one hand, we could ban the children. Now, if we ban the children, do we tell them why? Or do we just risk sounding unreasonable? If we do not want to sound unreasonable, do we have to consider whether we are being unreasonable? If we give our children the information we have on the Marchons, our children will perhaps give us counter arguments, such as, 'We can play with them and not do the bad things,' or they'll accuse us of not trusting their judgement. In my experience, we'll lose such a battle and find ourselves inserting a very unreasonable adult argument, 'It is right because I say so.'" Isabel paused to breathe and take in a pinch of snuff. She tucked the snuff box back inside her bra and continued.

"On the other hand, our children are quite innocent and lead protected, regulated lives. How can they understand what is happening in that House of Sin? I feel innocence is the domain of their childhood, and no argument will convince me to deprive them of that. There will be time enough for that. They will discover the world and become jaded, undoubtedly," at which point she glanced at me, almost speculating on whether I had arrived. "But for now, we must allow them that joy of being children, the joy of innocence, the hallmark of being a child. Otherwise we would be stealing their childhood, so to speak." She sighed. "Our choices now may have far-reaching effects, and yet, on the other hand, we cannot have the *Marchons* introduce them to life! Then yet again, we must consider the Marchon children. Must we penalize them and deprive them of the good our children can bring into their lives?"

Brevity not being one of Mother's strengths, she went on, but not before another pinch of snuff appeared between the thumb and index finger of her left hand. The air swirled around a few particles, and Mrs. Fernandes gave a controlled sneeze. Isabel, ignoring the interruption, continued,

"So I would suggest, let the children play with each other, but we can lay down some ground rules. They should never enter the Marchon household." She finally stopped to catch her breath and once again took in a pinch of snuff, almost like a tic.

And so the verdict got writ in stone: *You may play with the Marchon children, but you will not repeat any bad language you learn from them; entry into their home is strictly forbidden, nor should they come to our home when elders are not around.*

Thus, Ivan, Francis, Anna and Susan were forbidden to enter the House of Sin. Anna naively thought that the ban stemmed from the girls' bad language and flirtation with the male gender. Every time I argued that there were more important reasons, she annoyed me by saying, "Peter, you are so negative. You see more evil than there really is."

"Perhaps you should talk to the Surves personally too," Mum said.

"Why?" Dad asked.

"Their children do not play with ours, and they do not speak English. So perhaps it is best you speak to them."

"OK, my dear. My Marathi is not great either, but I will be able to convey my message, I suppose. Of course I think it is quite unlikely they will attend."

"Why not? They are equally affected."

"I don't know, my dear. Not everyone likes to bell the cat."

"I don't suppose that Catholic couple on the first floor will come?"

"Quite unlikely, you know, especially after the gate episode, dear."

The first floor belonged to another world. Dad talked occasionally to Mr. Surve, who worked in the same office—often they walked to the railway station together. However, one could not really call that 'together.' Dad took long strides and Mr. Surve took little running dance steps to keep up with him. That made it difficult to have any bonding or conversation with each other.

On Diwali each year, the Surve family sent us sweets. We returned the gesture every Christmas. Perhaps that could adequately sum up our relationship with them. That is, if one ignored the occasional Christmas when Mr. Surve joined the men, specially invited by Dad, as they went from home to home, drinking—"Just one peg, my dear"—till they came home, ate the large dinner and fell on the bed in a drunken slumber, snoring for the rest of the day. I think Mrs. Surve was happy that her husband socialized with the men only one day of the year. They were the only non-Catholics in the building, other than Ali's family and Miss Ezekiel, and of course the Madrassi bachelors. Mr. Surve had one son and one daughter. I must shamefully admit we did not speak or play with them. How could we? We only went down to the first floor when Peter and Ivan, in the middle of a bored afternoon, would creep up to Miss Ezekiel's door and bang the knocker while the rest of us looked out from the other side of the L to see her reaction. Of course, she never opened the door, but we could hear the angry sounds of Kek, kek, ke. Most often, after such forays I slipped a guilty little "sorry" note through the slit under her door.

Mr. Surve did not talk to any of us kids, nor did his children, though his daughter was my age. Sometimes I think it was because we spoke English and she went to the municipal school and spoke only Marathi.

Actually, I would have loved to be friends with her. She was very pretty and she knew how to make Diwali sweets, our favourite treats. I sometimes stood near the stairs when I knew she would pass and smiled at her, words not part of our repertoire 'cause we were so different.' Mr. Surve's son would stand at the bottom of the stairs, and very often I got the impression that he wanted to talk to me. I would have rather it was his sister, but he would stare at me and sometimes I felt embarrassed. I did not tell the others, because you know how one tells a friend and they get all angry, then confront the person and the person then denies it all, leaving you feeling stupid. Telling mum and dad would only cause a similar problem. Dad would go to Mr. Surve and he would ask his son and his son would deny it, and of course, really, looking at me is not a crime; no, not really. So I did not tell anyone.

The Mitchells, old and crumpling, lived next to the Surves. Their apartment was directly below ours, but they did not mix with us either. After the gate episode, even their occasional hellos stopped completely.

When Francis was little, he crawled all over and pulled down the utensils in the kitchen and anything else in sight. Dad decided the only way to deal with this was to make a gate between the living room and the kitchen. Dad was a closeted handyman and spent endless hours on holidays stitching the tears in our shoes, or mending broken chairs. So one Sunday morning he sat down with wood, nails, and a hammer. Barely had he started on the gate when Mrs. Mitchell came knocking.

"Mr. Fernandes," she angrily quivered, "you are making too much noise with that hammer."

"Mrs. Mitchell," Dad responded, a bit sarcastically I thought, "I invite you to hammer nails into this gate without making a noise."

She stalked off, muttering about men who had no right to be in society. I think "uncouth," "brash," "mannerless," were some of the adjectives we heard quiver in the distance. Never again did the Mitchells speak to Dad, nor to us. Not even to little Francis, who dutifully said, "Good morning, Mrs. Mitchell," or "Merry Christmas, Mrs. Mitchell," or "Happy Easter, Mrs. Mitchell." Our own affectionate Francis, who as a child got so attached to everyone who came visiting that when they stood up to leave, he latched onto their ankles, bawling and pleading, "Don't leave, don't leeeeeave..." Not unlike the leaches that clung to our legs when we walked through our grandfather's overgrown land on the far end of the estate in Mangalore, it took all of Susan's and my strength to extract him.

No, not even to Francis, whose sensitive soul always hurt to encounter such a lack of warmth, did Mrs. Mitchell soften.

Dad finally decided to make a list of residents that Ivan could take the notice to and, on Mum's suggestion, the residents where Isabel, limping, might persuade them to go to the meeting Dad had called for, and a separate list of those that he could do himself.

Ivan's list excluded Glenda's mother who lived in room No. 1, who was put on Isabel's list along with Mr. Mitchell and Jacob Olivera, who had at some time or other fallen out with us. Ivan's list also excluded Mr. Surve from the first floor, the Marchon household, and the Madrassis on the first floor. None of the tenants in the offices on the other side of the building were included, and the others, with the exception of the Madrassis, fell into Dad's list.

"Will you have time for this, dear?" Mum asked.

"A man has to do what a man has to do," Dad said, looking stern and focused.

The Madrassi men were a sort of club or chummery. All the girls were forbidden to go near their apartment. They were very dark, naked to the waist, oily-skinned and oily-haired, with white cloth lungis—Dad called them mundus—folded up from their ankles, knotted, and tucked at the waist to make for easy leg movement.

There was no need to caution us. The men showed no interest in us, nor did they mix with anyone in the building. Our doors could all be latched from the inside, or from the outside by a lock attached to a latch. But the Madrassis always kept their doors wide open, and when I went down to slip apologetic notes under Miss Ezekiel's door for Ivan's and Peter's trespasses, I had to walk past their rooms.

Their darkness always startled me. The men seemed always to be squatting on the floor in front of two primus stoves with a heavy black tawa, a pan of cast iron, making chappatis. They shared the work between them; some of them cut vegetables, others rolled out the chappatis, frying them, and all sorts of very domestic work. "Madrassi bachelors," Peter said. Their floors were not the smooth black-and-white tiles of the second floor, but rough Shahabad stone.

One day, perhaps in an overwhelming urge for privacy or almost as if in error, they closed their door. Peter and Ivan, always on the lookout for a prank, slunk down to the first-floor verandah and silently locked them in. At about four o'clock, perhaps after waking from an afternoon nap, they tried to open their door and found themselves trapped.

We all made for the window of the common passage near the stairs. Doubling over the window ledge that looked out on the outer perimeter of the building, we elbowed each other for a prime place to watch the drama ensuing below. As we had expected, after much shaking of the door on the other side leading to the verandah, they gave up on it, and not much later one black leg came over the window sill, followed by a white lungi and a naked black body, and as we watched in bated anticipation a second leg swung over. He walked along the ledge on the outside curve of the building, which had windows, and climbed into the passage near the stairs on the first floor level. He then went through to the verandah and unlatched the door. Never again did they shut their doors, which were instead kept wide open for all to peep in as they passed, only to quickly look away, embarrassed by the unseemly vision of twelve near-naked black bodies.

They were not invited to the meeting.

Jacob and Gina Olivera were 'progressive parents,' Mum said, echoing their own opinion of themselves. Irrelevant and quite silly, I thought, especially because Aaron Olivera, who was Ivan's age, beat us up every time he saw us, and our complaints to his parents met with an almost vulgar disinterest. Every other evening we ran to Mother, the three of us, Ivan, Susan and I, complaining, and perhaps what Aaron would have described as whining. Finally, Mum paid a visit to the Oliveras.

Gina Olivera, her salt and pepper hair tied up in a bun above eyes that were soft and attractive, spoke sweetly. Her husband, Jacob, a wiry, weak-looking individual, was gruff, belying his appearance. Both of them, of one mind, said, 'Children should settle their grudges amongst themselves without adult intervention.'

Mum came home dissatisfied. Mother herself, considered to be a beauty, with a long thick braid below her hips, did not look very pretty right then; more like a wild cat protecting her cubs. She looked at us and weighed her words.

"Try to be friends," she told us. "Try not to fight."

"But Mum, we do not fight. He hits us for no reason."

Mum was silent.

The next day Aaron, irritated with us for complaining, and encouraged by his parents' reaction, walked up and said, "How about this?" He pushed Ivan's head. Before he could get to Susan, she had run home. "How about this?" he said, shoving me. Off-balance, I reeled and banged my head against an empty drum left in the passage by the Olivera family in case they needed to store water in times of shortages. I cried all the way home.

As with all aches and pains of both body and mind, we waited to dump it on Mum. That evening I sobbed, "Mum, we can't be friends with Aaron. He hurt my head today."

"Yes, Mum," Ivan said, "He hit me too. And Anna cried all day because she hurt her head." Mum looked at us speculatively and finally said,

"I don't understand you children. There are three of you. Does Alice join Aaron?"

"No." Alice was Aaron's older sister, who did not play with us.

"Well, all I can say is that you are three and he is only one." Mum left to make dinner.

We looked at each other. Ivan said, "Let us make a plan."

"What plan?" I asked.

"Mum is right, Anna. He is alone and there are three of us. Tomorrow when he walks by us we will rush at him. Anna, you hold down his legs, and Susan, hold down his hands, and I will hit him for all of us."

"Good plan," said Susan. I was not so sure. What about turning the other cheek? Was that not our belief? But right then, with an

aching head, I thought that turning the other cheek would be even more painful.

And thus it was that one Saturday afternoon while our parents had their customary weekend siesta—"I don't want noise in here, so go out with your games," from Dad—we went out into the passage. Aaron had become so arrogant and confident that he strolled up and down outside our apartment whistling as the three of us waited for the opportune moment. Shirlen, Miriam and Carlton Marchon watched, feeling certain that something would happen. On his third march towards us Aaron was indeed startled when I ducked for his legs and he fell down. Susan sat on his chest and Ivan took a deep breath and pummelled him with his fists. Aaron cursed and threatened as he tried to set himself free from under Susan, swearing dire consequences to the three of us till Susan, in an attempt to stop his bluster, let free one of her hands and stretched her chewing gum across his mouth.

"Shut up," she said.

The Marchon children booed him all through the fight. "Sissy, bully, beaten by girls," they sang tunelessly. That afternoon Aaron went home bruised and crying. Gina Olivera, ominous and threatening, a giant version of Aaron, marched down the verandah towards us, her intertwined eyebrows foreshadowing a cloudburst. I ran in and dragged Mum outside.

The two women stared at each other. Aaron was still sobbing.

"Nathie, your children attacked my son, three of them against one. Completely unacceptable, and so unsportsmanlike!"

"Oh no!" Mum said, shaking her head from side to side. "I am so sorry to hear that, Gina. But what can I say? Children will be children. We cannot interfere in their affairs."

So Gina and Jacob Olivera went on Isabel's list, not Ivan's.

Isabel persuaded Glenda's mother, Mrs. Alphonso, to come to the meeting. Glenda was much older than the rest of us, though I think she was younger than Peter. When they first came to live in our building, mother and daughter arrived with only two small suitcases. On occasion, when Glenda's mother stood out on the balcony, we noted her clothes. She generally wore a navy blue dress, under which another dress, flower-patterned, peeped out. Not a very clean one, either. Peter said, "She does not change. She *just puts one dress over the other."*

Nobody ever turned down Isabel. Nor did Glenda's mother. She even showed up before anyone else at the meeting in the passage. Dad rushed out after we informed him Glenda's mother had already arrived.

Glenda attended the convent school over the bridge. Her mother washed the nuns' habits and did other odd jobs for the convent, not only for a salary but to ensure that Glenda got admitted and studied at that school. Peter said that it would do her good to wash her own clothes at least once in a while. Sometimes she brought the habits home to wash and hung them in our corridor, where she had tied clotheslines between the pillars. Anything hanging unattended was Sammy's next drink. But even Sammy did not steal the nuns' habits, for who could he sell them to?

That day Mrs. Alphonso walked into the meeting, her floral dress peeping out of the navy blue one that hung below the red one. Dad greeted her. I think she must have run away from her husband, rather than been a widow, because she particularly disliked men. Her face, at once swollen and a maze of wrinkles, resembled the surface of the moon, craters and all. Right now a fly walked drunkenly over the surface like a lunar rover, till she swatted it, skilfully maiming it so it fell on the floor. She turned her face away from Dad disdainfully. Dad, of course, never noticed such things. He was unstoppable, and waiting for the rest to arrive, continued to be energetic and bubbly.

Isabel, who we thought had the most money—after all, her husband was a police inspector—came up to Dad and whispered, "Bhovoji, maybe I can provide some biscuits for the meeting. What do you think?"

"Dev bare karo, may God bless you, Isabel. That would be nice."

Isabel returned with a tray of biscuits, followed by Joe and Sammy Marchon, Mrs. Cabral, Jacob Olivera, our next-door neighbour Anthony Vaz, and Ali, the fourteen year old son of our Muslim neighbour, Mr. Farooqui.

Dad looked pleased. This was more than he'd hoped for. Mimosa peeped out and, noticing the crowd, joined them when she saw the biscuits.

Dad told Ivan, "Please tell Mr. Surve that we are ready to begin the meeting." Ten minutes later Mr. Surve came upstairs with the drawstring of his underpants dangling through his buttoned trousers. As one, the women moved away from him. Mr. Mitchell came slowly up the stairs, dragging his feet, and Dad began the meeting.

"Thank you for coming. As you know we have several problems as tenants of this building."

Everyone nodded and Joe would have said something if Dad had not launched into his next sentence while we listened from behind the passage door.

"Let us first start with our immediate problem. Isabel, could you come here?" Isabel took a quick pinch of snuff from her little box, stuffed it back into the top of her dress, pushing it to some secret depths of her bra, and limped forward.

"As you all know, two factors led to Isabel's limp. Number one, the banana skin on the stair." Dad loved to talk in numbers. We spent endless evenings with him and our math books. "If two trains enter a tunnel and the length of the tunnel..." at which point our interest waned considerably. However, out here everyone listened intently.

"Number two, there is no light in the passages."

"Number three," Ivan whispered, "what was she doing at that hour on a dark stair?" We giggled. Dad looked at us sternly.

"This meeting is not for children." We slunk back behind the door of the passage once again.

"As I see it, we need, number one, a waste disposal system. We need dustbins." Anthony Vaz, to the right of Isabel, started sneezing, having inhaled her snuff. He moved next to Joe.

"Number two," Dad continued as if there had been no interruption, "we need to have well-lit passages and stairs." He looked around. Everyone seemed interested but looked helpless.

Finally, Mimosa asked, "Mr. Fernandes, how do you propose we get that?"

"We should form an association and then meet the landlord."

"How much will it cost us?" Glenda's mother asked.

"What do we do with an association? How will it get us the dustbins and the lights?" Mrs. Cabral asked. "Isn't that the duty of the landlord?"

"Yes, true," Dad said. "But Billy will not listen to us if we go separately. However, if we are an association he will have to meet with us."

"Do we have to pay to be part of the association?" Glenda's mother asked.

"There will be a small monthly fee."

"What for? If we are forming the association to get Billy to do the job, then the association does not need to collect money."

Dad tried not to look impatient. "In case Billy ignores our demands then the law allows the association of tenants to carry out the necessary repairs, lighting or the duties of the landlord and recover it from our monthly rent payments. But we need some capital to begin with."

"Then if it involves any money I am not interested," she said.

"Nor me," Mrs. Cabral said. The others kept silent.

Disappointed, Dad looked around, his eyes settling on Ali's bored face. Standing to the side, Ali had bit little half moons around the edge of his biscuit till it looked like a star. He was holding it up at nose level and gazing at it.

"What are you doing here?" Dad asked softly, though we who knew him well could detect annoyance in the question.

"I have come for the meeting," Ali said, unfazed. We were always surprised that Dad, who we all treaded so carefully with, was not seen as intimidating to our friends.

"Where is your father?"

"Working."

"Your mother?"

"Mother not come to meeting, she no speak English," Ali said, still watching his star.

Dad's eyes moved away with what our trained eyes could recognize as frustration. Our eyes, which had barely moved from the plate of biscuits for that minute, watched impatiently as Sammy Marchon stuffed his pockets. At last, his pockets full, he sidled out. Why was he at the meeting anyway, when Joe, his dad, was already there? He'd taken the leftover biscuits we were hoping to get.

Anthony Vaz from No. 15 had finished his biscuit and, ever since, kept glancing at his watch, his forehead creased with tense impatience. Earlier that evening, we'd heard through the thin wall the strident voice of his wife, Lolly: "Be back in fifteen minutes."

Anthony seldom, if ever, disobeyed anyone. He gradually took a step back, then another, and slipped away without a word. Ali soon followed.

Mrs. Cabral had not finished.

"Besides, I don't think this concerns us. We never go out in the dark ever since Mr. Cabral expired."

Joe laughed. "Well, Mr. Fernandes, no one can say you did not try!"

Dad shrugged at that and tried to hide his disappointment about the others. He gave a half-scornful laugh.

"I will do it myself."

As she collected her tray, Isabel said, "Bhovoji, I will share the cost of installing the light with you... and the waste bins."

Early the next day, Dad set out to Mohammed Ali Road to buy electrical wires and returned home around noon. On a Sunday, lunch was always late. It was the day we ate beef. The rest of the week we ate fish, except on Fridays when we had either egg curry or a vegetable curry. It is a Catholic thing we do.

Dad sat in his easy chair for a while and then pulled out his toolbox. Ivan, Dad's little helper, put out the high stool for him.

At around one p.m., Dad started the wiring near our kitchen switch, which had a plug point. He fixed the wire on strips of wood that he had nailed to the wall, on which were clips made of metal strips with a T-loop. Half an hour later, lunch served, Mum called out to Dad to come to the table. Dad had wired only a little way outside our door. He left the coil hanging up on the ceiling, where the last clip held the stretched wire, and Ivan brought the stool home. Dad led the grace before meals, and we ate silently while he rested in the easy chair until we finished. Then Mum and Dad ate in silence.

Another Sunday afternoon siesta—a dream of the adults! The parents in the noisy neighbourhood were indoors, strictly instructing the children, once again, not to disturb the neighbours, who were all napping. Dad said, "On second thought, I think all of you should sleep too," thus confining us indoors. It was the only day of the week that all doors remained closed and latched from the inside in daylight.

After evening tea, Dad and Ivan, armed with a high stool, went out onto the verandah to resume their task. Dad stared at the ceiling where he thought he had left the coil of wire. Gone was the huge coil of wire that he had left hanging!

He knocked on 19 to look for Sammy. But Sammy was not in and no one had seen him. Dad said there was no point in waiting, *because Sammy would have already sold the wire.*

Isabel came running.

"Bhovoji, I heard about your loss. I will pay for a new wire, but please do get us a light."

So Dad, Ivan and Isabel went to Mohammad Ali Road once again. They came back with four large waste bins, chains, locks, a cage that could be locked to encase the bulb in the passage, and Ivan came back with a bar of chocolate that Isabel had bought him. Dad insisted that Ivan bring it home and share it with the rest, and Mum put it away for "after dinner."

Dad went out with Ivan and the tall stool. This time he worked without a break with hammer, nails, and rivets. Soon it grew dark and Isabel brought a large torchlight, the kind that watchmen or security guards double up to use as weapons, and stood near the tall stool and directed the beam at the ceiling. Three hours later Dad was affixing the bulb and its cage to the ceiling. He did not stop till he had locked the cage and climbed down from the stool that Ivan was holding steady. He rubbed his hands together in loud claps as if to shake off the dust, but conveying a sense of a job well done. When he entered the home, he looked at Mum for approval, just as Francis used to do after he'd finished colouring. "What is it, Francis?" I'd ask, pointing to a wriggly line across the page. "This is the fish," he'd say, pointing to the bottom of the line, and then moving upwards with a stubby finger to the top of the page. "He died, and now he is going to heaven," or some such thing.

Dad gave that self-satisfied look at Mum and invited her to stand by him.

"Well, dear, now what?" she asked.

"You get to switch it on for the first time."

Mum put her finger on the switch, and then changed her mind.

"Let us say a prayer of thanks," she said, drawing us into a circle,

"Dear Jesus, who has been the light of the world, we thank you for the light on our stairs. Please let it work. Amen."

"Amen," we chorused.

Mum pushed the switch down with her index finger. We walked to the stairs, followed by Isabel, Miriam, Shirlen, Mrs. Cabral from the other side of the L, and even Sammy, who had returned from his mission.

We applauded. Mum looked at Dad with pride, just the way he wanted her to.

"Thank you, my dear. We really needed that light."

The next morning Mum looked at the four large waste bins sitting in the centre of the kitchen floor.

"You will have to take these out today, dear," she told Dad.

"I will, tonight after work. They need to be chained and locked so that they do not disappear."

That night Dad hammered holes on the bins near the top rim to pass the chains through. We kids sat outside No. 19 huddled in a tight circle, waiting for Joe. He bounced in, jumped over Dad's outstretched legs and headed straight for us.

"Joe, how was the day?"

"I had a very good day, till I set out for home." He paused and looked around the circle. Satisfied he had our attention, he went on. "It was 8.30 p.m. Time for my last round of the day. I started from the front gate of the factory and moved along the main building, way down the manufacturing unit where I'm stationed. It is a very long walk there—almost a kilometre. Halfway there I felt this tap on my shoulder."

We waited, sixteen round eyeballs.

"I turned, my hand on my gun." We gasped. Joe was the only one in our acquaintance with a gun. Though we had not seen it, we were impressed nonetheless. After a satisfied half smile at our wonder, he carried on. "I could barely see the outline of a man through the fog...Maybe security, I thought. 'What do you want?' I asked him. He was more discernable now, though I could not really see him. He asked me for a light... A hand stuck out from the mist with a cigarette..." Long pause. "I opened my lighter and looked at the man in front of me."

We gasped. The suspense was killing us. Francis put a shaking hand in mine. Joe lit a cigarette, watching our gaping mouths.

"Dad, Mum wants you," called Miriam, his daughter.

Damn, we wouldn't hear all of Joe's story tonight. He would not dare to disobey Chickpea.

"You kids," he said, wagging his index finger, "if you are here tomorrow at this time, I will tell you what happened.

Hold that thought, and good night. I must run. My Chickpea wants me."

Now Dad finished his hammering and set up the bins at various points in the passage. He passed the chain through the holes and around the balustrade and locked the two ends.

"We have to find a way to empty the bins," he said to Isabel, who was looking over his shoulders at the bin. Isabel was much taller than Dad. I think she was the tallest woman in the building.

"We can ask Soni to clear the bins every morning when she comes to clean the toilets," he added. "You and I can share the extra wage we have to pay her. As you know, the others are a dead loss. Pretty much a waste of time asking them, if you know what I mean."

Isabel agreed. The next morning Soni agreed to dispose of the garbage for an additional ten rupees per month. But Soni drank like a fish and did not come to work every day. On days she did come, she just tipped the bins over the balustrade into the compound—defeating their purpose.

"Where do you expect me to take the garbage?" she asked, to which no one had an answer. Dad, of course, did attempt to answer, and opened his mouth to Soni's vanishing behind.

We had no system of garbage disposal, the toilets always leaked and were never maintained, and the compound was filthy as ever, collecting what the tenants threw over the balcony. Now, with the bins installed, the garbage disposal merely changed hands but not geography. We still lived atop a giant landfill!

Chapter Fourteen

Thursday, the 2nd October 2008, I woke in the stifling heat to a sweat-soaked t-shirt and a noisy fan, my dreams cut short. I'd been standing with Anna in a passageway right outside a door with the number two on it.

"My apartment is no.3," I said as I took her hand and walked down the passageway. We could not find no.3. There was no door where I had imagined it would be, and I walked with her, searching for my apartment.

"Let's go back to the beginning and start the search again," I said to a silent follower.

We retraced our steps and stood in front of no.2. We took three steps to the right and there, just where it should have been, was no.3. I opened the door with my key and we stepped in.

The October heat, the noises of the morning...why don't people talk softly, and who was it, anyway, chattering away in my living room? The unmistakable smells of the creek and the fertilizer plant mixed with coffee brought me back from my dream...Anna's arrival was just ten days away. Thankfully, I had no lectures that day; though non-violence was no longer an ideology in this country, at least we still celebrated Mahatma Gandhi's birthday on 2nd October with a public holiday.

I dragged my caffeine-addicted body to the living room and found it filled with Dr. Apte and Premibai having a lively argument on the value of turmeric as a cure for a cold. It is surprising how two diminutive individuals can fill up a room.

"Ah, Peter! Finally you wake."

"Aren't you supposed to be in Jaigad?"

"Aaarey, Peter, I left you that day and went home. As I packed my bag I found Naqvi's invitation for his daughter's wedding sitting forgotten on my side table. It is three days from now. He will not forgive me if I don't attend."

"So you did not leave. Gosh, Doctor, do you sleep? When did you come here? It's only 7 a.m."

"I thought I would spend the holiday with my good friend Peter, so I walked over."

"Walked? You live ten kilometres from here!"

"I wake at four, Peter."

"Premibai, get me coffee," I sulked. Mornings are not good for entertaining noisy visitors.

She left the room and I pulled the armchair under the fan and settled down in its folds. This was going to be a long day. Dr. Apte, much as I loved him, would not let me be, so I stopped my pushing-him-away thoughts and gave in. 'If you can't stop it, just enjoy it,' they say of many such intrusions.

"Doctor, give me some time to get awake and shower. I had a late night. I need recovery time from this early-morning assault on my senses."

"Oh, don't worry about me, Peter, just make yourself at home. I have not read the *Times of India* today. You shower and get dressed and that way I can finish my reading."

October is the hottest month in Bombay. I shower every three hours. Maybe I should just install an air conditioner...I suppose the air conditioner itself is affordable, but the electric bills are phenomenal with an air conditioner, I am told.

Dr. Apte combatted the heat of the October morning by stripping his trousers and shirt off. He sat in my armchair, his bony legs stretched out in front of him, wearing just his *Kulkarni chaadis,* a blue-, grey- and orange-striped loose Bermuda shorts kind of thing with a drawstring to hold it up. A white vest, a bit yellowed with age, but clean, covered his bony ribcage. His palms behind his head, he stared at the ceiling, contemplative. My entry had no effect on his posture...He did not move, except to roll his eyes to see me better. I sat at the dining table and waited for Premibai to serve our breakfast.

"Had your breakfast, Doc?"

"No, Peter, I'm waiting for Premibai to serve me *poha*. Besides, I thought I should wait for you."

"Does she know?"

"Yes, I told her. What will you have?"

"Same as you, I suppose."

We waited in silence, buried in ourselves.

The silence was broken by a low mumble: "A Hindu."

"A Hindu?"

"Naqvi's daughter's marrying a Hindu boy. Not really boy... She's old now, nearly thirty-two, and he may be fortyish."

"Doc, don't I hear you call Rashida *beti*, daughter, and now you are upset she is marrying a Hindu—or should I say a Hindu is marrying her?"

He sighed. "She's like my own daughter, Peter, but I'm not for these inter-marriages. There are many unmarried Hindu women. If this goes on then our women will start marrying Muslims. Hobson's choice... Don't you see? The tradition of marrying one's own caste is not as unscientific as you may think. The country has so many cultures, religions, languages, customs... Bad enough, marriage is a major adjustment, but if you have to adjust to more—language, religion, customs—the chance at success is really challenged."

"So though you don't like the idea, you will go to the wedding?"

"What's that got to do with me going? I say, Peter, you are a strange man." He pulled out a *pothi*, a small cloth bag with a drawstring, which was tucked in his *chaadis* for convenience, and began putting together a *paan*. He looked back at me contemplatively.

"So why didn't you do it?" he asked

"Do what?"

"Don't be obtuse, Peter. Why did you not get married? Thirty-seven and unmarried, with an apartment, a good job, education, a car... everything a girl could dream of, mostly anyway. Maybe you should install an air conditioner..." He tipped back his head and popped the paan into the recesses of his left cheek. "Surely, it is not because you cannot get a girl. Besides," he added, as if it had anything to do with it, "you're not bad looking either."

With a groan, I ignored this pest and returned to my bedroom to retrieve Anna's notebook. And talking about marriages…as in all bad fiction novellas, I coincidentally arrived at Anna's memories of Ali's marriage. I place this before you since Ali is almost central to what took place that year that Anna's family left for Canada. I looked at the calendar hanging on the wall just behind Dr. Apte's head – little over a week for Anna to arrive in Bombay.

The angle of the L at 10 Nesbit Road seemed stacked with Muslims. Yes, that too, I discovered in my teenage years. The restaurant on the ground floor was an Irani restaurant. Though we always called it "the Irani restaurant," we never thought of the owners as Muslim. The room directly above the restaurant belonged to Sadiq Ali, Advocate, High Court. We did not know who he was since it was an office and we never went anywhere near the offices in Billimoria Building. Directly above Sadiq Ali's office was our own playmate Ali on the second floor.

It was the end of the monsoons. Five of us gathered to play in the passage near the stairs. Peter made a soft ball with a stuffed sock, and my brother Ivan invented a game that he called handball. He drew a circle on the wall with a piece of white chalk. The game had a batsman and a bowler, except there was no bat involved in the game. The batsman—for lack of a more inspired word—stood near the wall with his fist in the circle. The bowler threw the sock ball and the batsman pummelled it with his fist. The scoring was very much like cricket, the batsman taking runs when possible, and if the ball hit the centre of the circle he was bowled out. In a sense, the batsman was the guardian of the circle with his fist.

It was my turn to bowl. I threw the handball to Ivan. He hit the ball with the top of his clenched fist and it arched in the air, following the high-beamed roof. Five pairs of eyes mimicked the trajectory. Before we knew it, Ali, who had appeared from nowhere, jumped up and caught the ball.

"You want to play with us?" I asked.

"No, but I want to give you some good news."

"Yeah?" we said, abandoning the game and clustered around him. "What is it?"

We never played much with Ali, and when we all went in one big team to the Mazagaon Hill Gardens he never joined us. I don't think he was much interested in games, really. He attended the Anjuman

Islam School over the Byculla Bridge and spoke with an accent very different from our own convent-schooled tones. On occasion when we ran short of a player for a team, we stood outside his apartment and called out to him. He was a reluctant playmate, but never missed joining our tight circle outside Joe's apartment each night.

We waited now, our eyes turned towards Ali. The game stopped, not because Ali, having caught the ball, stood stroking it in his hand, unwilling to let go of his audience, but because of his visible excitement.

"What?" Peter impatiently prodded.

"I am getting married!" Ali said as he threw his head back and watched the ball, which assumed a life of its own, pop out of his hands and make its way toward the ceiling of the passage.

It is always a moment of shock when someone your age makes an announcement like that. My Catholic upbringing made us feel uncomfortable with marital aspirations, even ashamed. We denied those thoughts as unholy and most certainly did not admit them to our families.

"What do you want to be when you grow up?"

"A nun."

"A priest."

And when our aunts and uncles teased, "You want to marry," we strongly denied such wayward dreams and replied, shy and ashamed, "No, No, a nun, a priest."

So Ali's news was a bit of a shock. He was sixteen. Only old people marry!

"To who?"

"Whom," from Peter

"Whatever, to who?"

"Mumtaz."

"Who is she?'

"I don't know. My parents know her parents."

"Where does she live?"

"Mohammed Ali Road."

"Is she pretty?"

"I think so. I not meet her but her photo look really good."

"But don't you need to meet?"

"No. She is girl, I is boy. Come to my house, I show you."

We all traipsed behind him. A small passage stuck out like a tangent into the curve of the L, with smaller apartment rooms on either side. We walked one behind the other in a single file, of necessity, down the narrow passage to the end, right outside Ali's door.

We entered for the first time into this little home where Ali lived with his parents. While we visited all the Catholic homes at Christmas and New Year, we had no occasion to visit Ali. On Eid, too, we did not get invited, nor were they on our list of homes where we sent Christmas sweets. Really, though Ali lived on the second floor with us, his family could have well been part of the first, those who were just not part of our active lives.

Ali's apartment was very different from ours. It was stacked on top of the angle of the L, and we stepped onto a linoleum floor of bright red, patterned with yellow, black and orange geometrical labyrinth designs. It was as if we had stepped into the Arabian Nights of flying carpets and wondrous colors. Our own homes had black and white stone floors on which we played hopscotch. Our floor was smooth and shiny and we threw talcum powder on it and pretended we were skating, sliding once every so often, on what to us was our ice rink. But so fascinating was the design on Ali's floor that I stood on my toes and tried to move through the mazes without touching the lines. We all took that on as a game, making Ali impatient.

"This is the marriage bed," he said, pointing to the only furniture in the room apart from two folding steel chairs standing in the far end. We were uninterested in the bed, but I was fascinated with Ali's mother, who for the first time I saw without her black burqa. Ali grew impatient once again. He pointed to the bed more emphatically and said, "That is the marriage bed."

We did not really see the special qualities of a marriage bed. Ali was strange anyway, so we did not pay attention. He spoke English like it was Urdu, a language alien to us.

We would have returned to our sock ball game had Ali's mother not intervened at that moment.

"Ali," she ordered, "give them some sherbet."

We all rushed to the bed and sat down, it being the only seating above floor level. Ali served us a bright green sherbet. This had an immediate effect on us. Sherbet was not common in our homes. Coffee, yes, tea, yes, milk, yes—sherbet, absolutely not! Not unless we had it surreptitiously from the hawkers outside our school gates, mostly *with money saved from walking home instead of taking the bus.*

We sat sipping the sherbet delicately, slurping it through our lips and savouring the very last drop. Ali's esteem had risen considerably in our eyes. We were even willing to discuss the marriage bed.

"So Ali, what is it about the bed you wanted us to see?"

"Don't you understand? It is the MARRIAGE bed," he said, now try-ing to make us understand, using emphasis and gestures which none of us could really get. Even Peter, who normally knew most things, looked away, embarrassed. The rest of us were once again convinced that Ali was strange, just not one of us.

"Don't you know 'first night'?"

Looking at our ignorant faces, Ali ushered us out of his house. We were just not the right crowd to share his excitement. I guess that went two ways. We were as alien to him as he was to us. As we walked back in single file, minus Ali, I asked Peter, "What did he mean, Peter?"

Peter blushed. "I don't know what he meant. Forget it, Ali is crazy."

A few months later, Ali, wearing long trousers, knocked on all the doors of the second floor. Another way in which he stood out from the rest of us, who still wore short pants long after our legs grew hairy and we could no longer bear being teased by the school girls as we walked down the bridge past our school. He had invited all of us: *Mr. and Mrs. Farooqui invite you, your family, friends and relatives to the reception of our son, Ali Mohammed...*

Our parents looked at the invitation card that Ali delivered to our hous-es. Since his parents did not come personally, as would be the custom, our parents did not attend the wedding—'child's play,' they called it. 'Really I mean, Nathie, one can't take this seriously, ' Isabel dismissed it, waving it in the air. Visions of the sherbet fresh in our minds, we dreamed of treats far beyond mere green sugar water: ice-cream, we hoped, such a rare treat for us, to be had only at weddings. Dressed in our Sunday best and armed with the sealed envelopes with rupee notes inside, given by our parents, we walked down the bridge towards the Saboo Siddique hall in Nagpada.

In retrospect, I wonder why we were astonished at the crowds that at-tended his wedding—family, friends, and relatives indeed! We may have been the only folk there who had not taken that clause seriously. Crowds streamed in and out of the wedding hall.

The hall, divided into two sections and separated by a curtain, kept the women and men apart. Ali, with a gold embroidered kurta and a head-dress that befitted a maharaja, sat there looking pleased with being the centre of all this attention—and anyway it was his party. We were not allowed to go to the bride's side, and even Anna and Susan did not get to see her, though they sat on that side of the hall. The boys in our little group, separated from the girls irrespective of our ages, sat on opposite side of the hall with the men.

Nothing was really happening. I mean no music, no dance, nothing to watch but the streaming humanity in various colours, like sunshine through a prism, some with burqas and others with long, brilliant-coloured clothes. We looked around for the waiters, for the ice-cream, for the sherbet, perhaps water, as we felt our throats dry. Finally, we got wind that nothing would be served and we looked at each other, Ivan and I, and down at the cash in the envelopes. Maybe we should get ice-creams for ourselves...

We left the rest there, took Susan and Anna with us, and walked down the other side of the bridge to Clare Road. What an unforgettable wedding! We had piyali, cups filled with chickpeas and potatoes with a lot of spices thrown in, sherbet at Johnny's, the cold drink shop at the side, and finally rounded up our evening with kulfi, an Indian ice-cream, a block away, though rumours had it that it was made of blotting paper.

Anna, not our conscience, asked, "Peter, don't you think this is wrong?"

"No."

"But, this is Ali's gift money."

"So did you get ice-cream, which all weddings serve?" I asked.

"No...but..."

"God helps those who help themselves," Ivan said, "And if you tell Mummy and Daddy, you are out of all our games, I hope you remember that!"

I was startled when Dr. Apte, now his feet down and alert, slapped his thigh, watching me through large, astonished eyes. It would not be an exaggeration to say his eyes goggled and his Adam's apple moved excitedly.

He pointed at the book in my hands. "There is a woman, there is a woman, I can tell."

Chapter Fifteen

The history of life on this planet may well be the history of the sun, the stars and the history of God himself. But more importantly to us, it is the history of mothers. They breed, they nurture, they dominate all we do, and, if we allow them, they would even take over our lives. Everyone has a mother, so you know what I speak of. I did not have a chance to answer Dr. Apte's question, for mine was standing on my doorstep at that very moment, seeming quite agitated.

Isabel looked at the partially naked skeleton draped in my armchair with a haughty distaste that only she could convey—a look that has prompted many a butcher to sheepishly put the extra gram of meat on the scale, or the unfortunate government clerk, who usually cannot find his corrupt little pen until a currency note is slipped onto his desk, to do quite promptly whatever this formidable figure has requested in her very quiet, polite tones. Dr. Apte, however, was made of sterner stuff. Women did not faze him at all. Yes, he would have been upset with a bit of extra salt in his food or the darker hue of yellow in his dal, but any disapproval his eyes might meet, completely lost its way somewhere between two opposing retinas. He said in his most friendly of tones, even perhaps, one could say, familiar,

"Isabel, how good of you to come visit Peter. I haven't seen you in a long while."

Mother may be disapproving, but she prided herself on her impeccable manners.

"Good morning, Dr. Apte. I see you are feeling the heat."

"So I am. I keep telling Peter to install an air-conditioner, but will he listen? Single, good job and everything...I don't know what he does with his money."

Isabel did not deign to respond. Quite unlike her. She walked out of the room to my bedroom with me in tow.

"Mother, are you upset?"

"Peter, why do you encourage that mannerless man into your living room?"

"Mother, surely you are not serious? It is very unlike you to be so inhospitable towards others. What is it that's agitating you?"

"They are back with their nonsense." She pushed a church bulletin under my nose.

"Who do you speak of? Who is back?" I say, ignoring the paper.

"We will never have peace. The communal and hate crimes have only increased over the years. First it was the South Indians, then the communists, then the Muslims, the north Indians, the Muslims, and now the Catholics. Peter, I am worried. All these hatreds, not unlike pennies dropped in the slot of a pink plastic pig, filling it bursting its banks, will one day fill their hearts."

She had obviously followed the news of the past two weeks, of the violence towards Christians in Mangalore.

"Mother, you are safe here. Just don't go out for a while."

"Peter, this is not about me. It is happening in Mangalore. Right now, Anna is in Mangalore. She flew directly there from Canada as I had informed you, that is, if you care to listen to your mother."

"Oh Mum, of course I know Anna is in Mangalore and arrives next week. See? I listen."

"And Maggie, your father's sister, writes that the Ram Sena, some moral police group, is targeting young girls in pubs and other public places. You know Anna is now Canadian. She has lived there for so long that perhaps she may visit these pubs or some such place, and as you know, that is the worst thing that could happen to her. Look at this picture." She once again pushed the paper to me. "They trashed the Milagres church. These Hindus will not rest till they kill everyone else in this country."

"Mother, careful, you may hurt our guest," I whispered. At which, as if on cue, she walked into the living room—strode, I should say, spurring apprehension and a mounting headache in my already greatly tried body.

Anna, with mathematical precision, had chosen to land in Mangalore on the 14th September, at the very time she'd have to hide her cross, strung on its black string—if she was still wearing it, that was. On that very morning, nearly 15 years after the communal violence of 1993 between the Hindus and Muslims and her departure to Canada as a consequence, we had watched with overwhelming horror and disbelief the images of the police assaulting the congregation around the Milagres Church. The year 2008 seemed marked for violence against Christains.

Our shock at images of the broken Crucifix at the Adoration Monastery reverberated around the Christian world; the media covered it live and it appeared on the BBC and CNN as their main headline for the next 24 hours. Anna, waiting at the airport for connecting flights, would later tell us how she felt not just horror but fear. When you are at an unknown airport, you have no option but to follow the path your baggage takes ahead of you.

To the Christians watching fearfully in that moment, the images of the cross, broken, seemingly defeated, were ones of the humility of Christ; a return of his life on earth so to say. The hatred we saw in the eyes of the Hindu fundamentalists as they shattered the areas most sacred to the Christian communities, as they enacted their cruelty and sadistic violence on its symbols, could only be surpassed by our own dismay at the shocking connivance of the state machinery.

Christian sanctimony aside, it was in that moment that I felt a sudden empathy with tax evaders. I have always paid mine diligently, but now I could see it being used to fund a bunch of bigots (for indeed the police and the administration are paid by our taxes) who were using it to crush the country's own citizens, instead of protecting them. How many people felt the same as I did? Did the Hindus feel the horror I felt? Did the Muslims feel outrage for us, or did they feel relief that the attention towards them had diluted? Does citizenship in this country mean anything? Do we have citizens or only private inheritors of all that is "Indian"? History has always been political and written by the dominant group.

Did I need to apologise for being Christian in a country that boasts of being the largest democracy?

Love, I think, is the denial of questioning, for along the path of my questions, hate welled up inside of me. It felt like pig's lard. As a child I loved the disgusting stuff, and one greedy Sunday I ate a plate full of it. The retching that ensued as punishment led to a self-loathing so palpable that I needed to look outside myself, pick an object, something that I could hate so that this disgust at my excess would disappear. I, of course, picked pork lard to hate. I never touched it again—not to this day. I think my hate lasted a week, but my words, "I hate lard," lasted a lifetime. This felt the same. It accompanied waves of revulsion I was now feeling for all Hindus, every one of them who were silent. Everyone who thought it was not their fault, and could do no more than stand aside; everyone who voted these bigots in. My revulsion was all-engulfing, and not much later had expanded to the entire country. India, I hate you...

Did Muslims feel the same?

By and by, I separated the perpetrators of evil from the goodness of all else: the joy of my Hindu friends, my continued friendship with Dr. Apte, and my love-hate relationship with India. Right now I could only think with concern of the way 1993 changed the direction of our lives—and now Anna, after all these years in Canada, away from these indignities, had landed right in the middle of a very upsetting situation.

In the living room, Dr. Apte, characteristically oblivious to the moods or tempers of others, fanned the flames of Isabel's already advanced state of annoyance.

"Isabel, don't leave. Sit down and have a chat with us. Premibai will make you breakfast."

Mother nearly spluttered. Being invited in *her own son's* home by this *Hindu man*, who at this moment represented all that was wrong in our world? She summoned all her reserve and years of grooming and sat down wordlessly, a feat of self-control for one who generally needed to achieve a fixed word limit each day. She swallowed several times, opening and closing her mouth as if to speak and thinking better of it.

Earlier, I had surrendered my day, and now I made ready to surrender my peace. Mother looked like a cougar ready to spring. Not in the fashion of the modern-day cougar, but the really old-fashioned family of *felidae, puma concolor.* This species is found not only in the hills and wooded areas, but amongst rushes and reeds. Though they are not commonly known to attack man, this was one of those rare moments on the brink. Dr. Apte, clueless of Mother's distaste, kept patting the sofa as if inviting her to sit. Mother turned to face Dr. Apte, transferring onto him all her fears and anger.

If one refers to the Encyclopaedia Britannica, *castir* to *cole*, 1959, right next to the information on cats, felidae, and only separated by *"Casus Belli—a situation said to justify a state in initiating war,"* one finds 'Casuistry.' The classic connotation is one of 'determining the morality of particular actions in particular circumstances, especially such as are apt to puzzle the conscience...'; a more modern definition might be 'specious argument.' From therein emerged the casuists; while most often seen in the Catholic and Anglican churches, our very own Hindu casuist sat right there in my living room, unbeknown to Isabel.

"Forgive me, Dr. Apte, for not particularly wanting to speak to you right at this moment. I am too disgusted with what you people are doing."

Now Dr. Apte, incapable, I'd thought, of bewilderment, looked at Isabel in wonder.

"Do you mean Peter and I? I assure you that my relationship with Peter is purely platonic. We are friends, Isabel."

"For heaven's sake, Dr. Apte, do not be obtuse. Of course I know that my son is not gay."

"You don't know that, Mother," I interposed. "I could well be."

"Be serious, Peter. Besides, I am addressing Dr. Apte." She turned on him once again. "I am talking about the attack on the Christians."

"Ah." He sighed. "Isabel, I sympathize with the Christians of Orissa and Mangalore, but what has that got to do with you and me?"

In the dictionary under the letter 'c' is a word that etymologists ponder over, a trifle confused as to its origins: Is it the early 13th-century French *coart*, from *coe*, tail, or perhaps from the Latin *coda*, tail; undoubtedly it reflects, though perhaps metaphorically, an animal retreating with his tail between his legs. 'Coward,' the dictionary explains, is 'a person who lacks courage in facing danger, difficulty, opposition, pain.' Ernest Hemingway refined the concept further: "...cowardice, as distinguished from panic, is almost always simply a lack of ability to suspend the functioning of the imagination." Mine was speeding from scenarios of loud accusations, to fisticuffs, to spitting, hatred, bloodshed—all as I looked at these two antagonists in my living room. I admit, too, that I was more than a little worried about Anna. I withdrew to the only sanctuary left, closed my bedroom door, and picked up Anna's book.

That night we sat once again outside 19 waiting. Waiting for Joe. Waiting expectantly to hear the end of his story.

He bounced in to a rousing cheer from us.

"Joe, Joe, Joe, Joe," we sang together in the tune of 'Daisy, Daisy,' holding each other and swaying from side to side. Joe smiled, and from where I sat, I could see his gold filling at the back of his mouth. It always fascinated us, the gold. I remember when I was little, Joe joined us and pretended to be sick. He gurgled and gagged, holding his hand to his mouth. Finally, he made a vomiting sound. He took his hand away, and in his palm, glittering in the bright moonlight, a small piece of gold rocked to and fro as if filled with its own life force.

"I even vomit gold," he boasted to a very impressed midget audience.

"Joe, we did not sleep—what happened when you lit his cigarette?" We had not heard the end of this story left untold a few days ago. Joe, not cluttered with too many thoughts, knew exactly where he had ended his story the last time we had seen him.

"The fog swirled in big strong clouds around me, as if escaping from giant bellows. Peeping through it, I could see sparkles of light through the swirls. He is puffing, I thought, as the light glittered bright and then low." He took a long pause and we held our breath...

"Suddenly"—he now put his hands between his knees and threw them outwards in the air above. We followed his action, all heads turned to the ceiling—"the fog cleared for a split second." Now his palms, flat, circled the nothingness in front of him like they belonged to a painted French mime. "I saw him, tall"—Joe was on his toes now, holding his right hand high in the air to indicate the height of the man—"well dressed"—at this point he put his index finger of his right hand to the tip of his thumb, and shook it—"chiknaa, good-looking, except..."

We gasped edging closer to each other.

"EXCEPT?" Francis screamed shrilly, frightened.

Now Joe paused for a long moment, slowly moving his eyes around the circle, making eye contact with each of us.

"EXCEPT?" Francis screamed once again in a wobbly voice.

"He was this tall," said Joe, repeating himself to prolong our agony. Standing up and raising his hands, he marked a spot on the wall. "At least through the fog I could see his neck shoot out from his collar."

"Except? Joe, except what?" Peter now piped in impatiently.

"Except...he had no head."

We clutched each other. "What happened, Joe? Tell us, were you afraid?"

"Ha!" He waved his hands in the air with a scornful look at us. "Ha!" he repeated. "Not at all... You see, I was born in a veil. I can see spirits. It's a gift."

The day Joe first got his job at the factory as a security officer, we all milled around him admiring the uniform, its lapels and buttons. That summer, the heat had reached giddy heights as we waited outside no. 19 for him to return from work. He arrived looking so important that we gulped our levity.

"I am now a security officer," he said, saluting. From agape we travelled to a new high of respect, everyone greatly impressed with the word 'officer,' not knowing what it really meant; no doubt something very important. Joe preened with our attention, but such irony... one would think with his police record it would be the last job he'd be eligible for! I have often wondered how real his jobs were.

"Something like the rank of a captain," he said.

All the younger ones, round mouthed, large eyed—how did he get such an important job?

"Well, I was a captain in the army," he said with a casual wave of his hand.

"Indian Army?" I asked him, disbelieving.

"No, the British Army."

"Why did you leave?"

Joe, silent, seemed far away.

"Tell us of your army experience, Joe," I persisted.

Gangabowdi ghosts forgotten, Joe launched into a new storyline.

"I was on the front lines in the Burmese war."

"Were you a general in the army?" I asked.

"Sergeant," he replied without flinching. "Late one evening, crouched in our bunkers, an uncertain quiet fell upon us. The air was heavy, the kind you feel when smells sit unmoving, when the heart feels the weight and your shoulders droop; the sounds of fire were the imaginary vibrations in our ears that never stopped twitching. We watched the sun dip and the sky turn to a strange red glow, bleeding with the battle it had witnessed just hours ago. We sat silently, thinking of our homes, of simple things like walking down the street; a street with ordinary people going about ordinary things; simple food, simple arguments with the wife; I missed Chickpea especially at that moment." Then he glanced at Shirlen and Miriam and added, "I missed your mother, though not just at that moment, but that instant was especially intense."

His eyes shifted to the group. We fidgeted, a bit uneasy, the moment solemn, almost real, as Joe sat still, his eyes moving around unseeingly.

"I had lost my best friend not long ago in the battle and I needed to be alone. I left the group, thinking, how does one tell a wife that she will never see her husband again? How does one tell their children? 'Sorry, your husband is no more?' 'Where is papa?' 'Sorry, your papa is dead?' 'Sorry, your husband will not come home?' 'Sorry, we tried to save him but he was already dead?' What would they want me to do? Is there any way it can be done without the inevitable pain for both the giver and receiver of such a missive? I walked a mile down the field, sometimes tripping on parched land cracked by the sun, like a giant puzzle being put together. Every once in a while I picked myself up or stopped to get my balance, not just from the broken earth, but from this mad, passionate questioning and the hot blood that was trying to burst out from the top of my head."

He sat on the floor like the rest of us; a faraway look glazed his eyes.

"War," he said, "it is a strange contradiction to all that you are brought up to believe in. When is it right to kill another? I stood there not really knowing what we were sent to die for. Who were we dying for? Strips of coloured ribbon decorating our lapels? Is there anything real to die for except for a friend or close family? And, then too, we should not be called upon to die for anyone. Live perhaps, but die? That must be God's decision." He looked heavenwards and added, shocking us all, "That is, if there is a God at all."

Nobody spoke in that moment. Joe had questioned our deepest

faith in country, sacrifice, and God Himself. Eventually, after an eternity, he went on, "Through the loud, heavy firing that reverberated in my mind, I could also hear the silence and my heart's uneven beating somewhere in my head. No, let me tell you, children, it is hard to lose your friends. One day you are drinking with them and the next you are praying that at least their spirits are walking by your side. But I don't think they are. I think they lost their spirits, because though I was born in a veil I never saw them again..." He lapsed into a long silence and we, entering into his mood, waited patiently for him to emerge.

"Too late...I saw someone walk towards me. I knew it was the enemy; easy to see that. His hat and height clearly shouted 'enemy.' I reached for my gun, but god-love-me, there were no rounds in it. I stood paralyzed in the centre of an open field and nowhere to take cover. He lifted his rifle..."

"What rifle was it?" I asked, hoping to catch him at his game.

"An M14," he responded without hesitation. "I'd recognize it even 100 ft. away. My heart pounded like the ticking of a grandfather clock. His finger tightened on the trigger. I watched helplessly while he squeezed it. The bullet hit me right here." He clutched at his heart, reeling back with drama.

"Joe, that is your heart you are clutching. If you were hit in your heart you would be dead."

"Ah," he said, "it missed. Because you see, at that very moment my heart was in my mouth."

Perhaps it seems imbalanced that I should give Joe so much space in my own story with Anna. But the Marchon family was to play a big part in the drama, and it is only fair to spread them before your eyes so you might understand their influence on our lives.

19ᵗʰ April, 1992

It was the summer holidays in mid April and Dad could not take us to Mangalore for vacation. Once in two years is what is decent, he said. They will welcome us, but if we go every year they will tire of us. The truth of the matter is that Dad could not afford to take us to Grandfather's every year. Dad never ever said he did not have money. It always was some very intellectual reason—'You children must learn self-denial,' 'You do not deserve it, look at your marks in Math—94? Where are the other 6 marks?' 'You will not have time for studies if you go to the movies,' so on and so forth... So while we wandered the passages of our apartment building this summer break, knocking on Ms. Ezekiel's door as she slept, throwing water balloons on passersby and going to Mazagaon Hill to play, Dad and the other men in the building were trying to pass their time too.

Easter descended on us once again I say descended because the Resurrection could only mean that Jesus died, went up to Heaven—we all know that Heaven is up above and Hell below—and coming back to Earth could only mean he descended. We waited eagerly for the Easter breakfast, when we could have that promised fried egg—Mum's special version of the Easter egg. Dad gave us options:

"Do you want real eggs for breakfast, or do you want a hard sugar shell with a yellow cotton ball chicken, which you cannot eat, sitting atop it, and boiled sweets inside, which in any case you do not like?"

"Sugar shell," said Ivan.

"Sugar shell," said Susan.

"Sugar shell," said I.

"Dad, you choose," said Francis, the most practical of us all. Of habit we knew that Dad, never serious when he gave us choices, had already decided what we would have.

"Do you want to go to Mangalore or stay behind for the summer holidays?" Dad asked every other year.

"Stay behind for the summer holiday club," we replied in unison. All this while Mother, already in the process of preparing for the trip, was measuring us for new dresses she would sew to take along. We could not look poor in the village we came from. We were from Bombay, the city of dreams!

So Francis took the practical route and gave Dad the choice. Of course Dad ignored our replies and took Francis's option, 'being the youngest.' Fried eggs it was. I realise only now as I write it that most of our traditions centered around Dad's purse and his belief in value for one's money. Nevertheless, I am not complaining. We loved the fried eggs that came our way once a year on Easter.

As I mentioned earlier, Easter morning we sat around the dining table, all glowing and grinning at no one in particular, the smell of eggs frying sending us into a tizzy.

"I am going to eat my egg very slowly so that I taste every bit of it," Susan said.

Susan had this very trying way of eating our favourite foods very slowly. She nibbled till we all finished our portions and then she began to slurp and relish hers in loud satisfied hmmms and ahhhs, enjoying not just the food but also the little picture she drew in her mind of us drooling as we watched her savour the goodie.

Not much later, that April, Dad saw an advertisement for a big poultry fair in Bombay. The advertisement had pictures of Leghorns and Rhode Island chicks—"highly productive layers," it claimed. Such industrial fairs were rare, or at least were not the kind we knew of, because they took place in far-flung suburbia, very much outside our world.

He went across to room no.18. It was much too early in the morning and Inspector D'Souza, Peter's dad—despite a slightly receding hairline, a tall handsome man, almost as handsome as Peter—opened the door, his face covered with lather and a razor in one hand.

"Yes, yes," he said, wiping the lather from his tongue with the back of his palm and trying to be brief under the circumstances.

"That's settled then, I will ask the others," Dad said, knocking on all the doors and asking whether the other residents would like to accompany him to the fair.

Mr. D'Souza and Dad often made a twosome—fishing and other such manly pursuits. They returned from such trips with fish they boasted about, holding them up by the tail like in the many trophy photos they had seen. Everyone knew they had bought the fish in the market, but the two boasting men had no clue that Mum and Isabel, though they extravagantly praised the men's fishing skills, knew their husbands had never caught a fish in their lives. Dad and Mr. D'Souza laughed, delighted to have tricked the kids and the wives, and none of us desired, even ever so slightly, to take away that pleasure from them. Such is love.

This hot April day begat yet another male sortie: Dad, Anthony Vaz and Inspector D'Souza set out early. Late that evening, all three of them came home with a chick each. All three men were excited with the prospect of having their own egg supply. For a month or so the chicks were kept sheltered in the apartments, but as they began to grow, the apartments crowded with the new members, so the men tied their chicks to the railing of the common verandah of the tenements, outside their own doors. They took the chicks indoors at night.

For superior egg quality, said the brochure that they had brought back with them from the fair, fortified chicken feed with "calcium and minerals" was essential. Dad wanted nothing less than the best eggs. Thus several sorties took Inspector D'Souza and Dad over 25 kms to

Goregaon, every month, to buy the feed. Anthony Vaz stayed home, being forbidden by Lolly to 'waste any more money on a bird.'

The feed acted like magic, and in two months the chicks had grown into full-sized birds. However, to Dad's dismay and our eternal amusement, we watched a magnificent comb grow out of a red and blue head. This was no layer…Whoever heard of a cock that laid eggs?

Dad put a brave front to the gentle teasing he faced in the family— gentle because we knew how much he wanted us to have the best he could offer. Gentle, because we were in awe of him. "We can have it for dinner when it grows," he said, and he continued to feed it with the special feed—"It's a Rhode Island," he boasted to visitors.

The chick grew into a giant cock. This was no ordinary cock, it was a giant "Rhode Island." Its fiery red and blue feathers stood high on its neck when anyone passed it. It needed very little by way of provocation. In the small confines of our apartment, we had to pass very close to it and dodge the furious pecks he handed out with boundless aggression. The four of us made a game of 'rushing past the cock' when Dad went to work. We did not name it, nor did we hug him or stroke him, as one does with pets. We were afraid of him. Our teachers sometimes said, 'You are a pet,' when we ran an errand for them. But this was no pet.

Anthony's chick turned out to be a hen. However, Anthony did not feed it the magic formula and it remained an average-sized bird; nothing spectacular like our cock. It was just as well. Billimoria Building could not handle so much aggression, much less from birds. Anthony took his hen to bed with him each night, till Lolly, his wife, gave a not so private diktat—Get rid of the hen; it's either her or me—loud enough for us to hear it through the thin walls that separated our apartments. We later learned that Anthony chose to sleep on the floor with the hen, till the following Christmas, when in his drunken inattention he ate his wife's meal of chicken, hidden under a heap of stuffing, and could not find his hen that night. Towards midnight, we heard Anthony's loud retching next door. Lolly said audibly in the otherwise quiet night, "You should not drink quite so much."

Four months later our cock disappeared from the verandah where he was kept tied during the day. We searched for him all over the building, knocking on everyone's door to ask whether they had seen it. 'No, we haven't,' 'Why should we know where your cock is?' 'Good riddance, one bad bird.' No one had seen him.

As I sat at the window after dinner, as I did most days, I saw him tied

outside the door of the restaurant across the street. His red and blue glo-
ry was unmistakable. It strutted up and down to the end of its leash and
back, moving its head to and fro as if pecking at some imaginary foe.
It surprised us that someone had actually picked up that bird without
casualty.

"Daddy, the cock." I stood, pointing at the road. I got no further. Dad,
out like a rocket, rushed across the street, and the cock came home. The
restaurant owner argued a while with Dad. He had paid Rs.10/ to Sammy
for the cock, but of course it did not matter to Dad—you cannot trans-
fer good value from bad—everyone in the neighbourhood knew Sammy
pushed stolen goods, so the restaurant owner should have known better;
taking anything from that no-gooder!

That was it. The masala was ground for a chicken curry I want no
memory of.

One very wet day in September 1990—wet weather-wise, but also wet
for Sammy, who came home that afternoon well hydrated, swaying on
his toes, rocking from side to side and front and back on an imaginary
swing, until he finally reached room 19—what transpired was nothing
short of a miracle; at least most people would look at it that way. In
Roman Catholicism, the working of miracles has been ascribed to its
saints or the Christ himself; Sammy Marchon conformed to only one
requirement: He was Roman Catholic.

That very morning, he had nicked the wall clock from the Marchon
home and sold it. Bruno and Oswald Marchon, despite their own advanced life of crime, had a strict code of ethics—one does not steal
from one's own home. Furious noises emanated from room no. 19. Bruno and Oswald took turns exfoliating their disgust at such despicable
behaviour, and Sammy giggled in between, not really getting what all
the fuss was about. When the altercation finally moved into their living
room, all of us who had closely followed the exchange moved towards
our windows. We hung over the sills, all the better to get a view or at
least hear the proceedings, which had now reached a crescendo. Sammy's head and half his body, helped forward by four muscular arms,
finally toppled over the window ledge in a bizarre double somersault.
A collective gasp resounded around the curved outer perimeter of the
building as Sammy bounced onto the pavement two floors below. We
rushed to our doors and ran out to the passage near the stairs. Was he
dead?

"He's gone!" someone cried. Peeping over the ledge of the passage window, we were stunned: Sammy's body had disappeared from the pavement. We disentangled ourselves from the collective knot and turned towards the stairs in shock. Sammy, grinning, not a scratch on his body, had appeared at the top of the stairs.

Not much is known about the progress of nature, for if it were, we would surely have known this to be a miracle. But the nature of things as they are, it is hard to define whether it was an interruption, a miracle, or just the natural flow of events. However, they do say that drunks and babies survive accidents—though I am not meaning to say that this was one (i.e., an accident).

Sammy went home giggling in embarrassment and bravado and we all went back to our homes with a renewed respect for him.

December 18th of 1992 was like every December 18th: Excited with Christmas round the corner and making goodies, we decorated our homes and sewed new clothes. That day, like so many others, we washed our hands after dinner and went to the passage, where Peter had called a meeting.

Every year around this time, all the buildings in our area made their own 'old man,' a stuffed straw man, very like a scarecrow, with firecrackers strategically placed within, to go off at well-spaced intervals and to blast even when the last ember had died down. For the face, many a year we used a mask of old Father Christmas left over from the Christmas party we had in the passage. Some buildings with their own twisted sense of humour put on a mask of the devil on their 'old man.' 'Imagine,' they giggled, 'the devil burning in a fire on earth, while he survives the fires of hell!' Every building on St. Mary's Road made one and hung the 'old man' over the street. We tied our 'old man' with a rope that went across the street from the second floor of Billimoria Building, to the second floor of the house opposite, with the 'old man' hanging high above the street and sometimes swinging in the breeze, almost as if sprung to life and wanting to escape his fate.

I felt a familiar bubbling in my heart when it came time for these activities. Peter, Miriam, Susan, Ivan, Aaron, Conrad, Gordon and Ali came to the meeting. The other children in the building never joined any such activity when their parents were home.

"We will make an 'old man'," said Peter assertively. Peter led all

the activities in the building. He was handsome, clever and we all looked up to him. He never disappointed. We asked him questions, however unrelated, and Peter never failed to have an answer. He was the only one of us who listened to the BBC news on the radio; always up to date on the events in the world, he planned, he executed, he created our fun, our pranks, even our morality outside of our parents.

"Yes, yes." Everyone nodded their heads.

"OK then, that's settled. Let us make a list of what we need."

"Old trousers, old long sleeved shirt, old socks, shoes and we will need a mask," Susan said.

"How do we make a head? Francis asked.

"A bag. One of those jute bags we use to buy rations with." I sometimes wonder what we would do in a world without Peter. I for one would not survive. "And lots of firecrackers, hay, and newspapers. We have to outlast the other 'old men' on Nesbit Road."

"How do we get this? We can give some newspapers, but the bag, socks, shirt, firecrackers, hay, blah, blah, blah...where do we find it Peter?" Susan was the practical one. At this point Sammy entered the meeting.

"I will get it," he offered.

"Sammy, I forgot to mention, we need gloves too, for his fingers." Susan, who was otherwise not really strong on anatomy grades, began listing body parts.

"Easy," said Sammy.

We all cheered and Sammy left the meeting quite happy.

Peter turned around and said, "Watch your clothesline till New Year's Day."

Chapter Sixteen

The Monday after the very volatile weekend with Mother and Dr. Apte was different from others. The alarm rang and I reached, to no avail, to clamp it down and stop its irritating buzz in my ear. Finally, I opened one eye to locate the offensive aggressor. Now get this—small things seem larger when unexpected. I stared into a giant glaring eye sharing my pillow. If you think beetles have a body, I would have, at that moment, strongly argued otherwise: it's only one large eye that makes up a beetle. An eye that can get you out of bed like no alarm clock can. I scrambled from the sheets in response.

But no, this is not the difference I speak of. Shortly after I arrived at the college, I encountered, close-up, another insect that I had spent the last five years flicking off my sleeve.

The staff room was quiet except for Ms. Raikar slurping her tea from a saucer in loud satisfied noises. I looked at her in the corner blowing the steam from the saucer to cool down the tea. Disgusting habit...reminded me of Billy—another disgusting memory. I am told that the students have set out a marriage in some imaginary heaven between Ms. Raikar and me. Nothing could be more repulsive to me—and I guess that she feels the same, unless I am reading too much into the rude way she turns her back. A shame, really, I think absentmindedly; I would quite like to run my hand through that thick, straight hair down her back, and that skin... clean and smooth; she's good looking, if one ignores that disdainful curl of her lips when she eyes me. I overheard her once say how "Western" I looked with my suit and tie. "Why can't he look Indian?"

I sighed. She was all that was wrong with this city, I thought resentfully, following as prejudiced a path as her thoughts of me.

"Good morning, Ms. Raikar." Still on formal surnames after five years of being on the faculty and sharing the staff room.

"Good morning," she said, without turning.

Exasperating! How difficult is it to be civil? This was not a good way to start the morning or the week. It was time to confront her, and so I walked up to her from behind and stopped just a foot behind her, prepared to— Hell. Were those teardrops blotting the paper in front of her? Nothing is more surprising than when you see someone you don't like exposing their vulnerability.

I pushed back my first instinct to welcome her to the human race, but spontaneity long having been suppressed by a mind absorbed in quadratic equations, I restrained my sarcasm. Surely my "good morning" could not have brought on the tears? Focus Peter, focus, it is not about you. I set aside my belligerent thoughts and stood still there behind her—as all creatures of my sex, not knowing what to do with a crying woman.

"Sorry," I said softly.

"Why?" she asked, but no longer in that sharp tone I was used to.

"Why are you crying? Do you want to talk?"

"Oh you won't understand..."

"I can try to."

"You are so structured and unemotional," she said.

When one delivers a comeuppance of someone who barely tolerates you, it helps if one looks good and dignified. Ms. Raikar, however, not so endowed right now, blew her nose loudly and turned her even less appealing red-rimmed eyes towards me. "Mathematical about everything," she added. "How can you understand true feelings?"

"I can try." My incomprehension of this illogical trend of thought, and my own repulsion of her suddenly changed. Here she was, vulnerable, not seeing my caste, community, but only me as a person. True, I have been quite unemotional, uninvolved and very distant from her at least; so I looked at this phenomenon with interest—I am a person to her...

"Ms. Raikar, can I ask you your first name?"

"Shiela," she said, now looking at me like...like, I don't really know, but differently.

"So, Shiela, let us start over,"

She smiled. Oh my God! Five years and I had never seen her smile. Her teeth, white and even, and lips now red with all the biting she had done... I swallowed.

"Peter," I said, holding out my hand.

She nodded, ignoring my hand. Ok, never mind that. At least she smiled.

"Now, that we are on first names, tell me what is wrong."

"Peter," she said, "have you ever been in love?"

"Let's talk about you," I said, not wanting to confront this issue, least of all to Shiela. One does not go to a funeral and have discussions about oneself, or one's views, with the grieving widow. "*You are important at this time.*"

"I am in love with this man."

"Love makes you cry?"

"No, but he is marrying another woman this Saturday."

"The bastard—forgive my language—are you telling me he has been seeing you and now marrying someone else?"

"Yes, but he says he told me right at the start that we could never get married even if he loved me."

"So why did you continue to date him?"

"I thought that he would want me so much that he would change his mind."

"Why did he say he couldn't marry you even if he loved you?"

"He is a Brahmin."

"Maharashtrian?"

"No."

Interesting. Maharashtra for Marathis, but not in love?

"You know it is best to forget him, don't you think? Need I say?"

"It is easy for you to say. You are a cold bachelor."

I must say this woman managed to alienate my sympathies just when I was warming up to her, but at least she looked more normal now. "You don't know that."

"So have you been in love?"

"Yes."

"Ah, she turned you down?"

"No. I never asked her."

Chapter Seventeen

On 2nd January 1993, Dad came home a very troubled man. Mother immediately talked—one may even describe it as babbling—about dinner: food being her solution to all of Dad's problems. It showed on Dad too. For a police inspector, he would have been described as portly if he wasn't as tall as he was.

"Sit down, love, and rest. I will make *chappatis*. I have kneaded the flour and kept it covered so that the *chappatis* become soft. You know you love soft *chappatis*. I bought the seventeen-rupees variety of wheat. I tried the fifteen, last time, and you did not like the *chappatis*. Maybe it is the level of gluten in the wheat. I will make the *phulkas*, the small puffed ones that you so like." Mum, delivering a monologue of uneasiness about the silence, immediately went into the kitchen and started rolling out *chappatis*.

Dad silently pulled off his socks, went to the small shower, pulled the shower curtain that separated the kitchen from his bath. We did not have showers or running water, and a bucket full of water was what we dipped a plastic mug into and washed ourselves. The kitchen dipped into silence, except for the steel spatula on the iron pan as Mum fried *chappatis* on it, and the splashing of water as Dad's shadow behind the curtain scooped water and poured it over his head in successive arm movements.

We followed his bathing silently sitting in the smoke-filled room, smelling fresh cooked dough on the pan and the spices blended in the fish curry Mum had put on the fire for reheating. Now occupied with soaping his body, we followed his bathing till we heard water splash once again. From years of experience, we knew not to disturb him with questions during this time. Dad did the questioning; maybe a fallout of the job in the police department. He did not take very kindly to being on the other side of the table. Silence continued till I broke the air with the BBC broadcast on the radio and Mum joined me in the living room, waiting for him to finish his bathing.

He stepped into the living room not much later and Mum once again bustled into the kitchen.

"Dinner is served."

"Can we sit a while, here? I have something to tell you both."

Standing in his office earlier that day, Dad had been seized by the dilemma of how to mitigate the tension in the city caused by the pulling down of the Babri Mosque a month earlier by Hindus who had claimed it stood in the sacred place of Lord Ram's birth. He'd stared at the falling plaster on the wall, making mental notes to get the maintenance department on the job. The f---ers, he thought, we have just renovated this building. Cheap f---ers, the walls are so thin I can hear everyone breathe in this bloody place. Then he realised the real source of his annoyance: his assistant in the next room talking incessantly on the phone!

"Yes, yes, we have the list," he was saying. "Billimoria Building?"

At which point Dad leaned against the wall to hear more closely.

"Yes, yes, one family. Where? Second floor, corner room, above the Irani restaurant. Yes, yes, I am sure they are Muslims. Farooqui, what do you expect them to be, Brahmins? Of course I am sure they are Muslims. Okay, okay."

Dad had no doubt that this was a call for a hit on the Farooqui family. He had been aware for a while that something was amiss. Chaos had set in. Cause and effect. Chicken-and-egg syndrome. If we don't get them they will get us. There seemed no end in sight— the panic of survival from the very beginning of time! Disturbed, he went back to his desk and began to change the blotting pad on his desk, too distraught to move. He did not know how to address this. He came home a very troubled man.

Mum said, "Ali?"

"His family and their property."

"Haven't they faced enough? His father has just been killed."

"These are not the best of times, love." Dad now stood to go to the dinner table.

"Can't you save them?" Mother, who had followed him as he sat to dinner, kept piling his plate with food now.

"This disturbance is more ground level, my dear. You know, grassroots, civilian. Leaders may instigate, but nothing happens without the participation of civil society. The police, though they have a role in maintaining law and order, are also part of that very same civil society. They form part of the same social fabric we are all woven from; same religion, same culture, same fears. They have families that are part of civil society. No, love, I don't think I can do anything alone."

Chapter Eighteen

"How good and pleasant it is when brothers live together in unity!"

-Psalm
133:1-3

The drunkenness, music, dancing and frivolity, the usual hallmark of New Year, had not happened that year; not even the 'old man.' The situation in the city being tense, none of the parents let their children freely roam the streets on New Year's Eve as we'd done every year. Too many things had burned in the past week and no, it was not safe to be out. The mood was dismal. The sun, unsympathetic with our mood, shone just as bright, laughing at us, daring us to go out.

The day after Dad's revelation, Mum made the first sortie next door, to Mr. Fernandes, the centre of all action. I followed her close on her heels, not wanting to miss out on the drama. Even at twenty one, and in college, my life continued to be lived between the Fernandes apartment and our own. Dad stayed back at home of course. It was just not right for him to leak any official information or anything he had learnt in the course of his job. Mr. Fernandes, unlike Dad, said, "Stop it. Isabel, this has to stop! We cannot let the Farooquis be attacked by these villains."

"How? We are helpless, *bhovoji.*"

"Let us have a meeting."

"This must be a more secret meeting. We do not know who to trust or when this will happen. We do not know who is the enemy."

"First," said Mr. Fernandes, who always liked to thrash out matters linearly, "let us inform Mrs. Farooqui and Ali. We have to take care of them now that Mr. Farooqui is no more. Besides, I promised Mr. Farooqui on his deathbed. I have no choice."

"Who will tell them? Don't forget, bhovoji, we have to keep the confidentiality of my husband's information. The matter is not only life-and-death but also involves my husband's job. All plans should take into account this issue."

"You can trust me." Mr. Fernandes, ever the saviour, reassured Isabel, who had implicit faith in him and never really disagreed with him on any matter. "Secondly, we must ask Ali and his mother if they have someplace to go to till the trouble subsides." Then, trying to cover all flanks like a good strategist, he carried on. "We will have a meeting and call a few people who can help us. No need to call everyone... Some of them are useless." He waved his hands in the air, disgusted with their expected inaction. "Isabelbai, can you work out a list of who to include in this meeting while I speak to Mrs. Farooqui?"

Mum and I departed, leaving Mrs. Fernandes looking very disturbed. Isabel sat down, pondering the list with one eye on the door waiting for Mr. Fernandes to pass. Dad sat quietly nearby, as anxious as Mother. Mr. Fernandes returned shaking his head. As he passed our door, which was left opened, Mother stalled him. Mr. Fernandes was as transparent and dramatic as they came. Deception would have been a challenge, what with his Catholic conscience screaming loudly within.

No, he said, they did not have any place to go to... No, we will need a plan for where to keep them...

Mr. Fernandes asked Dad and Mum to come over and discuss the matter. We went over to their apartment. Everyone sat around silently, each of us mentally engrossed with how to get the Farooqui family to safety. Let us first have a plan before we invite anyone else to the meeting, Mr Fernandes proposed. He was a very methodical man. So once again we went into numbers:

"Firstly, let us define what exactly we want to do." He looked around the circle for answers.

Mrs. Fernandes, who generally waited for him to make the decisions, now looked around at each one of us and said, "We may have very little time. We need to act fast. So I think if we are in agreement that we have to save Ali and Mehroonisa then we should go directly to the point, but the first consideration is: do we want to save them despite the danger to our own families? I mean, isn't there a big price to pay here? We are not experienced in secrecy and deceit, lies and discretion, and our children—just look at them—they are so simple, though loving. Are we really equipped for this task? Can't we just hand it to the police?" She now looked at Dad.

Dad looked a bit embarrassed. He put his head down, thinking how best to word his reply; he focussed on the centre of the floor between his two shoes.

"Mrs. Fernandes, I agree with you in most part. I would like to agree with you completely and yes, I would also like to believe I work for an organisation that will uphold law and justice. So yes, logically it should be the work of the police to protect Ali and his mother. However, the force is riddled with men at this time and not police officers. Men with the same hatreds, anger, fear as you or any other person in society. They are operating as men and not police officers. Don't get me wrong. I would be unfair to the hundreds who actually do their job and do it well. But these are special times; the normal rules of social engagement are suppressed by this madness."

Mr. Fernandes looked at his wife. Then he looked around at his children. Then he looked at the altar that was above the chest of drawers: a small wooden shelf with a carved bracket that held a cross with a statue of Jesus nailed to it, and statues of Mary and St. Anthony on either side, with a small night light that always stayed on, flickering, pretending to be a roaring flame.

"Darling," he said, using a word we never heard from him; trouble can bring out the soft core as well as the strength in men. "It is our Christian duty to help our neighbour."

"Yes, we do have to be good to our neighbours and so we are. We are not part of the rioting or the bigotry. So is that not enough to be a good Christian? How far can we carry the neighbourly duty? Are we responsible for even those we barely talk to? I mean, how far can we stretch our responsibility?"

"Darling, in other words you want to limit and define the world into small circles of people—us, them—but that only separates us. If you recall Jesus' answer when he is asked by..." He stopped and groped for the biblical reference. "Umm...someone, I forget right now but it will come back to me. Anyway, the question he asked is, 'Lord, who is my neighbour?' and Jesus responds to it with the story of the Good Samaritan, I think it is in Luke. The essence is that the one who helps is the neighbour and it is not defined by caste or creed or proximity. How could we reconcile with our Christian consciousness if we did not help them? How can we face our children, whom we constantly remind of the teachings of Christ, if we are not good role models for them ourselves?"

"Is it not enough that we do not contribute to this madness? Must we be sucked in ourselves, to justify our Christian beliefs?"

"There are errors of commission, but there also errors of omission. Can we turn our faces away while our neighbour gets killed? Ali is merely a boy, not much older than our own Anna. 'Do unto others as thou would'st like them to do unto thyself,' as you know, that is what the Bible says."

"Yes, dear." She looked directly at him and said softly, "All I am saying is that in case you want to take them into our home it would endanger us all and may not achieve its purpose in any case."

"I was not thinking of having them here, but now that you mention it, yes, I think we have to move them out of that room." He looked around the room and at the decorated Christmas tree. "Take that down," he told Ivan, "and take the star down, this is no time for rejoicing."

Every year our Christmas festivities continued up to 6th January, the day of the Epiphany, or as most Catholics call it, the three kings feast. We finally take down our stars that we hang outside our windows, the nativity crib and the Christmas tree on the 6th of every January. Mr. Fernandes' diktat set Ivan in motion. While he took down, ornament by ornament, mostly cheap Santas made of egg shells carefully cracked at the top, with cotton beard and moustache and painted faces, with red caps made of cheap crepe paper, Mr. Fernandes continued the meeting.

"So at least we are agreed that we have to move Ali and his mother to a safe place."

There was a general silence only broken by Ivan's noisy dismantling of the tree. Some of the eggshells cracked with the operation and Ivan was making a game of smashing them further into smithereens by stamping on them. Everyone else looked around at each other, dumb with the enormity of the task... I mean, where could one be safe and where could we fit two adults? I should say two adult strangers, because our interactions with the family had been minimal. They lived so differently from us. Thankfully Ali's wife was not yet sent to live with him since she was too young. Still, how could anyone hide in this building when we had such small apartments? Why, our postal addresses did not say apartment number or flat number, they only said room number. We lived in rooms... Any such move would definitely involve endangering ourselves, because others would for sure know we had hidden them. Besides, Ali's mother was conspicuous with her black burqa, and she would never consent to taking it off, especially if she lived where another man lived. We were not only facing danger but something that had become a physical and cultural impossibility in our minds.

A silent room is the noisiest one imaginable. The clock screamed almost like a drum, tick, tick, tick, and the fan above whirred violently. The children in the Municipal school down the road sang the national anthem in loud, unmusical tones. The trucks on the street below were unusually laborious, their engines gruff and gritting their teeth; the street dogs were barking. An occasional aircraft thundered above as we glanced at each other. But above all this noise, we could hear our fear in the room.

"There is no sanctuary here in the building," said Mrs. Fernandes, now on the verge of tears. She, from experience, knew that Mr. Fernandes would take it upon himself to move Ali and his mother to the only place that would have them: the Fernandes home.

"Except Ms. Ezekiel's room, where nobody expects to look," Anna piped in. We all snickered. Just another impossibility added to the pile.

"No harm in trying," said Francis, who unfailingly aligned himself with Anna.

"Well, Ms. Ezekiel is out of the question." Mr. Fernandes waved it aside, not a sweeping wave but one with a loose wrist, fanning it around like he really needed several sweeps to get rid of it.

"Anna, my child, that is such a wild suggestion." Isabel tried to make up for Mr. Fernandes' disrespectful dismissal. "She will not even open the door for a discussion. You children have been harassing her and we will never have her consent. Besides, she is Jewish and Ali and his mother, Muslims."

"Isabelbai, let us not even go there. Being Jewish or Muslim has nothing to do with being a neighbour." Mr. Fernandes snorted. Then he looked around the room and realised how stupid that sounded under the present circumstances. "Well, at least it shouldn't..." he said in a more uncertain tone.

"Well, my dear, if it didn't, we would not be discussing this as it is," Mrs. Fernandes said kindly.

"Be that as it may, I feel that we should take them in, darling. How would you want it to be if the shoe was on the other foot?"

"Catholics do not interfere with anyone, dear. Why would the shoe be on the other foot? Besides, we do not have space here."

"But it is never always about interference, darling. This is mob madness we are talking about. It is Jesus' teachings: do unto others as you would unto thyself."

"Dad, may I ask Ms. Ezekiel in private?" Anna and Francis, whispering to each other, had totally ignored the conversation that had just taken place. "Besides, she does not speak with anyone, so it will be as good as a secret," Anna persisted.

"Ok. Take care that no one knows what you are doing," Mrs. Fernandes said indulgently, and I think, mostly to get rid of the two kids. She succeeded, if that was the intention. Anna and Francis left the room to do whatever they could do, or thought they could. The rest of us sunk back into the depressed silence, quite impoverished for ideas or solutions. Dad sat apologetically in his chair, wondering if they could shift Ali and his mother to another location. But where was it safe for a black burqa to be?

"Damn the woman," he finally said, "does she have to be so conspicuous in such troubled times?"

"Mr. D'Souza." Mrs. Fernandes spoke with gentle admonishment. "That is the identity she has been brought up with. Should she be deprived of the last vestige of what she is?"

Dad sunk back into guilty silence.

Anna, in the meantime, undeterred, sat penning a letter to Ms. Ezekiel, aided by the adoring Francis. In the view of Mr. Fernandes, such childish solutions should be best left to children to work out. He took a break from this dismal activity to caution that no one should know anything of the discussions taking place within the confines of their home. Susan, seeing that there was no role for her, picked a book and leafed through its pages, uncertain whether she wanted to get lost in its folds. Mrs. Fernandes left the room to resume her cooking and other chores interrupted by this meeting, and Mother and Mr. Fernandes sat with a crease between their foreheads indicating that they were still searching for solutions. Dad left for work. "I will keep you informed," he said.

Anna had come up with the letter after many scribblings and scratches and flinging several drafts into the waste bin in the kitchen. "May I read it aloud, Aunt Isabel?" she said. Mum looked at her and said kindly, "Sure, darling, I am sure it is fine, can we do it later? I am thinking right now."

Then Anna turned to me and said, "Peter, do you want to hear what I have written?"

"No, Anna. This is only an exercise in futility and I have better things to do." I decided to go back to my album of stamps which I had collected over the last few years and not engage in this hopeless optimism Anna displayed by placing confidence in someone so disengaged from society – as Ms. Ezekiel so obviously was.

"You are so quick to judge. Just because she does not mix with us does not mean she is unwilling to help when called upon."

"Whatever. Anna, do as you may."

So we never really knew what Anna wrote.

Chapter Nineteen

"A friend loveth at all times, and a brother is born for adversity"

-Proverbs 17:17

Anna had a very long relationship with Ms. Ezekiel—that is, if one could have a relationship without the other's participation or consent. (I am sure there is some impossible-sounding word given to this phenomenon in either Law or Psychology, no doubt accompanied by some deeply convoluted explanation.) Anna had for years—feeling that Ms. Ezekiel was very lonely and must thus be very unhappy—tirelessly conducted such a relationship with her. Every once in a while when she remembered, or by chance visited the first floor, she would stop outside Ms. Ezekiel's door and say, 'Good morning, Ms. Ezekiel,' or 'Good afternoon, Ms. Ezekiel,' or 'Ms. Ezekiel, I am quite well today and I hope you are too.' Such was her relationship, mostly with a closed wooden door painted dull beige and remaining ever shut to the world.

Anna had severe asthma. So for most of her childhood she stayed home from school. She did what none of us could: spend time with Billy, who none of us liked; talk to Ms. Ezekiel, who none of us had really seen or talked to. Through the closed door, Anna apologised for us and for our transgressions with little "sorry" notes slipped beneath, or sometimes a plate of cake left outside the door. The cake was a bit of a sacrifice since it was really very rare that anyone in Billimoria Building could afford a cake.

But our romantic, loving Anna left her share out there like she was feeding a puppy or a bird.

Did the cake get to the target? Ms. Ezekiel might be a recluse, but her sweet tooth did not move in the same direction. Anna patiently stood outside, plate in hand, and announced that she would love to share her cake and would Ms. Ezekiel please open the door? But of course it didn't work. The door never opened. Then Anna would say, I am leaving it outside and moving away, so please enjoy it. Faithful to her promise, she would walk away before gnarled fingers reached from behind the door and slid the cake inside.

I guess the eating of the cake did constitute a relationship. Words can distort and change emotions, feelings, can deceive or give meaning to what the heart thinks. But the heart thinks what the heart thinks. By that measure I guess Anna did have a relationship.

Now Anna, with her great penmanship, had written a long letter to Ms. Ezekiel. The Fernandes family ignored her naive attempts to find a solution, but did not discourage her. "Ensure that no one downstairs sees what you are doing, darling," said Mrs. Fernandes to the retreating back.

Putting a letter under the door seemed like an easy task, but Anna had to make two trips to the Ezekiel door. Her first trip was aborted by Surve's son.

"Hi, beby," he said in a very stilted English accent.

"Hi, but don't call me baby."

"So what you doing here? Come to meet me?"

"No, that is conceit."

"Cuntseat?"

"Whatever," and she turned around and came back upstairs considerably huffed; if blushing under a dark tan were possible, Anna would have been bright red.

"Stupid, stupid, s-stupid..." she stuttered with outrage.

Second time around, Francis said he would stand on watch while she went and slipped the note. And so, an hour later, they tiptoed down to the first floor as noiselessly as possible. It was 2.30 p.m., and tiptoeing was completely unnecessary—the coast was all clear. Anna slipped the note beneath the door halfway and waited for it to be pulled in. Shortly after, she returned and stood on the second-floor verandah at the other side of the L waiting for a response...hopeful.

Predictably, nothing happened, and we all went to bed that night wondering when and how to hide Ali and his mother—none of us wanting to face that it might be too late if we did not come up with a plan soon enough.

Chapter Twenty

Dad, who had most of the inside information, came home the next morning looking like hell. He said he did not want to talk and needed a short nap. We sat listening to his uneven snoring while we waited silently. The night before, someone had taken a knife to a Muslim in Dharavi. Though this was not Dad's jurisdiction, his police station, located in a Muslim area, was on high alert. They'd also received information that a group of individuals posing as officials of the Maharashtra Housing and Development Agency were making the rounds in Antop Hill, noting the residences of the Muslims.

Dad was trying to postpone confronting the real danger Ali and his mother were in. Finally he woke, walked to the mori silently, splashed water on his face, took down the towel from the clothes line and patted himself dry. He then walked out without saying a word. Mum and I followed him next door.

"Mr. Fernandes, I think we are running out of time. We have to find a solution as soon as possible. There is real and imminent danger to Ali and Mehroonisa. Everyone is looking at each other, distrustful, thinking they have to get the other first. Good, ordinary people are joining. I fear a complete breakdown of civil society. Much is out of the hands of the police. I fear for Ali and his mother. I fear, above all, we will never be able to live with ourselves if we don't do something."

From the other side of the L, where he'd been peering over the balustrade, suddenly Francis came running in. He rushed to Anna, who was cutting up some greeting cards, preparing to write a second plea to Ms. Ezekiel.

Ms. Ezekiel's door, it seemed, had sprung to life. Francis described the way a fraction of a paper stuck out of her door and kept moving to and fro, slowly, from the left to the right of the door and then back to the left. "I am sure it is a signal for you, Anna!"

"Calm down, Francis, we cannot have anyone see us if what you say is true." She stood, looking ready to run, but stopped short and walked slowly out of the door with Francis in tow.

Ivan and Susan walked over to the other side of the L to watch the proceedings, trying to look as casual as possible under the circumstances. We all agreed that secrecy meant safety for all concerned.

That was a very busy day for Dad. The violence had escalated and both sides were now actively 'protecting themselves.' There were reports that a big mob of Hindus, led by a bunch of self-styled keepers of the Hindu faith, and consequently of Hindu safety, had taken over the work of the police. Dad received a summons to report back at the station. The mob had attacked the Jogeshwari Police Station in protest for the lack of security for Hindus. Some enthusiastic mobsters had attacked Chacha Nagar Masjid, and the more zealous of them had thrown a few Muslims into the destruction, injuring them. Several Muslim huts in Magdum Nagar were subsequently set on fire by Hindus.

While Dad was gone, imparting strict instructions to all of us not to leave the house and not to be indiscreet with the information we had, Mum and I once again sat down with the Fernandes family. Mrs. Fernandes, who generally looked upon Mr. Fernandes to make all the decisions, not only in the family but in all matters, now showed an unusual firmness. *No dear, you will not go to work this week. I will be very unhappy if you do and I will not forgive you if you do not keep yourself safe. Do not forget we have four children and you have a wife.* Mum, not wanting to be left out of any conversation, said, "Yes, Mr. Fernandes, there is us too. We all depend on you and so do the neighbours. I read somewhere, 'safety saves,' so I completely agree. You have to be safe and we have yet to decide what to do with Ali and Mrs. Farooqui."

Anna and Francis burst into the room at that moment, Anna waving a sheet of paper in the air. "She said yes, she said yes!" It took them at least ten minutes to calm down and breathe evenly. Might have been less, but for those of us who were waiting in suspense, it seemed like a very long time.

"Calm down, children," Mrs. Fernandes said in her gentle voice. "Anna, my child, who said yes?"

"Ms. Ezekiel."

"To what? Anna you are not making sense."

Anna pushed the sheet of paper in front of her. "Look, she said yes!"

Mrs. Fernandes looked down at the paper, which had one word on it. It had, surprisingly, a very well written word, singular, mathematically centred on the page. Yes.

"Anna, can you take a moment and breathe in, my child. You know it is not good for your asthma. Ok, now, breathe in...breathe out..."

"Mu-m..." Anna, impatient to move on despite the loud wheezing that came through the silence, was interrupted by her mother's resolutely calm voice.

"Breathe in...Anna, slow down, I said breathe in, ok now breathe out..."

Anna stopped talking, sat down and began breathing consciously under her mother's direction like a metronome. Finally relaxed, she spoke.

"Mummy, I wrote to Ms. Ezekiel that the situation in the city is very bad and that they are targeting the Muslims, and we have special information that Ali and his mother are on the list. They could get killed if we do not intervene. I wrote: 'Ms. Ezekiel, you will recall the plight of the Jews in Nazi Germany. I beg of you to help us. I apologise for all the times we have hurt you with our childish games. It was boredom and not malice. Please forgive us and help us now. Let me remind you, painful though it may be to you, that so many Jews were killed by such prejudice and injustice as is happening right now in this city. But then, who else could better understand Ali's plight? Would you please consider keeping them in your apartment? We will provide the food they will need and they will be only grateful. Your apartment is the only one in this building that is above suspicion. Nobody will ever expect them to be with you. Not meaning to be disrespectful, but everyone knows you do not mingle and live completely cut off from the rest of the world. But I know in my heart, you have the kindness and love that every human is capable of, and I am begging you to once again find that part of yourself and help us. You are aware, I am sure, that many Jews survived because of their very generous neighbours who helped hide them...'"

"I am so proud of you my child," Mrs. Fernandes said.

"You are indeed a good writer," Isabel said, ready to praise everything Anna did. "Our Anna will be a famous writer one day."

"So if we are to understand right, you believe that her yes is to your request to hide Ali?" I asked, not believing it could be so simple. "Are you sure you can trust her? Is she really going to have them?" All my questions were greeted with silence and frowns. Anna even looked pityingly at my scepticism, moving me to say, "So what next?"

"We need to plan this move carefully," said Mr. Fernandes. "Do not forget we have the Surve family down there, and though they are our neighbours and very decent, these are unusual times. Muslims and Hindus who never did think like that are now looking at each other with suspicion and hatred. We do not know how the Surves are reacting to the problem."

"Dad, what do I tell Ms. Ezekiel?"

For the first time I saw Mr. Fernandes hesitate. He just did not know. Then all of us began speaking at the same time, each feeling we had to fill in the gap in conversation. Finally, Mr. Fernandes held up his hand.

"We must send an interim reply. Anna, ask her if the night of the 7th will suit her. Word it in your own way. We need at least a day to get her response and perhaps a day or two to plan and get Mrs. Farooqui to agree to move. Isabelbai, will you convey it to Mrs. Farooqui? I cannot handle her tears, especially because her eyes are the only exposed part of her face. Today is already the 4th. We do not know if Ms. Ezekiel would agree to the 7th. In the meantime, we plan how to move them and what to do, and then Isabel will inform them."

Chapter Twenty-One

D ad did not come home on the night of the 4th and continued to work into the next day. The situation had not eased. He returned for a quick lunch and rushed back to the police station. The night of the 5th, a Hindu *Mathadi* worker was killed. The unfortunate man, who worked at the warehouse of a transport company spent that night in the warehouse. Sometime in the night he went out on to the street in front of the warehouse, quite believing that urinating on Bombay streets was a truly innocent occupation, and not anticipating he'd be killed for it. As he relieved his kidneys against the wall outside, a small band of vigilantes, or maybe just a bunch of troublemakers, relieved him of his life. His friends rushed out from the warehouse to help him and met with the same fate. How does one really understand mob fury, fear, survival? How does one recognise the changes in one's neighbour and brother of yesterday? There must be a mathematical, numerical solution, some certainty to human behaviour...

The Mathadi workers' deaths set in motion events that made our mission to save Ali even more urgent. The Mathadi workers' union called for a *bandh*, closure. This heightened tensions further. On top of the fears of religious enmity were piled the tensions of the unions— and they were never a recipe for peace or calming of emotions. Speeches flew across the city. Mathadi union leaders held large meetings and vehemently and dramatically condemned the police and government for not providing adequate protection. Impassioned speeches calling upon the Hindus to prepare themselves with swords and defend themselves should the police fail them, flew in the already bloody air. Anarchy, no longer a subterranean, unspoken option, took a bolder form. Fear propelled it along, helped by those who saw an opportunity to achieve political mileage. The local fundamentalist political party stepped up the frenzy. The Union Leaders pressed for action. Though uncertainty prevailed and no one knew who the assailants were, the Muslims were accused—for who else could it be? These were Hindus who'd been killed...

A call for a *bandh* of the wholesale markets where the *Mathadi* workers contracted their labour pushed the idea further. Seemed like a no-brainer. Muslims were the culprits; Hindus needed to protect themselves because the state had proved it could not. The already tense situation spiralled like smoke from a fighter plane in the midst of manoeuvres.

Dad came home briefly. Mother, as always, bustled around him till he lost his cool. He had worked tirelessly, and from lack of sleep he dared to say to her, "Isabel, can you just sit down awhile?" Mother tried not to look hurt and sat down silently. He went on to say, "The situation is getting out of hand and we should make the move as fast as possible. I cannot foresee the timing, but violence is a great possibility. All of you, stay in the building. I cannot be here, but tell Mr. Fernandes to please work it out. We have not much time if we want to live in peace with our conscience." He rushed out of the door.

Mr. Fernandes did not go to work, as really there was no point. For one who worked near the airport and had no car, he would have to use public transport. The call for the *bandh* at the transport company, though generally illegal, was obeyed out of fear—and for safety, as miscreants would stone any disobedient vehicles. As always, public transport was taken off the roads to prevent loss to public property. Private vehicles and taxis, not wanting to incur losses either, stayed away too.

Mr. Fernandes and Isabel led the new discussion. *If we have to transfer Ali and his mother on the 7th, in case Ms. Ezekiel agrees to the date, how best can it be done? Do we need to involve others?*

Mrs. Fernandes and Mother both thought that calling a meeting would be a good way to start. Now that it seemed more concrete on where they would be moved, we knew that there would be more planning and execution required to move them to the first floor than merely moving them into our homes. Ferrying their luggage, and taking them down without anyone noticing, would be the biggest challenge in Billimoria Building.

"Isabel, who do you think we should invite? I myself am of the opinion that the fewer the people that know about it the better. We cannot maintain secrecy with too many people in the action. But we need more than just our two families. You know how curious neighbours can be. Will you go and inform Ali and his mother to be prepared?" Looking at mother's doubtful face, he added,

"She is not comfortable with a man. Tell her that she will have to take off the burqa. We cannot transfer her secretly if she is in that garb. The building opposite will see her come out on the verandah—especially in the night, we will not know who is at their windows watching. Then we have the Madrassis below. We will have to pass their room to reach Ms. Ezekiel's, and they are Hindus. Then there is the Surves' apartment at the end. We now know that his son has been part of the youth roaming on the streets in the vigilante gangs. He has been openly walking on the streets with them, even right here in our neighbourhood, brandishing a sword. We must first ensure that Mrs. Farooqui will not wear that god-awful outfit while we make this move."

Isabel went to Ali's room and the rest of us waited patiently for the next response to come out from under Ms. Ezekiel's door.

Chapter Twenty-Two

From the droop of her shoulders and her gait we knew that Isabel had returned with some very worrying news. The lines in her forehead were deep grooves, a veritable network of waterways as she dripped sweat and took a nervous dip into her snuff box.

She had set out to Ali's room, labouring to make the journey surreptitious. It was a challenge for one such as her, with a tall, imposing figure that was far from discreet. Mother attracts attention; not just her size but also her very friendly relations with all around. Mrs. Olivera, who had not gone to work, stopped her as she passed their doorway.

"Isabel, how do you make veal with green curry?"

Isabel, trying not to sound impatient, said, "Veal tastes best with the traditional beef curry. I suggest the regular curry you make, Gina."

"Isabel, is Mr. D'Souza on duty?" This from Mimosa, who, next door to Gina, was idling in the verandah and wanted the latest news on the rioting.

"Yes, Mimosa." This was the briefest Isabel had been in a very long while.

"Any news on what is happening in the city?"

"No, Mimosa."

"So where are you going?"

Isabel, normally a very patient woman, was trying to look at this new pest with patience and not arouse her curiosity in any way.

"Mimosa, I must excuse myself, I am going to look out from the passage window, I think I saw a friend pass," she lied.

Mimosa stepped aside. Isabel had a clear run after that. She went to the window of the passage and looked out, tapping her foot impatiently till Mimosa went indoors, and then made her way to Ali's home without any further interruptions.

Ali's mother cried for the first twenty minutes. Ali and Isabel attempted to console her, but she was inconsolable. Her husband, a statistic of the casualties of the riot, and now to find themselves in a similar danger...it was too much for her to take.

"Mehroonisa," Isabel said as she started to calm. Mother seemed to be the only one who addressed her by her first name. "You have to listen carefully. We are going to help you. You have to let us help you, do you understand?"

Mehroonisa nodded. Ali nodded too, to confirm that she understood.

"You will have to pack some clothes and food for you and Ali. You will be staying on the first floor in Ms. Ezekiel's home. I don't know the arrangements yet and we are discussing the details. You do not have to concern yourself with that. Please see that you take your potty; we don't know how long you will be holed up there and you should not be using the common toilets if there is anyone in view. We will give you precise instructions later. For now, can you get this ready? And..." Isabel paused, not knowing how to do this painlessly. Anyway, this was no time for Mehroonisa to be offended by people who were trying to save them, so she just went ahead and said it. "Please do not wear the burqa. We do not want you to stand out so blatantly as Muslim."

Isabel was in for a shock, because hardly ever did anyone say no to her.

"*Nai ho sakta*, not possible," Mehroonisa said firmly. "*Marne ke liye tyar hai*—I don't mind dying, but I will not take this off."

Isabel had not anticipated this hurdle. "She refuses to take off the burqa," she told us. "The black garment is so obvious and so dangerous. Even if we move them without anyone seeing us, how would she avoid being noticed when she goes to the toilet? How do we help her if she will not cooperate?"

"Dad," Francis said, "at least if she had a white burqa she would look like a nun."

Sometimes the simplest suggestions are the most logical. While we adults – and though I was often included with the children, I thought of myself as an adult – were engaged in re-criminating thoughts, fighting with our frustration, some of us even going as far as cursing the oppression of tradition, the children, not so encumbered, imagined a solution. From thereon the conversation turned to the different colours of burqas and how they compared to a nun's habit. No, not the same. The design of the burqa, the lace trimming, especially in the coloured ones that the Boris, a Muslim sect, wore...no, not the same as a nun's habit.

"Maybe we should get a nun's habit, in that case," said Francis, once again the problem solver...no cluttered screen there.

We all looked at him more carefully then. He had no doubts. Unlike us, he seemed to think it was all so simple. Here we were, all the adults, with brains being exerted and looking at every solution but the obvious...at least, obvious to Francis.

"How," I asked, a tad sarcastically, "do you propose to find a nun's habit?"

We all looked at each other with one image in mind.

Chapter Twenty-Three

G lenda's mother, Mrs. Alphonso, had continued to work even during the riots. Sister St. Claire, the nun in charge of the convent's housekeeping, under whose thin, wiry nose Mrs. Alphonso worked, had seen no reason why not. She'd said something that began with, "You see, in Ireland..." She was originally from Ireland, where they gave their sons and daughters to the church as a career. Having known no other life from the age of fourteen, Sister St. Claire, not burdened with compassion, had turned her very blue eyes from her task, looked down her thin nose at Glenda's mother and said, "Here." She held out a giant cross that could be worn around the neck. "You will be safe."

It was a wonder Mrs. Alphonso survived the weight of the cross around her neck without developing a form of spondylitis. Truthfully, if she did have spondylitis we would never know. We knew nothing about her. "This is a Hindu-Muslim riot—no need for you to stay home." So Glenda's mother put on a red dress over her flower-patterned one and walked down the street, sloppy, glum, disconnected, her head cocked to one side and her hair screaming for a comb.

She spent well over two hours washing the nuns' habits and other miscellaneous clothes they gave her, and finally, not wanting to stay late at the convent, she carried a large bag of clothes home to iron. Sister St. Claire stopped her at the door and counted the habits—much to

Mrs. Alphonso's disgust—reminded her that they would require them the next day, and then allowed her through.

Who the hell would steal a habit? No one wears those bloody things but those witches! thought Glenda's mother. They were supposed to be above such pettiness. I have never thieved or slacked, yet they continue to count and check me every time I leave. Trust is definitely not their strong point, these women of faith. No, she definitely did not have the perfect job... If not for Glenda, I would kill myself. This is a shit life.

Mrs. Alphonso slowly made her way home. No mob would want to kill her. Mobs were on a rampage, and kindness was not their job. No they would never be kind enough to relieve this depressed, dowdy specimen of her life. It wasn't necessary to. Catholics were not part of this madness. And so no one interested themselves in this almost invisible human being trudging down the road, a huge cross swinging around her neck.

We watched Mrs. Alphonso come up the stairs, all of us waiting for her to return. Mr. Fernandes and Isabel discussed whom we could share the information with and whose help we needed. Mr. Fernandes went next door to Anthony Vaz's home. Anthony Vaz looked at his wife. Her face stern, she said,

"Sorry, Mr. Fernandes, I do not see how it is our business."

"Mrs. Vaz, what if the roles were reversed and they had to save us?"

"Mr. Fernandes, that will never happen. We are Christians and we do not interfere with other communities. We mind our own business and we do not engage in anti-national and illegal activities."

"Mrs. Vaz, in other words, are you saying that Ali should be condemned to die because he is Muslim and some Muslim may have committed some offences? You say you are Christian, but where is your Christian charity?"

"You are better advised to mind your own business. Besides, you are not my spiritual guardian and I will work with my Christian conscience without your help, thank you very much indeed."

Mr. Fernandes now looked scornfully at Anthony Vaz, who sat in the corner, cuddling the kitten that had replaced his hen. Anthony Vaz looked away. Mr. Fernandes walked out of the Vaz household very discouraged, but taking comfort from the thought that at least he had not told them what the plan was. He wondered why, after all these years, he had actually expected them to do anything outgoing. Optimism ran strong in the Fernandes vein, he concluded.

Meanwhile, Isabel returned from a failed campaign with the Oliveras, who really didn't see how they were involved in this at all. *I mean, we are not even friendly with them. I mean, they are not even Catholics. I mean, our children too are not that friendly with Ali.*

Failure was beginning to get to Isabel. For one who very rarely failed, this second disappointment almost brought her to tears. She returned to the Fernandeses' sniffing at her snuff several times in that short distance from the Olivera household. Mr. Fernandes, much used to the building's apathy, found strength in recalling all those times others had not joined in and yet he had achieved his aims nonetheless.

"Isabel, do not be disappointed. Not everyone sees this as their duty. Somehow Christ's teachings are not practical for everyone. There is so much confusion—'love thy neighbour as thyself' and then there is 'charity begins at home,' but is that from the Bible?"

"Mr. Fernandes, do you think we should go ahead on our own?" Ignoring his ruminations on the confusion of being Christian, she brought him back to the issue on hand.

"Isabel, if you recall, we have made a good team in the past. Going from the cooperation we have received from our neighbours, I think it is a bit far-fetched to expect Glenda's mother to lend us a nun's habit, let alone expect her to stop to listen. We will have to consult the Marchons."

Both Isabel and Mr. Fernandes went to the Marchon household. Mrs. Fernandes, Susan, Ivan, Francis and I were not far behind. It was the first time in years that we'd entered the House of Sin; our parents were too seized with the problem to bother about such a matter at a time like this.

At the entrance was an old non-working Bosch refrigerator with no door, being used as a clothes cupboard. There were no obvious signs of the sinning life, just a very crowded home. Shirlen, Miriam, Oswald, Bruno, Carlton, Colleen, Mili and Joe were all seated in their living room, now crowded out of space with Isabel, Mr. Fernandes, Ivan, Susan, Anna, Francis and me. We could not see any of the room beyond the faces around us.

"Joe," Isabel said, "we have special information that Ali and his mother are in great danger. Never mind how." She raised her hand to preempt any curiosity for the source of such information. "We have decided to move them tomorrow into Ms. Ezekiel's home—if she agrees—at night. We need to ensure that no one sees this happen. We also need someone to ferry their baggage and food over. Right now we have a problem with Mrs. Farooqui, very real, though it is silly. She refuses to take off the burqa. We don't need to elaborate on how dangerous that can be. So we thought a nun's habit would be better to make her less conspicuous. That could work, especially since very few people have seen her face completely." She stopped for breath, took a pinch of snuff, and left it on the skin under her nose before resuming, "Francis came up with the idea of dressing her in a nun's garb, the clever child, but we cannot find one." This addition came only because Francis was tugging at her sleeve. "No use asking Glenda's mother, no help there. Only God knows how we will execute this operation safely."

She stopped to take a breath once more, and at that very moment Sammy staggered into the room. Riots were no deterrent to the small home-brewed liquor joints scattered all over the city, and Sammy had guzzled up to his nose. This did not affect him seriously, except in his gait; his body was long used to the fluid.

We turned on Sammy like he was an answer sent by God himself, all ten people in the room with the very same thought in their heads—or at least Isabel and the Fernandes family thought it was God's answer, and the rest of us thought it was logical.

Oswald and Bruno dragged Sammy to the mori. Bruno held his head forward and Oswald poured cold water on his head. Sammy, of habit, did not protest; he knew he was no match for his brothers. Instead, he giggled—*what are you guys doing?* hey, hey, it is cold man, stop it—and they stopped and sat him down. Mili, who had put a pot of coffee on the stove, set down the hot fluid in front of him.

"Drink," she said, briefly though not unkindly. He was her son, after all.

Sammy, sitting down, smiled amiably at his neighbours, quite uncomplaining of the rough handling by his brothers. In a sense it was an acceptance of who he was and a lack of embarrassment at it.

"I did not steal anything," he said, denying any responsibility in a very sweeping way, to cover all missing items in our homes or his own home.

"Ok, sure," Mr.Fernandes said placatingly, "sure, but we want you to," he added, nodding his head

Sammy giggled, quite sure this was a joke. He kept giggling without saying anything. Oswald and Bruno stood him up once again and took him to the mori. "What are you doing now? I am sober, stop it, Oswald," he protested, and stopped giggling.

"Sammy," said Mili, "we want you to steal a nun's habit from Glenda's mother."

"What?" He looked at the hopeful faces around him—this definitely was a joke.

"Yes, we want you to steal it, since she will not part with it if we ask her," Isabel explained.

If Sammy hadn't been used to not understanding most of the processes around him, being too drunk most of the time, he would have asked why. But he refrained. Whatever the reason, it seemed really important to all of us, for us to be looking so kindly at him. *Of course, anytime*—he was ready to steal it, but there were some important questions he had to set to rest first.

"For how much? Who's paying?

"Ten bucks, and I will pay," said Mr. Fernandes. No sooner had he offered to pay than he felt sorry. Sammy acquiesced so quickly that he felt he would have gotten away with five. But errors will cost money and so he agreed to put the ten rupees out.

"It should be done today, and in utter secrecy. Do not go around trying to get more for it," Oswald warned, knowing his brother, "or you will not only not get the ten rupees but you'll have hell to pay."

Sammy sat in the passage waiting for Glenda's mother, who was now labouring up the stairs, to return to her room. The Alphonsoes had two doors to their home, being the last room near the stairs that led down to the street on Nesbit Road. So Oswald went to the front door and Sammy went to the back. Sammy knocked on the door leading to the stairs and waited for Glenda's mother to make her way from the front door off the verandah to the back.

Glenda's mother was not very athletic in her gait. She ambled slowly towards the door. Barely had she pulled down the inside bolts when there was an urgent knock on the door leading onto the verandah. She sauntered back without pushing up the latch on the door.

Opening the front door, she encountered Oswald. Now she looked really annoyed. What did this man want? She had nothing to do with the Marchon family—why was he here?

"Is Glenda at home, ma'am?" he asked, respectfully and politely.

No inquiry could have been better designed to throw her into a fit. It is a burden to have a daughter to support without a husband, but a daughter who is a young woman is a challenge to any parent. Keeping them from getting pregnant is every mother's concern. Oswald, young, handsome and eminently ineligible, sent blood rushing into her creased face and got her stuttering. "W-what, d-do y-you w-want with m-my ddd-aughter, y-you no-gggood w-waster? I-if you d-dare to l-look in h-her ddddir-rection I w-will h-hit y-ou w-with a brrroom." As if to illustrate her point she went in and came out with a broom, giving Oswald just enough time to peek around the wall and see that Sammy was gone. When she came out, Oswald had also vanished.

Satisfied with the results, Mrs. Alphonso closed the front door and went once again to answer the back door. Finding no one out there, she locked the door and went back to making dinner for Glenda, blissfully unaware that she was minus one nun's habit.

Chapter Twenty-Four

It seemed that the city had swallowed Dad. Involved in all kinds of cases as he was, the situation growing worse, as the 6th of January dawned we did not know his whereabouts. If one looked out of the window, which in our present confinement seemed the only thing to do, one noticed that nature continued, in its very insensitive fashion, to be what it was supposed to be, despite the unrest in the city. One almost felt angry with the sun, shining like all was well. But then if nature followed the city's mood, we would never be able to predict the weather.

The mood in the city fast deteriorated from fear to hatred that very bright day. Dad's job in the Nagpada Police Station became never ending. Seven cases of death by stabbing had been reported, and none of the deaths were random—all seven were Hindus who had unfortunately found themselves on either secluded roads or by lanes, where they were stabbed after the attackers had confirmed their religious identity. We heard on the radio that there were 18 stabbings in the city, and casualties in the Hindu community exceeded those of the Muslim. Paranoia mounted.

These deaths of strangers not even remotely connected to us, our neighbourhood, or our lives, unfortunately brought to our attention how time was running out...

We hadn't heard from Ms. Ezekiel yet; we were now doubtful

that we ever would. Maybe, just maybe, she'd been playing a return prank on us. Anna and Francis, however, had not yet passed the age of faith. *I'm sure, I'm sure*, Anna said, and Francis, forever her echo, added, *yes we are, yes we are*. It was drawing near to dusk and they still hung on the verandah's cast iron balustrade, hopeful.

Closer to 9.00 p.m., the situation in Mahim, at the edge of Bombay, right beyond which the suburbs began, was reported to have gone out of hand. It was an area populated by a large concentration of Muslims. Muslim and Hindu mobs clashed violently, both in fear and in hatred. In various lanes and roads throughout the city, both sides, enraged largely by what they saw as lack of security protecting them from the other, decided to be proactive. In the confusion and rapid deterioration of civilization, it was hardly certain who or what or how. Who cast the first stone? Is that even relevant when people are killing each other? From a distance, it seemed like the question to ask. Who deserved to die depended on who cast the first stone. But we had missed the point. No one needed to die; no one should have; why were we fighting?

Excited voices emanated from the first floor as Surve's son stepped out of their room with a sword in his hand and stomped noisily down the stairs to the street in front. He paraded up and down, brandishing the sword high above his head. This was the first time I had seen a real sword, not one made of plastic and sold in toyshops. He strode with a gang of other young men who carried sticks and hockey sticks and whatever weapons they could muster, as if protecting the neighbourhood. It seemed like a war dance, or the martial art dance Chhau of Orissa, except lacking culture and grace. And while everyone at their windows held their breaths in expectant voyeurism, the moon—leading towards the full moon calculated to appear on the 8th January—as if joining in our occupation, shone brightly on a thin line of white paper moving frantically under Ms. Ezekiel's door.

Anna and Francis, still on vigil, froze. They looked around furtively. Anyone watching them would have been moved to investigate. But thankfully Surve's son was now on the streets doing his dance; they ran down the stairs to the first floor. Anna whispered, 'I am here, ma'am,' as respectfully as she could, hands folded in prayer, hoping that it was not a trick. It is the hardest thing to hope that the person you've victimized will come through for you in your time of need. To be fair, Anna was not the transgressor; I take full responsibility. I cannot even blame Susan and Ivan, who only went along with all my pranks. I was the elder brother, friend, and mentor. Right then, I felt the pain of asking someone who I had taken such pleasure in penalising, to give up her privacy. *One picks up lessons along the way, I suppose,* I have reflected since, wanting to be forgiving of myself.

Anna and Francis came straight to Isabel, and she ran with the paper to Mr. Fernandes. Hidden behind a cloud, the moon smiled.

We sat looking at the paper, not knowing what to make of it. Once again it was brief. *Don't knock. Enter after 7 pm.*

We did not know whether to be excited or worried. *What if we take the Farooquis down there and she does not open the door? Do we have a backup plan?* All heads turned towards Mr. Fernandes, who in turn looked at his wife.

"Nathie, darling, you know if we were in the same position we would go to anyone who would help us. But what if those we seek help from refuse us? We have brought up children with precepts from the Bible. How many times have we repeated to them, '...do unto others as you would unto thyself.' I would not be able to live with myself—and besides, how can our children keep the faith if we are lax on our own principles? I suggest that Ali stay with us, and his mother"—he turned—"Isabel, would you keep his mother?"

Isabel looked at me and nodded. "Mr. Fernandes, you can fully rely on me. As it is, Mr. D'Souza will not be home with all this trouble in his precinct. So she can stay with me. She will be more comfortable at my home... not because your home is not comfortable," she added kindly, always mindful not to make enemies over petty misunderstandings. "I mean, with fewer people around her, she will feel more comfortable. I am thinking of that disguise in black that they wear..."

With plan B now in place, we set to working on making room for the Farooquis in our homes. Mother bustled back and forth from our home to the Fernandes household, making space in the closet and taking out the mattress from storage under the bed to air out. Mr. Fernandes asked his wife to decide what Ali would need to be comfortable. "Same as Ivan, dear," she said and went about the cooking.

We decided to make the move late at night, around ten the next day. First Ms. Ezekiel's door would be tried at about eight to ensure that it could be opened. We planned to work surreptitiously with the transfer later.

That night we slept fitfully.

Chapter Twenty-Five

Nature, ever detached from our worldly turmoil, ever separated, almost indifferent, made the day seem like any other. The sun rose a little off the coconut tree behind the B.I.T chawl, spending a good one hour sitting on the terrace of building no 3, and then finally disappearing in one blurred splash of brightness in a clear blue sky. Thank God for that. Would we want darkness to engulf us for the time our hearts were down? Or the birds...should they join in our madness? The crows continued their morning routine. Sitting on our windowsills, they cawed, sometimes facing into the room and sometimes into the far distance, but at all times following the routine they had set for us. They did not reflect our fear, or our disgust at what we had done to our city. The mild stench of garbage went unnoticed, our minds on the task of the day.

The situation on the 6th and 7th of January in the area around Nagpada, Belasis Road, and Clair Road was so tense that we knew that our plans would have to be executed without dad's help. The Marchon boys, mainly Bruno and Oswald (we kept Sammy's role to the minimum, right man for the right job and all that) would take Ali's baggage and transfer it to Ms. Ezekiel's room. Then the two of them, Ali and his mother, would walk down separately when signalled and enter the Ezekiel room without knocking. We

171

would be on watch and ready to distract any attention from them; our main concern being Mr. Surve's son, who seemed to be the only one who kept moving in and out. Knowing that he was part of the vigilante Hindu group that was patrolling the streets quite boldly now made our task even more precarious. But expedience was demanded by the daily statistics that streamed in to Dad's police station. For the past two days the number of Hindus killed had overtaken that of the Muslims. Neighbours had ceased to exist; all that remained in their stead were neighbourhoods of religious divisions. Fifteen million people rubbing against each other in single separateness—everyone a potential threat. We felt safer with our crosses conspicuously around our necks, but our neighbours, the Farooqui family and the Surve family, were both under threat.

Intuitively, both families should have been safe had they remained inside their homes. What had started our crusade, however, was Dad's report that some elements in the city had access to the voter lists and were targeting Muslims inside their homes. Our fears for Ali, more than the Surves, stemmed from Dad's suspicions, reinforced by the telephone conversation he had overheard, that Mr. Farooqui's murder had, in fact, been pre-planned and that the family continued to be in imminent danger. Mehroonisa and Ali were defenceless—making it our call to stand by them. We termed our operation 'Saving Ali.'

Meanwhile, the violence and the riots had spread to further parts of the city and all the police stations around us were flooded with cases of stabbings and serious riots. Dad's police station at Nagpada, and now others, were suddenly registering more cases of Hindu deaths than Muslim. The news sparked a Hindu mob to attack a *dargah* in Pydhonie and another in V.P. Road, and mobs of Hindus and Muslims in various areas—depending on who were in the majority—put up roadblocks to prevent police or fire brigades from bringing calm to the area. All kinds of rumours had struck fear in the city, and finally, a curfew was called for.

The Angelus bells at St. Anne's chimed as they usually did at 7 p.m. I doubt this call for the Angelus had been responded to anywhere in Billimoria Building that day, except by the Fernandes family. Isabel and Anna went down to the first floor to try Ms. Ezekiel's door around 8 p.m. as planned. Isabel could never go unnoticed;

something we had overlooked. While they stood at the door, Mrs. Mitchell opened hers and peeped out.

"Isabel, what are you doing here!"

Her tone of wonder was less a query into purpose than the sort of rhetorical exclamation when one sees an unusual sight. Columbus had the same question—*What have we here!*—when he landed in America.

But Isabel, never overwhelmed, neither at a lack for words nor resourcefulness, whipped around promptly and said, "Ah, Mrs. Mitchell, just the person I wanted to see!"

"What about?" said Mrs. Mitchell, both curiously and hesitantly, as though she'd initiated a conversation she did not really want to continue.

"We are looking for a contribution to a lending library we want to start for the residents. Would you like to join the library?"

The question received the exact response it was designed for.

"Sorry, Isabel. We have no time to read and we are not interested. We wish you well in your enterprise, and thank you for thinking of us." Not wanting to prolong the conversation further, she scurried back into her room.

"Aunt Isabel, are we planning a new library?"

"No, Anna, but save the thought. We could do it sometime in future. For now I think we should push open the door and see if it is ok. If it is open, you go in and tell her we will be back at 10 p.m."

Anna leaned against the door and whispered, "Ms. Ezekiel, I am opening your door," and waited for a full minute, looking around furtively and trying to act casual. Seeing the coast clear, she gently tried the door. It opened a little; it was indeed unlocked, and she pushed it ajar a bit more and slipped in, while Isabel stood outside, leaning on the balustrade and looking up at the full moon that lit up the three coconut trees in the compound. On the second floor of the building opposite, a violin cried under the bow of a very new violinist, almost eerie amid the intermittent silences in the air.

Two minutes later, Anna rushed out and pulled the door closed behind her. She looked startled, pulled on Isabel's hand and rushed towards the passage with Isabel, unresisting, in tow—up the stairs and into the apartment, where we were all waiting for news.

Anna's asthma had kicked in and we had to wait until she could speak again.

"She's gone, she's g-gone," she said.

"Ok, slow down my child," said Nathie soothingly. "Breathe in... hmmmm, ok, now breathe out, hmmm, breathe in...."

"Mum, Ms. Ezekiel is not there. Her apartment is open and the rooms are empty. She has disappeared..." She began to cry.

We all were totally silenced. Where did she go? Had she sacrificed her home for Ali? We looked around at each other. She had put us to shame—despite our Christian conscience we had found it so hard to make the decision to host the Farooqui family. She, a Jew, had never spent a day in friendship with us, yet had made the ultimate sacrifice, had given up her home.

Our awe turned to concern. Where did she go? Did she have relatives in the city? When did she leave? It was now 8 p.m and the curfew had been enforced in our neighbourhood. Had she made it through the riots? We could not be happy with this turn of events.

Chapter Twenty-Six

We had not come very far from the medieval ages, when the curfew bell reminded everyone to turn out their lights and smother their fires before bed. Maybe even regressed since then, because the call for curfew that day was not to put out the fires that kept us warm or lit our hearths, but to quell the violent, raging fires of hatred. The city burnt in sporadic flames, as business establishments torched down by unknown hands lit up the horizon. The order for curfew should have gladdened us; the hope of establishing order in the city gone mad should have lifted our spirits; but it brought only worry in our little circle.

A curfew meant that Surve's son would be home and stalking around in the building. How could we safely handle this? Though we had tried to plan on all fronts, trying to cover all scenarios, we had failed to visualise this one. Mother, Mr. Fernandes and I, stood on the verandah outside No. 19, consumed with the problem. The Marchons, Oswald, Bruno, and Miriam joined us. Oswald and Bruno, always ready to suggest a speedy solution, offered to clobber him and lock him in one of the toilets. Mr. Fernandes said, "Can we leave violence out of this? How different are we from these animals?"

The time now advancing towards nine, Surve's son entered the building with a loud clatter on the stairs, not unlike the footsteps one uses in forests to warn the snakes of one's arrival, hoping they leave. Snakelike, the boy hovered on the first floor passage, legs apart, a stick in his hand, ready to strike.

Miriam finally broke the silence with, "Leave that horny b-----d to me," opened the top button of her blouse and walked out of the room. Mr. Fernandes, not exactly happy with the new turn of events, kept silent nevertheless, knowing we had no time for moral judgement. We had to start the operation.

Mr. Marchon went first, followed by Mr. Fernandes and me. We walked to the door of Ali's home. Mehroonisa looked like a cloistered nun sitting on Ali's marriage bed, her tears streaming. Ali pointed to the packed bags and boxes on the floor and we silently picked up one at a time and went down with them. I could only imagine how much more complicated this would have been had Ali's wife been here. With the violence spread across the city, no place was entirely safe for Muslims.

Thankfully, there was no one outside as we made our way to the first floor—Miriam had found a way to keep Surve's son out of the way. We did not ask, nor did we want to speculate on how. Quite unknown to the Farooqui family, this was an evening of sacrifices all round.

After we reached the first floor, Oswald and Bruno picked up a second lot of boxes, being all that the Farooquis owned, except for their furniture and some of the glassware. The Farooquis left their room in the centre of a tight band of people. Mr. Fernandes led the group with a cross in his hands and Nathie held a candle that, though lit, was really no help with light, being so short of wick. Instead, the light of the almost-full moon lit their path, and to a casual onlooker they would appear to be a group of fervent Catholics, a nun in their midst, praying for peace in the city. The little Catholic procession made its way across the verandah and past the Madrassis' rooms. As they passed Mrs. Mitchell's door she opened it to see what the shuffling feet was all about; the first thing she saw was Mr. Fernandes standing with the cross, and she immediately shut the door on his face. That little drama allowed Mehroonisa and Ali to slip into Ms. Ezekiel's room and lock it from the inside quite unnoticed.

Chapter Twenty-Seven

All of us were silent, as if waiting to exhale; waiting, but not certain for what. We had moved Ali and his mother two days ago, with adequate food, asking them not to show their faces or do anything to be recognised. We sat in long silences trying not to talk about it. Spending most of the time indoors, sitting at our windows, we looked out onto the road and beyond, sometimes praying, sometimes blankly listening to our heartbeats. Loud wails and moans emanated from the old cobbler's house. His very large wife, who could barely walk, sat on the charpoy on the pavement wailing and wiping her eyes with a bright green sari pallu.

A stray paper that looked like the front page of the *Times of India* flapped and twirled as if caught in a whirlwind and flew a few feet above the road, travelling past the cobbler's wailing wife and up St. Mary's Road. As it flew past the municipal school, it stopped for a brief second, surprised by the silence and the emptiness, and finally disappeared, leaving us with nothing to follow except the wails of the woman down there mourning her husband.

We children were all fixed at our windows. Our thoughts crowded our heads, which occasionally we stuck out to look at the neighbours. We nodded at each other, reassured that all of us were holding our breath. Comforting, in a way; it seemed to bring us closer.

At eight o'clock, as if just one aspect of our life had maintained its routine, all heads disappeared inside for dinner. However, not much later we were back. Our parents hoped we would study during that time. We were expected to study every day of the year except Christmas, New Year's day, and summer holidays in May. But they were all absorbed in their own thoughts as we hung out of the windows in silence for a second day in a row and no one wanted to talk.

Suddenly, from the south end of Nesbit Road, we heard a low rumble—a small band of people coming up the road. They were very near Bad-rud-din/Sad-rud-din Building: twin buildings named Bad-rud-din and Sad-rud-din. Not knowing which was which, we referred to them generally as Bad-rud-din/Sad-rud-din. As the group passed the twin buildings, we could see they were brandishing choppers and sticks in the air, which glinted under the dull streetlight and the full moon as they passed beneath it. Closer now...about ten of them—and one of the more enthusiastic waved a sword in the air. We all ducked below the wall so as not to be seen and peeped over the sill to follow where they were going.

They approached Billimoria Building, and it seemed like they were continuing onwards on Nesbit Road. They did not turn onto St. Mary's Road and were soon out of sight, allowing us to exhale—for we had held our breath as we followed their path. Within minutes, however, loud shouts and commotion shook our relief. It sounded like hundreds of hooligans had come up the stairs on the other side of the L of our apartment building.

The shouts grew louder. We felt terrorised, trembling behind locked doors, wondering whether the mob would break them down. We thought of Ali below us and shuddered. Even though Dad was a police inspector, he knew he could do nothing at this point.

All of us, too scared to open our doors, stood still, helpless, alert, trying to visualize the turmoil a few feet away, trying to follow what was happening. The mob had made their way straight to Ali's apartment in the angle of the L. It seemed like they knew exactly what they wanted. The sounds of banging, pots and pans being flung around, breaking glass, screams, shook the verandah that had, up until now, only reverberated with sounds of children's laughter and play. Never had we heard such noise; even when the Marchon family fought with each other, their shouts seemed like purring in comparison to this.

Just as sudden as the interruption was, the sounds died down with the last of the footsteps running down the stairs that led to St. Mary's Road, the opposite staircase from where they had ascended. We rushed back to our windows to see the figures of the thugs streaming into the distance and disappearing into a lane that led to the B.I.T. blocks. As if their presence had been only an illusion—a collective overactive imagination in a time of discord—silence cut through the cool air, and calm took over once again.

Suddenly Mr. Fernandes stuck his head out and asked me whether Anna was in our apartment. No, we said, instantly panicking. "Maybe the toilet," I shouted, and then his head receded, presumably to search for the key. Finding the key, which normally hung on a cord near the door, missing, he realised that Anna had chosen to go to the toilet just before the commotion, and had perhaps held back, crouched there, when she heard the noises.

Barely had we made this discovery when Anna's scream, shrill above the unnatural silence, startled us. One of the men who had trashed Ali's apartment, still hanging around, had seen Anna come out of the toilet. Still full of adrenalin, excited and considerably aroused, he grabbed her. She struggled and screamed, both of which only served to excite him further. He dragged her into the passage near the stairs, where the space was more permitting.

The Oliveras' apartment adjoined the passage. Aaron dragged a chair and stood on it to peep from the top shutter of their door, to investigate what was transpiring. Alarmed with what he saw, he then stuck his head out of the window and yelled, flailing his arms, "He has Anna, he has Anna."

In a nanosecond, Mr. Fernandes picked up the nearest weapon, a thick, cricket-bat-like wooden piece used to beat clothes while washing, and ran to the passage. All of us on this side of the L stepped out of our doors and followed in his path. In a fury, Mr. Fernandes swung the clothes beater at the man and nailed him in the head. He achieved that just moments before I had raised my own cricket bat to do the very same thing. He grabbed Anna and lifted his sobbing daughter, her clothes ripped, her hands covered in bruises, and ran back along the verandah towards their room, moaning with the horror he felt for her.

He rushed past where I was standing agape. Anna's clothes,

ripped from the top, had bared her right breast. And in that fleeting instant as he passed me, a stray moonbeam that had squeezed through the palm trees and building opposite lit a gleaming nipple—oh my God, Anna has breasts!

Isn't it startling how a moment can change the way you look at someone?

Chapter Twenty-Eight

You might imagine this to be the main event I've wanted to recall, but it was subsequent events that defined the life and fortunes of the Fernandes family and, consequentially, those of the rest of us.

Sammy, Bruno, and Oswald Marchon rushed to the passage where the attacker lay face down, a deep gash on the back of his head. Imagine their shock when they flipped the body over and found the son of Mr. Surve lying there, his blood slowly spreading on the black and white tiles of the passage floor. It was hard to tell if he was alive. Not only had he sold out the Farooquis, he had attacked our own sweet Anna in his youthful lust. They picked up the bleeding body—dead or not, they didn't care. No one could violate the neighbourly code and get away with it. Bruno and Oswald, who had their own code of acceptable behaviour, knew exactly what to do. The loud splat on the pavement below splintered the body into a few severed parts.

Dad, now Inspector D'Souza dressed in uniform, exited the apartment and went down to the pavement. He called the local police to come down to the building (after the blood on the floor of the passage had been mopped up and the rags put in paper bags and disposed of in the garbage bin in the compound, by the Marchon family, who were obviously very experienced in such emergencies).

The local inspector arrived with his team and inspected the meat on the pavement. He realised he could not draw a chalk outline to mark the place of the body and so prepared to begin questioning. He spotted Oswald near the scene and walked up to him.

"So you are here too?" he said. Oswald was, of course, well known to the inspector. "So what have we here?" He looked down at the splattered road and kicked a piece out of the way with his shoe.

"He's dead," said Oswald, quite unnecessarily.

"I can see that, but what are you doing here?"

"I live here." He pointed to the second floor. "We saw him fall and came down here."

"Did he jump?"

"Don't know. We were at our windows when a group of youth stormed the building with swords and choppers and trashed our neighbour's apartment."

"Which neighbour?"

"Farooqui."

"Never mind that," the inspector said, brushing off the incident. "How did this happen? Did the Farooquis do it?"

"No, they are not there. They went away on a vacation. The hoodlums who trashed their apartment may have done it."

"Did you actually see it happen?"

Oswald shook his head. "I was in my apartment, heard the noise, and we looked out of the window and saw this."

The inspector glanced around at the small crowd. "Who saw this happen?"

Everyone turned on their heels and dispersed. Inspector D'Souza was left staring down at the road.

"Inspector, do you know how this happened?"

My father looked weary. "I have the same information that you have. I think we have to put it down to a casualty of the riots. The city unrest has to stop. Anyway, I would suggest that since we cannot recognise the body we will have to wait for a missing person report before we ascertain whose it is." He shrugged. "Since the city morgues are full and so are the hospitals I don't know whether we have the space for one more. But this is your jurisdiction and you will have to take a decision."

Dad returned home, showered and went to bed without talking. We did not disturb him.

There was total silence in the building; we were all in shock. And we all shared a secret.

Chapter Twenty-Nine

The next morning a crow kept cawing in between pecking at a small piece of leftover meat, pleading for us to awaken. Last evening's report of the riots seemed like nothing compared to our own drama. A mob of 3000-4000 Muslims had damaged property in Dad's jurisdiction while he had been at home after three days of continuous work. Soon after, a Hindu mob set about trashing Muslim properties in retaliation. The larger activity dwarfed the events of our small building in the eyes of the police. They lacked the manpower, will, or courage to investigate.

Nobody hearkened to the cawing, incessant as it was. Nobody got out of bed till 10.00 a.m Nobody went for Sunday Mass. Nobody wanted to even peep outside their door. But we finally came out onto the balcony, tiptoeing, responding to the wailing sounds we heard from room no. 6 on the first floor.

Apparently, the Surves' son had not returned home. Mr. Surve filed a missing persons complaint and the police asked him to identify the blood-soaked trousers that they had kept from the remains. The trousers were unrecognisable, but the belt that held them up had a buckle so like the one his son owned and had worn the previous day, that Mr. Surve was convinced it belonged to his son. There was no body to claim, the police informed him; since it had been found in several pieces, they'd had to cremate it. No, they could not provide him with the ashes, since several bodies had been cremated on the same pyre.

Mr. Surve returned from the police station and broke the news to the family. Mrs. Surve wept shrilly and we all went back into our apartments in silence. None of us spoke or came out that day. We heard nothing from the Fernandeses' room. Even Mother, who ordinarily would have gone to console them, stayed home, needing consoling herself. Our lives, tainted with attempted rape, murder, violence—all that we had never encountered or expected to in our sanctimonious world—seemed broken, irreparable. The secret that we all shared weighed us down.

Ali's matrimonial bed had been chopped into firewood by the vandals; it seemed significant, almost handy, in the cremation of the Surve boy that the family held as a symbolic gesture of sending their son away in dignity. None of us attended, nor did we go downstairs and sympathise with the grieving family. I suppose they must have felt the differences in our cultures in that moment. Neighbours who do not mourn with you...no shared grief, no shared happiness, no shared expectations... does not make for a good community. No. We seemed ghettoised. And communal lines and ghettos create bitterness, as history constantly reminds us.

The Surve family left soon after. They moved out of the building a few months later without saying goodbye to us. We were relieved. No one wanted to speak to them. Nobody wanted to remember.

The blood in the passage that had seeped into the grout could not be washed off easily. The Olivera family was left with the unhappy task since it was practically outside their door. Everyone else had shuddered, not wanting to touch it or clean it. The family boiled water, poured it on the floor and left it there to soften the blood so it could be cleaned. When that method proved unsuccessful, they bought a bottle of hydrochloric acid and applied it by dipping into the bottle a piece of cloth tied to a stick, and painting it over the grout. Mr. Fernandes, who would have normally taken the lead to solve this problem, had withdrawn into some netherworld, unreachable. 'Isabel what do we do?' the Oliveras asked Mum when the acid failed to work. So Mum hired Soni to clean the passage. She asked questions: 'Kya hai, memsaab, khoon ki tra dikta hai?' 'Kya hua?' 'Koi gira kya?' But Dad, now in his uniform as Inspector D'Souza, told her peremptorily that she should clean and leave since it was not in her place to ask questions. She silently returned to the task.

The clothes beater had mysteriously disappeared, and there was no inquiry about any weapon. There was no inquiry about who had killed the boy or how. There was no search for weapons. Officially, the boy had committed suicide, jumped out of the window. No one knew why—no suicide note, no goodbyes. Case closed, the police moved on to more pressing matters, trying to contain the riots that raged around the city.

Mr. Fernandes finally came out of his room on Monday morning and went to work. He nodded absently at all those who stood outside and wished him well. None of the children went to school for the whole week. There was silence till our ears hurt with the noise of the traffic. No children's laughter, no sounds of balls being thrown against the walls, not even our evening gathering for stories from Joe.

After that week all seemed normal in Bombay. The cobbler's wife took over her husband's business. She sat on the steps of their home ordering her eldest son who now had replaced his father at the awl. The city seemed to bustle back: early morning clanking of pots and pans in a million sinks around the city; the sounds of milk bottles tinkling; trucks rolling down the streets. The stables, some of them burned down and others shut, belonged mostly to Muslim owners. Had they fled? We were too absorbed in our own silence to know. We just did not hear the hooves on the macadam roads anymore, and we no longer looked down on the first floor from the other side of the L.

Ms. Ezekiel had disappeared somewhere into the unknown, like vapour merging unnoticed into the atmosphere. She sometimes flitted into our dream moments: a brightly patterned dress through a taxi window or a large brimmed straw hat pulled low, climbing the upper deck of the red BEST bus. I run, arms outstretched—*Ms. Ezekiel, Ms. Ezekiel, wait, wait, I am sorry, I am sorry,* I shout behind a disappearing figure; disappearing without a backward glance, old, tired, wonderfully generous. I am sorry, I am sorry, I am sorry...where are you? How do you live? Sorry, sorry, sorry...

The needle of our lives gradually swung back to normal. In our attempt to forget, all the older children, who knew that something evil had just happened, took to reading. We read book after book, comic after comic. We exchanged books. We smiled at each other. But laughter seemed the sole preserve of the younger kids. Their games returned. And occasionally they tapped our doors in the afternoon and ran away.

The Farooqui family disappeared, leaving the door of Ms. Ezekiel's room locked. They did not say goodbye either. No one knew when they'd left or where they'd gone. Somehow we all wanted to live in silence, occasionally acknowledging each other with half smiles or nods. I guess we were all afraid of what we might find beneath the surface if we did speak.

Two weeks after the incident, Anna finally emerged, looking all normal and sweet. I could not look at her, embarrassed as I was by my own fantasies of her. She, I think, sensed the change in our relationship. She assumed a shyness with me that hadn't been there earlier. Mr. Fernandes dropped her at school every morning and picked her up every evening. He did it for the next three months till it was summer vacations. He went late to work and left early for those three months, even staying home on occasion.

And in March, that is precisely what saved his life.

Chapter Thirty

A gentle breeze played with our hair as we sat on the verandah outside Joe's door. Today, March 10, 1993, was the last day of the S.S.C. exams: Anna's finishing year. We had a tradition of celebrating the last day of exams, the group of us, sitting out late and talking, singing, and wherever our hearts took us on that day. So we wondered—would Anna want that? Would she come out and play, laugh, love?

All the children who usually sat outside Joe's room, except Anna and Francis, waited. Shirlen and Miriam were there too. They brought the guitar out. Francis came out and looked at us.

"If you are waiting for Anna, she is reading. I don't think she plans to come."

"Not today," I said, "Francis, can you convince her? It is her day today."

Francis went back in. He came back almost a minute later.

"Nope. She says no. Maybe, Peter you should ask her."

Susan and Ivan nodded. So I asked my mother to ask her.

Nobody really says no to Isabel, and ten minutes later, Anna came out smiling at us. It was the first day she'd smiled after that fateful January night, at least at the rest of us. Yes, we spoke in monosyllables in the toilet queue, but this was the closest to normal we'd come. All of us clapped, and Shirlen strummed the guitar

189

while we sang, '...she's the jolly good fella, so say all of us.' Anna was here and she seemed like she was recovering from her shock. We went on to sing songs that we were all familiar with: Boney M, Cliff Richard, Abba, the Beatles. Shirlen and Miriam took turns playing the guitar and Miriam led the singing. The Marchon family had it all: theft, prostitution, murder and crime, but also talent, and love, and loyalty. We looked at them and thought, how wonderful to have them with us. They were our connection with the big, bad world out there—outside our bubble. They were also our means of survival...

Joe came home an hour later. We clapped for him and then put our arms around each other in the tight circle. Even I, who normally sat outside this circle as I grew older, now wanted the comfort of hugging these, my friends.

Joe stood smiling down at us till we could see the gold tooth at the back of his mouth from down below. He suddenly went serious and wagged his finger at us.

"So what do you think happened to me today?" he said.

"You saw a ghost?" we chorused. He smiled once again. Joe had a white smile in a very dark face. His smile and manner of speech made him really distinctive and tall from our low vantage point, though with hindsight now, I think he was shorter than average.

"Tell us, Joe," we begged. The suspense was killing us now, even more than before. He looked at our faces one by one.

"I finished my duty and came out of the factory gate."

"Where is your factory?" I asked, to check whether he'd vary the place today.

"Close to Gangabowdi Street," he said.

"Never mind, Peter, let Joe tell us what happened," the others shushed me.

Joe sat on his haunches, slowly moving his eyes round the circle. We huddled close. The moon had waned and the light was very low. His shadow on the wall and ceiling looked ominous as he bobbed on his haunches.

"I finished work at 7.00 p.m., a bit later than usual. A tiring day, so I stopped to have a cup of tea at the canteen. I walked from my office to the factory gates, and it took me a while to get to there."

"Why, Joe?" Susan asked. Small details are very important to her.

"Why, what?"

"Why did it take a while to get to the gate?"

"Because I work in a very large company. The gate of the factory is nearly a mile away from the building where I am stationed."

The younger ones were impressed, as Joe intended. I nudged Ivan, who nudged Susan, who nudged Anna.

"Coming out through the gate I noticed him for the first time. A tall, dark man, the same shade as Peter..."

"Peter is not dark, Joe," Francis piped.

"Yes, he is," Miriam said.

"Oh never mind, black, brown, white, who cares," I said, "Just get on with the story, Joe."

"Same shade as Peter, right behind me, I guess following me. I turned into a side street...if he turned I would know he was indeed following me." He stopped and smiled his golden grin.

"Did he, Joe, did he?" Francis asked, moving his body, anxious to reduce the suspense to the barest minimum. I guess these were not exactly the stories we should have been exposed to at this time in our lives, but the very normalcy of sitting and listening to Joe's adventures made us forget our own tragic secret.

"You betcha...he turned too." Joe stopped once again and made some gargling sounds in his throat, coughed a bit and carried on. "I was not sure what to think. Being born in a veil, I sometimes confuse the spirit world with this world, and what with all the trouble in the city and all..." He swept his arms in a big circle to engulf the entire world. "I started walking briskly." At this point we heard a clanging of a bicycle chain coming from Joe's apartment, followed by a spoon banging on a pan. Chickpea, for the first time, was participating in our storytelling night, hidden behind the door of the apartment.

"Were you afraid?" Francis asked. I could see Anna's muscles tense. I don't think we'd chosen the right entertainment for the evening, but nothing could be done now; everyone, rapt, gazed large-eyed at Joe.

Joe shrugged. "Of course not, frightened? You must be joking! I had my pay packet in my shirt pocket, you see?" He patted his shirt pocket. "It is bad luck to talk to strangers with your pay packet in your pocket."

"And then what happened?" Ivan asked, impatient at this digression. But Joe wouldn't be rushed. He pulled out a bright yellow comb, smiling widely enough for us to see his gold tooth, smoothed down his sparse hair, and then continued.

"The stranger quickened his pace too."

The younger ones gasped. We hugged each other tighter, showing our anticipation and fear. Anna began to shake but stayed there, waiting.

"I started to run." He paused and looked at our scared faces. "He started to run... I started thumbing vehicles that were passing."

"More likely to stick them up," I whispered to Ivan, who giggled.

"Cars just whizzed past... Damn, if you need help in this city... Indifferent bast—" He stopped short, suddenly aware he was talking to a bunch of kids, and went on. "He was nearly three feet away from me... Now, I don't like to admit this, but I began to get a trifle anxious. Sweating. I wondered—maybe the heat and the exercise was getting to me?"

Francis now lost patience. "Joe, get to the story. You are frightening Anna."

The truth was that all the kids were now quivering. Joe looked at Anna and decided to be merciful.

"I saw a car slow down and I opened the door, got in, and sat there panting... The car kept moving and I finally felt safe as I glanced behind us and saw the stranger disappear into a side street. And then I looked at the driver."

We were thankful Joe made it in time. Colleen, Joe's youngest, sighed in relief.

"But...there...was...no driver!" Joe paused and looked each of us in the eye.

Our grip around each other tightened, the circle getting smaller.

"The car continued to move. I saw a hand on the steering wheel, no body." We sighed. Ghosts were preferable to humans, at least now.

"Don't panic, don't panic, I told myself. Look ahead, Look at the road, there is an answer out there. I did not turn my head, just looked at the road, waiting for the opportunity to jump out. We reached the top of a slope. Then, just before we started rolling downhill, the door opened and a man jumped into the drivers' seat."

The circle got smaller, we sweated and held our breath in the still, hot summer night.

"'What the devil! Have you been sitting in my car all the time while I was pushing it to start the engine?' the man yelled at me angrily." Joe looked around at our pale faces. "Gotcha!" He grinned.

"You tricked us, Joe!" we shouted, almost together.

Chapter Thirty-One

It seemed like the earth had taken one full trip around the sun since 9th January that year. We were beginning to forget, except for Mr. Fernandes, who did not speak to anyone but for Dad and Mum, in very brief sentences. He no longer had to drop Anna to school and pick her up. But he continued to come home early and go to work late. On the 12th of March he decided not to go at all. He invited Mum, Dad and me to join them for lunch. Dad had gone to work but would be home for lunch, and Mum, of course, could not stay away and just be a guest. She flitted in and out of the Fernandes home. *Nathie, do you need help with anything? Do you want me to make the dessert? Peter and I could help on some thing?*

It all seemed like we were back again to our earlier days of being one large family, familiar and loving. Mrs. Fernandes gently turned down all offers of help. No, Isabel, you will be our guest today. Mr. Fernandes sat on a stool at the dining table chopping and slicing the meat and Mum talked ceaselessly while we, adults and children, played rummy with two packs. Mr. Fernandes allowed us to play cards only in the summer vacation and never for money. Francis, not allowed to play, hung around, whispering the cards into Anna's ears.

Dad returned around noon. He showered and dressed for lunch.

Today was special, obviously, so Mum, Dad, and I dressed up in our Sunday best. It seemed important, since it was not a festival, nor was it a birthday, and yet we had already seen that the cooking was elaborate in the Fernandes home. So, though we knew nothing of the reason for this occasion, we anticipated something special.

The apartment was too little to celebrate a sit-down lunch, so it was a buffet and we all served ourselves. Ivan, Susan, Anna and Francis sat on a colourful striped dhurrie around the coffee table. We ate with a lot of banter and small talk flying across the room. Francis was sucking loudly on a bone to extract the marrow. Susan arranged all her meat in rows on one side of the plate and pro-ceeded to arrange her vegetables like a garden on her plate. This was the first time since January that we were eating together like this, or for that matter, sitting down with the loving companion-ship we had always shared. The adults concentrated on the food, and mother sneezed once or twice till she got rid of the excess snuff under her nose with a handkerchief pulled from somewhere deep within her blouse. At peace, we all relished the fare, laugh-ing, nudging, competing and slurping. Finally, with the last of the plates cleared, and now nearly 2.30 p.m., Isabel could not hold it any longer.

"So Mr. Fernandes, what is the occasion?"

Everyone turned their attention to him. He took his napkin and wiped his mouth, cleared his throat and asked Nathie to get him a glass of water. It had been a big meal and Francis burped loud-ly, moving us to laughter, except for Mr. Fernandes who had just gulped down the water Nathie had given him. He waited for the laughter to die down and then in a very sombre voice said,

"We are leaving in May."

Mum was stunned. She never believed that the Fernandes family could ever surprise her. She believed she knew everything that went on there, sometimes before it happened. So to be fair, yes, she was not surprised. That indeed was not the word—but stunned, stunned, stunned! She opened and closed her mouth several times, her words sticking somewhere in the epiglottis and escaping back into her lungs, making her splutter and gasp for breath, bringing tears to her eyes. Finally, having received a fresh gust of oxygen by her continuous rubbing of her chest, she exhaled one gust of words that had mixed up in her lungs and could only sound like 'whooooa' maybe a 't' at the end of it but we could not hear it. She got up, erect, stern, and said in a more discernible syllable, "Where?"

"Canada."

"Canada?" She sat down once again, and if Isabel D'Souza could look defeated, this was it. She was losing her family...we were losing our family—they were losing their family, I could see, from the total silence we sat in for an eternity.

Then Francis said, "And we are going in an airplane!"

I think he was the only one who did not really seem affected. The airplane, and all the other things Canada stood for in his mind, made up for leaving us. Suddenly they looked different: Susan, Ivan and Anna sitting together, their arms over each other's shoulders and I, the stranger outside that little circle—redundant, an unwanted comma that needed editing. They had each other, and till now I'd thought in my deluded mind that I was part of them. At twenty-one, of course there were my friends, but siblings? Didn't they see it that way? Didn't they feel the dull pain I was feeling? Maybe they had an unknown world to look forward to—a new life—but I, sitting there, taking in this scene of a stunned mother, a father who sat stoically, and the Fernandes family looking at us like we were already strangers, I felt alone. I looked at Anna now. Her body slumped, her eyes looked back at me guilty, apologetic, pleading for forgiveness. In that moment, I knew that she felt my dismay and was asking for understanding, asking for forgiveness, blaming herself for this separation that had been brought about by her inability to overcome her fear, her horror, her weak succumbing to shame.

I looked at her, feeling a strange kind of excitement inside me. I did not see the little sister who had followed me, adored me, hung on every word I spoke...I saw a woman, neat, that cute little nose, her fingers that lay still on the table were long and shapely, artistic hands, the hands of a beautiful woman, a stranger. We were separate, she and I. I looked at her remembering that shiny nipple in the moonlight. I had to leave...

Mum and Dad followed me, but I did not look back at them. I did not go home; running instead to the passage and down the stairs, I walked hurriedly towards the one place I went to when in trouble, St. Anne's Church, down the street. The church, closed to the public at this time, the sacristan perhaps gone to lunch, had its huge doors barred and locked. I sat on the stone border at the grotto at the back of the church. Looking up at the statue in the rocky niche, the Madonna holding the child protectively, I wept, mindless that men don't weep... I felt abandoned.

When one takes stock of all the hurts that one faces, abandonment is by far the worst. Does one learn when one is still in the cradle to remain emotionless, distant, uninvolved? Along the way, the little abandonments of life keep piling into the big decision sometime in life. I did not know whether this was the small or the big touchstone of my life, but I did not like what my body felt right now.

Eventually I returned home, making my way slowly down St. Mary's Road, looking at the buildings, past Bad-rud-din/Sad-rud-din, the deaf-and-dumb institute, and to Billimoria Building. The building looked worn out, old, the façade neglected and the inside bloody. I walked up the stairs and in the passage near the stairs, our social space, I found Anna waiting. She held out a notebook in her hands, an offering, as she looked at me silently with what I could only take as intense longing and love. I believe it was longing for me as a man, as I longed now for her as a woman. Love, I feared not. We had forever loved each other; as brothers and sisters did. I took the book, never taking my eyes off her. So many feelings mixed up inside me then. Hope, longing, love, and as a tear streamed down her face, despair. I knew then that she was suffering too.

Billimoria Building had changed, or perhaps, only we had.

Mr. Fernandes was not the only person who had exploded a bomb that day. Dad had been summoned back to work. Several bombs had exploded around Bombay: at the Stock Exchange, Air India Building, Juhu Centaur Hotel, Plaza Theatre and Lucky Petrol near the Shiv Sena castle, Worli, the area around Century Bazaar, the Passport Office, Katha Bazaar, Hotel Sea Rock, Fisherman's Colony in Mahim Causeway, Zaveri Bazaar, and finally but not the least, Sahar Airport, where Mr. Fernandes worked.

I went next door with Mum. In the Fernandes household, they had suddenly discovered how important the events that took place that December through to January actually were. Mr. Fernandes, who had skipped work that day, was alive, and Anna once again the heroine.

Chapter Thirty-Two

That March marked the change in our summers. We no longer sat outside on the balcony huddled together like an overturned basket, our arms intertwined over each other's shoulders in a circle. Joe disappeared on that 12th day of March, like so many others in buses, cars, buildings or merely passing by the places that had exploded. He did not return home and something told us he never would. The police could not trace him, and like many other families in Bombay, the Marchons eventually gave up searching.

But the Farooqui family did return. They came home one Sunday morning in early May, unloaded their belongings, amongst which was a new bed, cleaned up their apartment and continued their life there, same as earlier. Mehroonisa wore her black burqa, despite the hot May sun, and walked straight to her home without as much as a hello to any of us. Ali had changed; we looked at him anew. He returned with his wife; a slightly pregnant wife. His earlier well-oiled hair, parted at the centre, had morphed into a combed-back, insolent sweep. He looked like he had added ten years to his age; he had become a man. He too, did not speak to us and, holding his wife's arm, escorted her to room no 26 in silence.

Mum wanted to leave too. She kept on at Dad, and we finally moved to Bandra—a Catholic neighbourhood, with the church

and market nearby, she said. We sold our apartment to a Muslim
family. They were from the Borah community and had their business at Mohammed Ali Road. They moved in from a predominantly Hindu neighbourhood and paid an obscene sum of money for
our apartment, which was small, in an old building with a toilet
that had to be shared. They were just grateful that some people in
the city still sold their apartments to Muslims.

The Olivera family moved too. Just as we had, they chose Bandra, for almost similar reasons and quite near our home. *Isabel, we
are so used to you that we would like to stay close by.* They sold to
a Muslim family too, from the Borah community, once again for an
obscene amount of money.

Our relationship with Anthony Vaz (who was clutching his kitten that had replaced his hen, as if it was all he possessed) and
his family pretty much disappeared behind the moving truck that
transplanted their home to a far flung suburb, Malad, where I do
not think we would ever travel to. It is a Christian suburb, they
assured us, as if it served to sanctify the decision to a bunch of
people to whom they did not really owe an explanation. They sold
their home to a Borah family too.

The Marchon family, we discovered, did actually have an inheritance. But Joe did not enjoy it, nor did his creditors of the past who
had hoped to get their bills paid. Joe did have a father, brothers and
a sister. For a man who seemed to have come from nowhere, and
whose relatives never visited, this came as a shock to us all—even
his own children. His father left behind a huge property somewhere in Bandra, which, once sold and divided between Joe's siblings, amounted to a tidy amount that even after being shared with
all Joe's children, still amounted to a big sum for each of them.

Oswald and Bruno let their money slip through their hands
like they were sieves with very large holes. Sammy's inheritance
was recycled into cirrhosis of the liver, which he did not survive.
Miriam left India in search of that evasive respectability that she
could never find here. I am told she did find it, marrying a rich
old man in Cyprus. He never let her out of his sight and she never
returned to India. Shirlen went back to school. She took drama
and literature and graduated with honours. She went on to write a
bestseller, *My Love, and Other Lies,* that is still being sold by young
street urchins at the traffic lights. I have never seen her in all these

years, but guessing from the sales at the street lights, she must be well. The Marchon family kept the apartment, something like a family home. It became a refuge, almost like a stop-gap arrangement for the Marchon children whenever they needed it.

Billy, the landlord, took over the empty apartment left by Ms. Ezekiel. He sold it to a Muslim, another Borah, with a shoe shop at Pydhonie, near Mohammed Ali Road. Ms. Ezekiel never claimed the apartment nor did she return, vanishing completely. With the kind of events that took place that day in 1993, none of us had the courage or the morality to report her missing to the police. We told ourselves that she did not want to be found, her being a recluse and all that.

The Madrassis continued their life in the building without interruption. They never made the mistake of closing their door again.

The Cabrals moved. Mrs. Cabral searched for a Catholic locality to move to. *Billimoria Building has become more Muslim than Catholic and I want my children to be exposed more to Catholics than Muslims*—so they moved to Goa, where the entire village they lived in was Christian. Mimosa had nowhere to go. She stayed in Billimoria Building till the very end of her days.

Chapter Thirty-Three

"Let me see: four times five is twelve, and four times six is thirteen, and four times seven is—oh dear! I shall never get to twenty at that rate!"

- Lewis Caroll
Alice in Wonderland

It was the 13th October, the day after collecting Anna from the airport, and I went to the college to gather a semblance of normalcy. I entered a very bright and airy staff room to find Sheila in the corner, smiling at me.

"So, things sorted out with you?" I asked.

"Yes, but not the way you think."

In the past this would have been her red flag to my bull, but we have come a long way. She is human, and I guess she sees me that way too. Smiling, I nodded. "You are going to tell me how?"

"I put him on the railway track and let the speeding train go over him; very therapeutic, that. I recommend you do it with this woman you are hung up on."

"There's a bit of a difference."

"Oh yeah? How's that?"

"We have not been seeing each other like you; she lives in Canada and she is a beautiful, kind, loving soul—you see, not the same thing."

"If she is not with you, it is the same. It is about getting them out from under the epidermis, changing the pigment colour, choosing an even tone. What use is a relationship at a distance?"

"She is in Bombay right now."

"Ah." She went back to her book, leaving me with my calculations.

There comes a time in a man's life when he sits back and appraises his history. I don't believe in History. I am a mathematician, and what is History if not the ramblings of oppressive men who smother the voices around them, giving colour, form, and life to events they were never part of? No certainty in history, no accountability for distortions—and yet its repercussions are weighty enough to distort minds and humankind.

Then there is God. He is history too; the kind that streams from man's imagination. Perhaps he'd lived once in some aeon, or perhaps he was the construct of some fevered mind drunk on opium, created and painted, sculpted and varnished and set atop our garden gates or altars to ward off evil. He is history, like every history: written about by many, painted in their own colours. It's in those differences that history keeps us apart; unlike animals, we elevate ourselves to the status of Gods, arguing that in his image and likeness we are created.

So what makes us superior? Mathematics? Calculating in light years of where we are; no certainty, no accuracy, based only on assumptions, comparisons and relativity; like the Cheshire cat in *Alice* who eventually disappears, leaving behind the grin all on its own, can we disappear while the numbers stay up there? Do they have meaning on their own? I mean, one God, two Gods, it's still about God, and the numbers are meaningful only with God present. For that matter, why "God"? *We all believe in one God, we just call him by a different name. Allah, Om, Jesus...*are they any different? Are they reason enough not to live together in harmony, in civility? Civilization is just another movement of history; of people making rules along the way to protect their own misdeeds of history. The 'Ownership of Property Act,' for example, to protect property previously stolen from the colonies. Truth—knowledge—is a shifting ground. Built on experience over time, with observations of the underlying consistencies of environment. So knowing when to plant rice, e.g., is knowledge of the weather timings. But with climate change, what is the world of experience to us? We have to wait for a long stretch of stability to know anew. The fears we have are about the fear of loss of centuries of knowledge. We need certainties. Is there any certainty in our lives? Or is reality uncertain?

I think of Anna, of our history, our separate lives, but the certainty of our love, unchanged despite the change in our environments and our separation. Love perhaps will have a formula, an equation to predict or calculate—someone somewhere will find it, but till then its existence is certain, and like the grin on the Cheshire cat's face that stays after the cat is gone, love will inexplicably hang around our lives; even when our oxygen is depleted and all earth is destroyed it will linger.

I guess what I am saying is that I believe in love.

Chapter Thirty-Four

Deep in the forest of the Sanjay Gandhi National Park, which surrounds the city of Bombay, and just beyond the point where the road for visitors ends, lie the Kanheri Caves carved into the basalt rock. Beyond the caves, as one climbs higher, taking the pathway on the left stamped out by a hundred feet, the air clears and the eye can stretch beyond the city through black rock and water bodies; through downy clouds on rainy days and bright sunshine on others. Climbing farther up the winding pathway, one loses the crowds and escapes the city where prying eyes are beyond where your own range of vision ends.

On either side of the pathway, trees of all kinds push upwards to the sky, lung-like, saving the city from choking in its own smog. If you are silent on foot, you might surprise a cobra in the middle of its breakfast. And spiders; spiders abound, hidden in the growth, waiting for their next prey to land on their gossamer hammocks—those maddening silken threads you have to wipe off your face as you make your way up. I'm half convinced the arachnids are taking over the forest, like Google's search engines crawling through your space and life, gobbling and spitting it out for some other predator to live on.

If you get past all this, you reach the highest point in Bombay. This is where, two days after her arrival, Anna and I walked, hand in hand, and sometimes she put her hand around my waist and leaned her head on me, pointing in wonder at the monkeys that darted in and out of our path, sometimes coming daringly close to grab the apple that she bit into every now and then. I could see Eve in her—the quintessential temptress who changed the destiny of mankind. But Anna, unselfconscious, laughing, happy, had learnt to live like the animals. In the moment. Not a trace of history that sent the Fernandeses off to Canada was visible; I was the only link to any history she remembered.

We made our way to the high point on top of the hill. Anna sat atop a rock like a Greek goddess, or Roman—the ones that sat thinking, looking beautiful as they did—and ate the rest of her apple, seductive, all together. I sat beside her, a bit breathless from the walk, and perhaps from her presence. Her crepe cotton skirt flared around her like a pretty Japanese umbrella, colourful but delicate, her skin smooth with health and her hair in affectionate curls: nature had been kind to Anna.

Suddenly, pointing toward the small glimpse of Vihar Lake, Anna said, "Peter, are you happy?"

I looked sideways at her, her nose little, her lips now red from all the activity with the apple, and wondered where all that seriousness came from. She continued to look at the lake and point as if the question itself had risen up from the depths of the lake and she, with her own special teleprompter, was asking me the questions that some water creature held up with dripping, spindly green arms.

Was I happy? Did I stop to think about this, ever? What did it mean anyway? Just a word that did not represent a single common, definable feeling. I had no answer. I did not understand the concept. I sat there silently looking at her finger pointing out: long, artistic fingers, fingers that perhaps created beauty; beauty I was not part of; beauty I did not know of...

It was some time before the silence was broken by a light wind that swept through her curls; time, in essence incalculable, relative—like happiness, notional. Our days represented the spinning of the earth around its axis, and if the earth took an eternity to spin around its axis, would that mean our day would be eternal? What would the year be like? Born and dead in a day, our life would be eternal. I had no answer for Anna.

"Peter, why are you still single? Do you have a woman? Or a man?"

"You, too, are single, Anna. Or are you? Do you have a man? Or woman?" I asked, not wanting to be the first to tell all.

She laughed. "I am quite as single as they come."

"Anna, are the men in Canada blind?"

"Perhaps. Maybe I have not been open myself. Something holds me back."

We sat looking at the lake. Anna finished the apple and threw the pip into the distance. A bird swooped down and picked it up, ever ready to eat the remnants of man's indulgences; this is what keeps the wheels of the world turning. And love? Where does love come into all of this?

"You did not answer my question," she said softly.

"No, Anna," I said. "I am single. I suppose I have never forgotten you."

Bold utterances, which all at once surprise and silence. We looked at each other, suddenly shy. Sitting atop this hill, she and I, shy; it was the strangest feeling—more so than love, for we had always loved each other in all kinds of forms. But shy?

Anna plucked at a weed, dried and looking like straw. She held it to the light as if trying to focus outside ourselves, forcing our attention away from this moment, and said, "Remember our New Year's old man, Peter?" as she held up a dried straw she had pulled up from the dry earth around the black mountain rock we sat upon.

Chapter Thirty-Five

Since Dad died a couple of years ago, Mother had taken to drinking a regular peg of scotch every night before dinner. Anna and I arrived home to a slightly sozzled Isabel, whose nervousness about our outing had taken her to her third drink. A crystal decanter and cut-crystal whisky glasses stood on the coffee table. A man taking to drink is intuitive—we are weak and crumble under stress and intense emotion—but Isabel matched most men in stalwartness and capability. Her nervousness seemed out of place.

Anna took the glass from her hands and set it down. Giving her a hug, she said, "Isabel, aunty, can we have dinner now? I have been dreaming of your cooking for so many years and I want to savour every taste before I return."

Nothing was designed to trouble Mother more than that last statement. She looked at me and then at Anna. Not knowing who she was losing, she poured another shot of whiskey from the fast-depleting bottle.

"I will lay the table." Anna, intuiting Mother's condition, glanced at me, then left for the kitchen.

"So?" Mother whispered, just as Anna walked in once again, saving me from having to respond. She almost sprinted in and out of the kitchen, either very hungry or trying to prevent Mother from developing ulcers from drinking on an empty stomach—or just afraid to let the conversation go on without her. We sat down in silence.

"Anna, we were hoping you would extend your stay for a while," Isabel finally said.

Anna put down her fork and knife and looked at her plate for what seemed like a lifetime to us who waited for the answer. Inconsequentially I remembered Joe's observation as we waited in the queue outside the toilets in Billimoria Building: 'Time is relative depending on which side of the door you are on.' He'd wagged his finger in the air, head to one side and gold teeth glistening in the sunlight.

I chuckled, but it was short lived as Mother took out her box of snuff and unscrewed the top, still looking at Anna's lowered head and the storm of curls that engulfed it. Absentmindedly Isabel laid down the snuff box on the table to steady her shaking hands, from drink or nervousness it was hard to say. The whirring fan above, circulating the air in the room, brought with it particles of snuff that set Anna and me sneezing into our plates. As we smiled at one another sheepishly, it served to ease the air, almost like releasing the valve of a pressure cooker.

"Isabel, it is hard for me to leave you. You are my second mother. But I have to get back to my life in Canada soon."

"I ask for a week, Anna. We have lived for so long without seeing each other. All I ask is one more week."

Isabel always knew how to get what she wanted. She did not have one style that said "Isabel." She used any trick that might work, and now she was playing on Anna's soft core.

Silence prevailed once again, broken only by silverware working on the porcelain dinner plates that Mother had taken out for the occasion.

"Tell us about your trip to Mangalore, Anna," I said, trying to lighten the mood once again. "What did you go there for? Did you have a nice stay? Is your grandfather's house still there?"

The next day, I went to work while Anna went to the travel agent to change her ticket. She decided to move her departure back a week. Isabel called me, ecstatic and rebuking all at once. *Can't you ask her? What's wrong with you? Do you have another woman in mind? Time is running out...She is staying one more week, thank God... If I have to wait for you to do anything it will be never... Some things have to be done by you... you cannot depend on your mother for everything.*

Unfair though that last comment was, I must admit that for once I was happy to have her interference. I was out of my depth with Anna—with romance—and could do with some help. I'd been reduced from Anna's childhood hero to a bumbling mass of nervousness. Surely this was not love? If love was so good and wonderful, why was I nervous, stressed and choking?

The train journey is designed for introspection. Smashed between bodies, body odours and microscopic views of skin, pores, and the anatomy of sweat droplets, the mind travels into oneself—implodes, so to say. This feeling within me was not unlike the feelings as I stood behind the door that winter night in January of 1993, listening to the screams and the silence, not knowing what to expect and frightened of what was happening out there, beyond my control.

But that was fear, anticipation of fearful, unknown happenings; happenings that would hurt me or those close to me. The very same feeling I had right now as I thought of Anna. Fear of love? Fear of Anna? Fear of what she felt for me or I felt for her? Fear of losing her—that which I have not? I could not answer those questions, but I was sure what I felt was fear.

Fear is a strange feeling. It accompanies horror, love, hate, and most emotions—like the shadow on the street at the crossroads. A painter understands light and shade, the light from the back casting shadows in front, almost as though foretelling who you will be as you walk ahead. My own shadow from the past was throwing distorted designs in front of me. I could step over it, and yet the fear stays around, ready to spring in all we do.

Near the window of the teachers' lounge, Sheila sits reading a book. I look at her now, anew. She is not an object of fear—but one of compassion? Friendship? It is hard to say.

"Asked her?" she said, without much ado.

"No."

"Well?"

"Well, what?"

The very history of mankind is rife with insects, though we're relatively new to their world, which dates from more than 200 million years prior to man's present mutation. Their persistence in survival is well known, transmuting from form to form, never really going away.

And right there, before mine very eyes, this insect transmuted.

Whether from irritation at the inquisition or a display of my own inadequacy, it is hard to say, my voice was gruff, unwelcoming—one could almost say rude. Ms. Raikar sniffled in loud bursts. Good heavens, didn't she know that men don't know what to do with a crying woman? What had I said that was so terrible?

"I'm sorry," I said after wrestling my irritation under control.

"For what?"

"Being rude just now."

As if by magic, her tears dried and she sat upright, looking at me as if I had just entered the room.

"You were rude? Why?"

"What were you crying about?" I asked, now certain I did not understand women at all.

"He called me last night."

Was this a game of guess who? I of course did not risk prompting another burst of moisture.

"He thinks of me when he is with her. He wants to continue seeing me."

"Is he not married?"

"Yes, but he loves me."

Finding it hard to reconcile this with my own Catholic conscience, and marvelling at the ease with which such young men keep women interested in them, I could barely conceal my revulsion toward him. "What's with you? You are settling for trash. How can you let this piece of excrement snack on you? You deserve better!"

"I love him."

There was that word once again to haunt me. *Love is a verb, not a noun*—over and over again, Ms. Faria, our third grade English teacher, explained that a verb is a *doing* word.

When, and what, would I choose to do?

"Marry me," I said.

Outside cave no. 44 at Kanheri, I looked it in the face, this fear to love beyond myself. As Anna stood chewing a straw she had pulled out from the crevice of the dark black rock as we ambled upwards, I knew that there was nothing more right than loving her.

A long silence followed my declaration; all the while, she looked at me. How have those before me gotten down on one knee and declared undying love? Does one need youth? Never a drinker, I was now longing to gulp some fiery tonic down my throat, which had suddenly dried up.

"Peter," she said softly, reaching for my hand, "can we sit down? I need to process this."

I sat on a rock facing her, my eyes never leaving hers, hoping that somehow this would help her make a decision, hoping my fears would be unfounded, hoping that Anna loved me like I did her.

Like Mother and her mother before her, I waited nervously, fingers entwined as if in prayer, as if everything I'd ever wanted in my life was at stake. Finally, an eternity later, with what seemed like a torturous fire in my belly swirling in rings, I knew Anna was holding my sanity right there in her wide-eyed gaze.

"Peter, will you understand that I love you? That I have always loved you in so many ways, as brother, friend, my hero, and mentor all these years?"

This did not seem right, though it seemed like the right words. There was something in her tone and the phrasing of the question that was once again tightening the muscles of my stomach. Out in the cave, two birds were doing a dance, more, I suspect, from landing their feet on hot basalt than a seductive mating.

"I must say no to your proposal of marriage, but I also must say it is wrenching my heart in several directions. I want you to know that. I want you to understand that my decision is rooted in the deepest love I have for you, rather than lack of it. Will you remember that, will you remember this as an affirmation of life and love of you, above all others?"

I looked down the hillside. The black of the rock was more apparent with dry grasses peeping through and the air, hot and heavy. Somewhere down there a million ants could be copulating while I struggled with confusion. Perhaps it was the environment. Perhaps I was not romantic enough? Should I have waited for the moon? I looked at Anna and my heart skipped. There is nothing more attractive than when someone loves you and looks at you the way she was looking at me. And yet I was confronting a parting from her.

"I don't understand this, Anna, but I cannot deeply trust you and yet doubt that you truly believe what you say. So I must too." Empty words. Silence can be graceful, it can be the beginning and end of music, but it can also be oppressive. Does one fill it with small talk, or carefree flippancy? Tears? Because right now I was dangerously close to it. I looked up and saw Anna's wet eyes spit one down her cheek. Needless, I thought. She could just say yes. Weren't we both single—hadn't we loved each other all our lives?

I cannot say I had dreamed of this moment consciously. In all those fifteen years we were apart I had never believed I would see her again—I had rejected thoughts of her, yet found every other woman wanting: they were not Anna. So I sat tongue-tied, trying to see the absurdity in my situation, trying to make sense of my destiny, my life.

"Anna," I said eventually, then hesitated, my lips opening and closing like a fish's. If I was trying to woo a woman with manliness and strength I was failing without doubt. I closed my mouth and sat still, looking at her—an impartial observer may even go so far as to say begging her with my eyes, my heart, my entire body. The alternative of not having her, wrapped a bony hand around that reported seat of emotion, my heart.

She shed steady tears while looking at me; not for herself but for me. She was feeling my pain and living its life with me, but she shook her head like it would never change. Like all those years ago, she read me, she felt me, and yet her strength moved her always towards what she deemed right, pure and unselfish. This was one time I wished she would take the lower road.

"Marry me," I repeated. My pride was no longer a barrier, nor my dignity; I knelt on hard basalt, pleading with every cell of my body. But she only sat there silently crying, every tear oozing pain—hers, mine. My heart left my body. I died, I hope I died, because my heart was not in there pumping blood to keep my body alive. Instead, Anna was holding it and offering it back, making choices that caused every cell in my body to scream with despair.

Eventually my flesh, aware of itself, began to hurt at the knees. In silence, I stood, pulling Anna to her feet after me.

"Peter, Peter my dearest...I don't want to inflict any hurt on you."

"You don't have to Anna. Marry me... or tell me if there is someone in Canada you have not told me about. If you love me, is that not enough to commit to a life together?"

"No, Peter, no. There is no one in Canada but Canada itself."

"Anna, right now, I feel like my world is ending. I need simplicity, something I can understand. What has Canada to do with you and me."

Anna moved away from me, releasing her hands from mine. She walked up and down towards the cave and towards me. There was emotion, but I could not tell what, for, in the flutter of her hands I saw oblivion.

"Our lives changed that year of 1992-93, when we really should have had nothing to do with it. We had built a safe world of Catholics. Yet, we could not protect ourselves from the larger events that sucked us in. Our worlds changed immensely."

"Can't we leave that in the past? We are grown, different and love... why, love can conquer all. And anyway, where does nationality feature in your relationship with me? Where does it figure in love and marriage?"

"Peter, all those years ago we should have understood how vulnerable we were, and are. We cannot just insulate ourselves from everything else taking place, no matter how little it has to do with us. When I arrived in Mangalore last month, it was the Catholics that were being targeted. I was there only to take over the property I had inherited." She hesitated. "But it was hot, and after dealing with the solicitors, I went to a pub. I downed two beers and of course I needed to go to the washroom, which was just as well. A mob of young men rushed in, dragged the women out into the streets and assaulted them. This was not an isolated mob; mobs all over the city were dragging women out from the pubs. Their point? Women had no business being in a pub!"

"Anna, you would be my wife. I would protect you from such encounters," looking at her, I remembered the readiness in which I would have swung the cricket bat at the Surve boy all those years ago.

"You see? I don't want to be protected as I live my life making my choices. I want to make choices because that is my right, my entitlement as a human, as you would have. I don't need to protect you, do I?"

"But Anna, that is the way of the world."

"Not my world in Canada, Peter."

"What is your world in Canada? Surely it cannot be greatly different. You will have issues there too."

"Yes, we do. But there is a rule of law that is respected and hence we have recourse." She shook her head. "Somehow I feel we have more rights there than we ever had here–a place we were born in. You see, Peter, growing up in India we made the best choices we had, but not really the ones we wanted to."

We were both quiet for a moment, and then I said, "Then let's make the choices we want to. We've been speaking of everything but ourselves: of you, of me, of love."

"Oh, Peter, there is nothing to discuss about love. We feel it and it will be what it is. But marriage has a physicality of presence. I could never live in India, not after living in Canada."

"I could live in Canada with you, Anna."

We both sat on the rock and looked towards the mouth of the cave. It had a dark, ominous emptiness. Did young lovers live there, unmindful of the world?

"Peter, we never did talk of our lives after we left. Immigration is not easy. Ivan, Susan, Francis and I were happy for most part. Our lives had renewed and we made friends easily. We were students, but Mum and Dad...their lives changed in so many ways. Dad never got a job. I mean a real job. Mum got a job and supported the family. You know Dad. It killed him not to be the breadwinner."

"Why did you choose Canada? If your dad had no job or a plan, it was a big risk."

"It seemed to give us hope that somewhere out there we would find the acceptance, justice, safety, and above all, overcome fear. Father never did feel safe after that incident with Surve's son. What if someday the inquiry was reopened? So we left. Who said 'home is where the heart is'? My heart was in so many different places, scattered around the earth, in homes I have never lived in and with people who I might never see again. Restless—as if there was another place I must be in all at once. Then finally we had to stop the tearing since it did not allow us to settle. We gave up the memories that tugged us and accepted our home in Canada. It is like a long exhale after an unconscious holding of one's breath."

"I could exhale in Canada, too, Anna."

"You would have to restart your career all over again. That is not easy. How could I condemn you to a life of an immigrant who could possibly never work as a professor of Math again? Time and time again I have seen people come to Canada with a light in their eyes. Hope lights up the darkest sky. But the light gradually dies out as they pick up any job they can, to survive. Maybe you'd drive a cab, or perhaps spend a few years as a security guard at some condominium, saying, 'Good morning, ma'am,' 'Good day, sir,' till that light of excitement in your eyes died too. Dad, Mum, those that come to the community centre, talking of their homes, 'back home' where they had maids and life was not so hard? If not for their children they would return. Too late, they realise that they came as immigrants and settled as exiles. That is survival, Peter. That is not living. Would our love be enough to stop living and just survive? I don't know. Is love a sufficient ground for uprooting your home and discarding your history and very identity? A man with no history or identity is a broken man. A broken man forgets how to love." Anna was shaking her head, thinking of private thoughts, and I stood outside that zone as a slight quiver shook her body. She turned back and looked at me and said with a finality, "I don't believe love conquers all."

She stood and pulled me up and hugged me, close, hard, as if she wanted to merge into me. Not wanting any more conversation to stretch this moment of total union and separation, we held each other. Anna was mine, and I was hers, even in her rejection.

We climbed down the hard rock of the Deccan Trap, which, ironically, originated from the ancestral Réunion hotspot that welled up beneath India in the late Cretaceous, killing dinosaurs in its wake, trapping frogs and other creatures in its folds, and cooling down into this porous, dark trap—dead, cold rock, as all molten lava is bound to become over time.

Chapter Thirty-Six

"To be or not to be: that is the question…"

- **William Shakespeare**
Hamlet

I had dropped Anna to the airport amidst tears shed by Isabel, who unashamedly wailed—not for me or Anna but for herself, her own separation from Anna, her daughter. I stood there waving at Anna, and she at me, while she got swallowed into the large bowl of partings and reunions.

We returned to Mother's apartment, driving through the streets silently. Mother nervously sniffed and kept fidgeting with the snuff box. The endless drive culminated in Mother's living room.

In the fading light of evening, Isabel and I sat at her dining table, drinking whiskey. She finally laid down her empty glass, after drowning at least three when I was counting, and picked up the snuff box. She inhaled deeply, some of it resting on the upper lip hairs she had grown in her later years. These details being unimportant to a woman living on her own, she sneezed, her disappointment in her son unspeakable.

Finally I said, "I tried."

"Yes I know. I am sorry not just for you but for myself. We have lost Anna all over again, but this time I know it is final."

"We can still hope, Mother."

This somehow seemed to trigger Mother. She stopped short, looked at me and jumped back into her skin.

"Peter, now you listen to me. You may have fantasised about Anna, and I admit, so did I. But that should be put behind. Hope is good, it gives meaning, helps us live. But find your meaning in something real and tangible. You can fight for love, but not with a country, not with geography. You need to find a girl here, marry and give me the grand-children any dutiful son would give their mother."

Picking the *Times of India* that lay carelessly at hand, she ignored the headlines that had smudged with some of the flying wet particles that sneezing sometimes ejects, and flipped the pages rapidly, stopping at the classifieds. Thumbing through the advertisements, she stopped at the Matrimonials, and began circling an advertisement here and there, sniffing and sometimes snivelling loudly, the crockery and cutlery on the table set for three quivering in response.

She looked up at the mantelpiece, a needless decorative structure without a fireplace, and her eyes fell upon the sculpture of a wooden sailboat that Joe Marchon had whittled from what was once a clothes beater. Staring at it for several long moments, she finally walked up to it, picked it up and carried it, like the offensive object it was, to the kitchen, where she dropped it into the garbage bin under the sink. She then washed her hands with soap and water several times before drying them on the tea towel at hand.

Soon after, I found myself on my last journey to Mazagaon, the cra-dle of our life together and the destroyer of our innocence. It was dif-ferent, devoid of memories, devoid of emotion as I looked around its familiar, yet unfamiliar roads, buildings and people.

I walked subconsciously towards the one place I'd always run to in the past, when in trouble: St. Anne's Church. My belief in the existence and essence of God, being a trifle weak, had steadily dwindled over the past few years. Making my way to St. Anne's was an act of expunging all memories and associations I had of this place and its history in my life. The church was closed, as churches are wont to be nowadays—no lon-ger sanctuaries but buildings of utility, conference halls of the faithful that must shut after the meeting is over. I sat on the stone border at the grotto just as I had all those years ago when my sense of abandonment had dominated any other feeling.

Now there is no feeling of abandonment. My overwhelming emo-tion at this time is one of loss: loss of hope that comes from belief. I did not know what I believed in, nor where I had lodged my faith. Anna's rejection made the world I had clung to for a very long time merely illusory.

All that I considered the basis of my life was the life I had shared with

Anna, and now, suddenly, I realised we had added to that reality in very different ways and separately. Knowing this, knowing Anna was not really part of me as I imagined, I felt bereft: not of a woman, not of a love, not of a lover; but of my own reality; my understanding of the very subjective selection I had made of memories to retain, people to value, love to feel. The colour I'd given my life so far, none of it was real—none of the life in my head could be real to anyone else but me.

I walked down Nesbit Road once again, looking around and seeing nothing and nobody familiar. None of them would be. Finally, standing at the foot of the stairs of Billimoria Building, I scanned the space. The smells were unfamiliar and the stone steps at the bottom that led to the wooden staircase were cracked in several places. I moved up the wooden stairs that I had spent years walking up and down, but the hollows in the wood no longer fit my footstep. No, this was an unfamiliar stair. I stood in the passage on the very spot Anna and I had, all those years ago when she handed me her book. I thought I had read love, and indeed it was love, but was it the romantic love I had dreamed of? Did Anna, in her kindness, look at me with love and compassion as one does a brother and a friend? I looked up at the high ceiling and at the pigeon's nest that had dried, old and unused, but not swept away even after all those years; and if it had remained because the pigeons still lived there, then they apparently had been the least affected by our history.

Outside the Marchons' apartment a young, handsome boy stood staring idly at Nesbit Road across the compound. I did not recognise him. The three coconut trees were still there, a bit taller, older, and lean from lack of sustenance, whispering in a language I did not understand. Finally I knew this memory I had hung on to, of Anna, of her loving me, not just as brother and friend but as a lover, had been spent. I don't know where, or whether I had suppressed it, and whether it would surface at odd moments, but for now it seemed like an uncertain reality of an uncertain memory. Isabel was right. I needed to embrace what was in front of me.

Chapter Thirty-Seven

Brushing the cobwebs from my forehead and lips, I felt I'd spent an age away from my apartment; really it was a short time away, entertaining and wooing Anna, running errands for Mother and working in between. Premibai had obviously decided to stay away too; with little activity in the apartment, the spiders had taken over. Dusky shadows danced on the ceiling, reflecting the plants in the corner as I switched on the light. I walked directly to the washroom and showered to take off the fatigue I felt. Stepping out with just a towel wrapped round my hips, I sat in the living room hoping to immerse myself in reading Dickson's, *History of the Theory of Numbers, vol. three,* and resurface as close as I could to reality.

As if on cue, I heard a key turn in the lock. Premibai, I suppose, back as if she'd been watching for my return. However, the bony frame of Dr. Apte slipped into the room.

"Doctor! How did you get in?"

"I have a key to your apartment, Peter."

"Only Premibai has one."

"Oh, she will not be coming for a few days and has asked me to inform you. She gave me the key."

I stifled a sigh. "She does some weird things, but anyway, Doctor, I am not in a very social mood so you will have to excuse me."

"Excused," he said with a wave of his hand and picked up a National Geographic and thumbed through the pages. I stood and walked toward my bedroom, knowing I would have to bear his presence in the drawing room.

"She said no, I suppose," he said to my retreating back as I opened my door, stepped in, and shut it.

Staring at the ceiling is therapeutic. If one concentrates long enough one can decipher patterns in the strokes of the painter's brush and even see the odd spot that escaped. Sometimes my attention leapt past the walls and ceiling of my room to the noise of the television playing in the drawing room. No, Dr Apte had no intention of letting me be. I knew he would even sleep on my couch and I would wake to loud snores at some early hour of the morning, and yet I felt unable to step outside and face him. Finally the noise of the television died down and all that I could hear was the horn of the traffic in the distance. Perhaps now I could get that glass of water that I so thirsted for.

Trying to be surreptitious, I carefully slid the door handle in slow motion, but the creak seemed so loud that I was afraid I would wake him. I opened the door to the realisation that my fears and caution were unfounded. Dr. Apte, far from being asleep, had stationed himself outside my door and was listening for my heartbeat or whatever he thought he would hear with his ear to my door. Of course he did not have the grace to blush; or perhaps he did and it did not show under his brown skin in the low light.

"What are you doing here?"

"Checking if you are ok," he said, like it was the most natural thing in the world to listen at doors. But in that action, perhaps, he had made it the most natural thing to do; set the standards for social behaviour, so to say. On many an occasion my ideas of good manners and boundaries had been totally pooh-poohed by this man, "Peter, you are so conditioned by the British who left this place so long ago. Who is interested in their standards on anything at all?"

I walked towards the kitchen in silence. Good manners, good friends, well meaning interest—who cares! Right, wrong, boundaries, privacy...close on my heels, I could hear him breathe down my neck.

"Leave me alone, Doctor."

"Not possible, Peter."

We sat in the living room, the two of us, keeping a great amount of space between us. He on a chair under the lamp and I in the far opposite corner in the darkness, where he could not see my face, at least perhaps not my expressions. I did not want to talk, I wanted to be alone, but I also knew Doctor Apte felt that I should not be allowed time alone at such a crucial moment of my life... Sometime during this evening I knew I would have to talk to him, or be burdened with his presence for the night and the next day.

After a long silence in which the clock could be heard ticking from the kitchen, Doctor Apte started wheezing, now challenging my irritation to guilt. I think I had fatigued him, but he did not give up. "Peter, I am waiting."

In fits and starts, I began.

"And that is the folly of my reality," I concluded many minutes later. Dr. Apte had let me go on uninterrupted, a phenomenon that I had never encountered in the past.

"And is that it?" he scoffed. "Your discovery. I mean, is that all it is—this construction of your life on an unreal premise? Have you no emotional sense of loss, disappointment, a disbelief in the eternal nature of love?"

"Love? Yes, I discovered love. In all this I discovered love."

"Ah Peter, interesting. But you speak without emotion, without the true feelings of one turned down by a loved one."

"But don't you see, Doctor, that is precisely the point. At first it shattered my world. When one builds a narrative inside one's mind, a narrative based on pre-lived experiences and imaginary projections, it is not built on the love I had for her. I had objectified her, wanted to possess her, legalise that possession, and all this was based on my fear. The strange feeling in the pit of my stomach...I thought it was my fear to love."

"Peter, you speak like a robot! Don't you think you are intellectualising a very basic human emotion?"

"I don't know, Doctor... perhaps. But then, that is how I am wired. I do not deny the feelings Anna brought on. Fear, then loss.

Loss of so many things. Loss of illusions can be a very great loss. The mind tricks us, our reality, our sense of creation. Everything is possible in its realm."

"You still speak of the mind, Peter. Love is not an emotion of the mind, it is an emotion of the heart."

"But if you speak of emotion, you still speak of the mind. Emotions, sensations are related to the neural system controlled by the brain. The senses need the presence of the object, but the mind can function beyond. Mine did. The direction I took it relied on a memory of Anna that had stood still since she left. So my emotions, corrected by the discovery of my folly, do indeed fall flat on their face."

"You say that the love you felt for Anna no longer exists?"

"I am saying the sensation and that emotion that objectified her, that stemmed from fear of losing her, of needing to touch, see, hear her speak, all that comes from the libido, is just that. Emotion is an event. It has been there in the past with other women, and I reckon will be there with other women. In your own definition it could not be love, since all emotion is of the senses linked into the nervous system, which is in turn controlled by the mind. If the loved one is physically removed from one's presence, would we then continue to love? How could love be eternal if so?"

Dr. Apte sat there looking at me in bewilderment, and I stared at the wall, trying to explore my feelings, my thoughts, and what went on in that body, the spirit and my heart. He waited patiently, my friend. Waited as if there was more, something I needed to tell him, so I went on.

"There is something that is running inside of me. Uncontrolled by the brain. Anna did not reject me, in essence. She said it was an act of love. Eventually, I did understand love. Not 'understand' in a thought process, nor a sensation or emotion, but my heartbeat, my blood circulation, powered from no object but within my own."

Dr. Apte waited a while. Finally he broke the long silence with, "So you admit you still have feelings for her."

"Yes, Doctor. The coursing through my blood is undeniable. Anna is definitely part of it, but my love for her is no longer distressing as when I thought, feared, and let my mind rule me. She's freed me from her, yet kept me with her in some strange way."

We both now lapsed into a restful silence. A silence that allowed us to hear the molecules of air jostling one another as we breathed the night; listened to larvae nibbling through the chrysalis to fly away as butterflies. Like Anna in Canada and me in India, their wings flapping on one side of the globe caused waves to beat ashore on some sandy beach in a far removed longitude. Above this noise, a kitten cried like a baby missing its mother; and out there in the cosmos the debris of a dying star passing through a cloud of gas and dust, millions of light years away, compressing to become a new star that would be seen only several millions of years later when its light travels into our solar system.

Amidst this loud din out there in the cosmic heaven: Muslim, Hindu, Catholic, Love and Hatred, Fear, Truth and Falsehood, Reality, Right and Wrong, Living and Dying—all of it seemed insignificant, almost a comical exertion set in motion by a God who has ceased to watch this repetitive farce play over and over again under what they call History.

Chapter Thirty-Eight

"The struggle itself...is enough to fill a man's heart. One must imagine Sisyphus happy."

- Albert Camus
The Myth of Sisyphus

A few mornings later, I woke as usual and swung out of bed, picked up the newspaper, read the not so unusual news of war, crime, disasters, and every depressing news that could be compressed between the pages of a daily. Life had resumed in a living room devoid of Dr. Apte, with the din of trucks, honking traffic and pungent smells from the fertiliser plant. Out there, crows and sparrows dug into bins, picking on man's excesses, unwilling to find the open air spaces where searching for food might tighten their muscles and build their voice boxes. They had rejected that life for one of greed and easy prey, filling the dull aches in their bellies with food that had just decayed.

Premibai, for who I seemed to be the ideal employer, had returned to her daily chores; she cooked, cleaned and packed some of my stores to take home. Somewhere in the distance the trains rushed in and out of Chembur station, and women furiously wove flowers for other women with oily hair or for businessmen to hang around a statue or a picture frame of some God or Godmen, as is their way of worship or appeasement, all for the few rupees that would feed their skinny bodies and those of their many children. Almost anyone could find work: cleaning streets, houses, dishes, roads and sometimes people's ears; almost everyone could find work and food, but shelter, water supply and sanitation? Right now, along streets and in open view, children,

women and men sat with little tin pots beside them, unashamed, doing what the body demands, some relieving themselves on the walls,
others just squatting.

It must be noisy out there if we stop to listen. There must be sounds
of distress if we can hear, but the cosmos shouts loudly somewhere
out there unheard, while stars die, meteorites spin out of control and
gas clouds implode into new stars and new life; and the earth, offering its north to the sun, brings down rain with the drafts that rise from
the oceans.

I put my coffee cup down and left my apartment, walking to the
station through hovels and hawkers, mud and slime and bodies that
look just like mine yet in different motion, walking to and from the
station. I entered the platform where I was pushed into and out of
a train, walked through the crowds, zombie-like; but for once, protesting this search for survival, I turned instead toward the sea front.
There I sat on its walls. The rain, selective as usual, had skipped this
part of the world, and its dry concrete wall was a temptation for many
a lover with no access to privacy in this city; they could peck at each
others lips, feeling secluded and private in full view, like ostriches
with their heads in the sands while they sat with their backs facing
the road. I walked along the wall, taking in the cool air, ignoring any
signs of sexual bliss emanating from the concrete.

A seagull sailed high, almost motionless, on one of the last monsoon drafts of the season—the monsoons, both longed for and dread-
ed, life-sustaining and destroying, chose this moment to beat down
in large, heavy drops, causing a sea of umbrellas to open along the
beach. I, lost in this hurry, rushed to the side of the road opposite and
hailed a cab—or perhaps several cabs, since I could not see whether
they were occupied through the rain that curtained my glasses. Finally, one did stop with much ceremony, splashing mud and water over
the cream trousers I had thoughtlessly worn.

"St. Xavier's," I said as I dried my head with a handkerchief.

"Through Churchgate/Dhobitalao or seaface, saab?"

"You decide, but just get me there."

The rains beat down as great chargers pounded against the seawall
on Marine Drive, through which my cabbie was inching his way. Help
me hear something above my heartbeat, God, I prayed. Don't let it be
the cabbie's voice, I added. Exerting Himself to listen to my supplication,

He kept the cabbie silent. Baby steps, I thought, building my faith in His existence.

I walked into the classroom and looked around. The students returned my gaze expectantly; I dismissed them with a project, giving them class time to complete it—a ploy used by Ms. Faria, my English teacher from a past life. At my desk, I opened L. E. Dickson's *History of the Theory of Numbers*, and stared at its pages, its memories of a past meeting with Dr. Apte and my own interest in Mathematics embedded somewhere in its pores as I rubbed the pages for comfort, direction, until the bell sounded. Meandering along the corridors to the teacher's rest room, I noticed the young nymphettes whose life had yet to be lived, their eyes on their nails, the boys and sometimes a passing glance at me, and knew that in all that lay my reality. Entering the Teachers' Rest Room where, on many an occasion, I'd glanced towards Ms. Raikar with disgust and intolerance, I now saw her once again at the table where she last sat looking out into the courtyard. Her delicate fingers tapped the table impatiently, nails painted coral pink. Her ring finger, which had last worn a sparkling sapphire, was now bare and a very slight pigment mark told a tale. No words necessary here...

Perhaps it was the seagull, the sudden monsoon, that shifted my vision, cleared the internal storms, made way for a new season. Sheila did indeed have very lovely skin, and her hair hung long and loose below her shoulders—a soft yet uncharted landscape; a challenge. In that moment, sensing she was being watched, she looked up at me and smiled. Her eyes were, surprisingly, a blue shade I had never seen before, and I stepped forward to swim in them.

Epilogue

Tukia, the keeper at the Borivali National Park, was assigned the task of feeding the panther. His experience with animals in general not being extensive, he was awarded the sole task of feeding this panther, who he had fed ever since its capture as a young cub back in 1968. He entered the enclosure while the animal, old and frail, watched from a distance waiting for his daily visit. Tukia was accompanied by a guard armed with a tranquiliser gun, though he had established a history of long friendship with the aging beast. The panther's meals were left in a small cave-like area in a corner of the large enclosure, usually in the mornings.

That morning Tukia, as he was wont to do every morning, walked to the enclosure's fence and looked for the animal in the distance. He circumnavigated the barricade, making clicking noises, like the one his grandmother made when feeding chickens, but he could detect no movement inside the enclosure. Puzzled, he and the guard cautiously entered. The animal could not be found anywhere, but what they did find surprised both men. Sitting atop an unusually large pile of faeces, a strange looking creature of a rat-like species peered back at them. Both men were nonplussed, never having seen such an animal before, though one would expect that they'd be familiar with most species living in that forest, having worked there their entire lives. Tukia's own parents were tribals who'd lived in the National Park, same as their parents before them.

The guard's response instinctive, he raised his gun and shot a tranquiliser dart into the creature, stunning it. Pulling out large rubber gloves that he always kept handy for just such an occasion—being prone to dreaming big dreams of adventure, at one time even going so far as to imagine a superhero, Dartman, who (in disguise, of course) worked as a forest guard—he scooped up the creature with one hand and they locked the enclosure, making off to the resident zoologist, Mr. Khan.

Mr. Khan shook his head silently. He seemed surprised—if he could seem anything but inscrutable, being blessed with an expressionless face, or having studiously developed it on the job. He'd spent many years training to view all creatures as specimens to be measured, weighed, analysed, classified, and that left no space for emotion or surprise. But he nodded as if talking to himself.

"Where did you find this creature?"

"On the top of the faeces of the panther."

"And the panther?"

"Gone..."

"Gone?"

"Yes, gone..."

"Disappeared?"

"Yes, disappeared."

He nodded, inscrutable once again. He prodded the pink and yellow skin with one gloved finger. Then he measured the creature, which did not look larger than 5 inches, and proceeded to weigh him, putting 30 grams in his balance, and adding another 5 grams to balance the scale. He took a small wire mesh cage, slipped the creature delicately inside, and locked the cage. He dismissed the two men and proceeded to his writing desk to file a report:

Date: 12th February, 2010

Time: 11:30 a.m.

The creature was brought in stunned by the guard. It was found on top of faeces of the panther. The panther's whereabouts are not known. No possible escape route found. On measurement and general appearance of the creature it could be classified in the genus Heterocephalus, what is referred to

as a naked mole-rat (Heterocephalus glaber). The creature
is not native to the Indian subcontinent and is largely native to parts of East Africa. Its presence in this forest is un-
common and must be further investigated. The animal is
only one of the two species of mammals that are eusocial. Its
physical traits allow it to thrive underground and it has no
pain sensation in its skin since it lacks substance-P, a neu-
rotransmitter responsible for sending pain signals to the
central nervous system.

Mr. Khan, stopping at this point in his report, assessed whether any further details should be provided. Perhaps this would suffice, he thought.
Who would read this report anyway? He reread what he had written and
wondered whether to erase the mention of eusociality. This would only
cause Mr. Marathe, his boss, to call him in for an explanation. After careful
consideration, though, he chose to complete the report with more detail:

The naked mole rat species have a complex social structure.
One female queen and two or perhaps three males have re-
productive abilities. The rest of the colony function as sterile
workers who gather the food and maintain the nest while
the larger workers handle security in case of aggression.

    I may point out here, as a matter of interest, that the
naked mole rat is born blind. The babies are nursed for the
first month by the queen and then workers feed them faeces
until they can ingest solids. Naked mole rats are copropha-
gous. Interestingly, they have the longest life span among
rodents.

Mr. Khan decided he had been elaborate enough and stopped at this
point. He went with the paper and the little cage to his boss in the room
down the corridor. On his way, he saw the two keepers still loitering near
the door.

"Are you sure that the panther is not lurking somewhere in the
enclosure?"

"Absolutely sure." Tukia, generally a mildly unsure man, nodded decisively.

Mr. Khan nodded once again and went onwards down the corridor. He stopped outside the room and read the nameplate as if to confirm that Mr. Marathe, his boss, still occupied that room. No reason, really, but for hesitancy borne out of long years of unpleasant interaction with this individual. He finally knocked on the door. Hearing no sound from within, he made bold to push the door open. Lying on his stomach, stretched on the sofa without a shirt, Mr. Marathe was enjoying a back massage administered by his peon, who would possibly be paid through overtime wages from the office budget. Hiding his disgust, which exceeded what he felt when he viewed the naked mole rat, Mr. Khan set the cage on Mr. Marathe's table and stood by, seemingly deferentially, waiting for the operation to cease. Mr. Marathe, unconcerned with his surroundings, in the throes of the massage, began to moan in small gurgles, quite unaware of the waiting scientist.

Pulling out a chair, Mr. Khan waited, now watching the rodent closely. Incredible, he thought, this rodent is spotted. Perhaps sunburn? Never having seen one before, nor having any opportunity to study the mole rat in live circumstances, he wondered. Maybe a mild suggestion in his report may have been in order.

Mr. Marathe, now aware of having company and seeing Mr. Khan through the corner of his eyes, turned and sprung up, looking superior despite the internal embarrassment he surely felt.

Aadmi gira tho bhi taang upar—Though the man had fallen his leg is still in the air, Mr. Khan thought resentfully. *I would like to wipe that silly look of superiority off his face.*

"You should have knocked. Anyway, why are you here?"

Mr. Khan pointed to the little cage, inspired. "The panther we captured in 1968 is missing. Instead, they found a naked mole rat in its place." He wondered whether he should ascribe this to a phenomenon of evolution, but thought better of it.

"What is a naked mole rat? I have never seen any such creature before."

Mr. Khan could feel a bubbling hysteria mount inside of him. He imagined Mr. Marathe, whose face resembled some lichen-covered surface, shaving in front of his bathroom mirror. Underneath that scraggly facial hair he could see the face of a naked mole rat.

"What are you giggling about?" Mr. Marathe cursed under his breath, something that amounted to *you circumcised butcher.* That served to bring Mr. Khan back to the present.

"The details are in the report, sir"—now feeling spitefully delighted at the explanations that Mr. Marathe would have to give to the government about the missing panther.

Mr. Marathe had sat at his desk and was scanning the report. He rang the bell on his desk for the peon who had just left the room. The peon, who stood just outside the door, was inside within a second.

"Yes, sa'ab?"

"Call Tukia immediateliy."

Tukia, expecting this, had stationed himself not far from Mr. Marathe's door. He entered, looking a bit apprehensive.

"Did you leave the enclosure open yesterday when you fed the animal?"

"No, sa'ab, it was locked even today when we went there to feed it."

Have you checked carefully for the animal? Is it lying dead somewhere inside the enclosure?"

"We checked carefully, but this is all we found," he said, pointing at the creature inside the little cage.

Mr. Marathe's mind moved quickly over the facts, the evidence, and his own predicament. There did not seem to be a furor over any escaped beast out in the city, nor had the forest dwellers reported any episode. There could be only one answer to his now spiralling stress. He took the magnifying glass that he kept on his table to sometimes read—his vanity not allowing him the more convenient option of wearing reading glasses—and peered closely at the creature in the cage. Yes, there is only one answer—and looking at the spots through the glass he had convinced himself beyond doubt that this creature was indeed the panther.

He rocked on his chair, one hand behind his neck now, ordering those around him:

"Tukia, take the armed guard and carefully look through the grounds and report back. Mr. Khan, we had a casualty with a snake from the display not so long ago, didn't we?"

"The snake did not survive."

"So I recall. What did we do with its glass display cage?"

"It is still in its place, minus the snake."

"Good. Go get it," he said, turning to the peon.

He sat for the next ten minutes pondering the creature, counting the spots. He wondered if he'd have to promote Mr. Khan to get his endorsement.

"Congratulations Mr. Khan," he said, when the peon returned with the display case, "you have made the discovery of the century. Who would have known that a panther could be reduced into a naked mole rat? Yet in our forest we have just that...a wonder of science and nature, such that no one has heard of—at least not in this country," he corrected, uncertain whether it had happened in other parts of the world, never having kept himself abreast of international affairs. "I will have to recommend your promotion."

Mr. Khan, unable to respond to this development, kept silent. Mr. Marathe handed the glass case to Mr. Khan along with the wire cage that held the rodent.

Put it in a glass case and have it on display. Let the world see that there, within, is what once was a panther."

Acknowledgments

If I list my thanks to all who have played a role in my life and in the writing of this novel, it would fill the pages of a book. How far back does one go? It frightens me to think I will have missed someone, however small their contribution, both positive and negative, that made this book, made me...

However, I must thank my publishers Mosaic Press, especially Howard Aster and Matthew Goody who have put in so much work to bring this book to readers, taking their role as a publisher with such dedication and above all sharing a respectful relationship which I am sensitive to as a writer.

Joyce Wayne, thank you for helping this process along and for your friendship.

I thank Sagorika Easwar, John Calabro and Sylvia Fraser for their friendship and reading the book and commenting on it and Caitlin Alexander for her editing which made the book so much better than the original.

I would also like to thank the Ontario Arts Council for their assistance.

Above all I thank God for staying so close to me in all I do.